CABAL

ALSO BY MICHAEL DIBDIN:

DOUBLEDAY

NEW YORK

LONDON

TORONTO

SYDNEY

AUCKLAND

MICHAEL
DIBDIN

CABAL

A PERFECT CRIME BOOK
PUBLISHED BY DOUBLEDAY
a division of Bantam Doubleday Dell Publishing Group, Inc.
666 Fifth Avenue, New York, New York, 10103

DOUBLEDAY is a trademark of Doubleday, a division of
Bantam Doubleday Dell Publishing Group, Inc.
All of the characters in this book are fictitious,
and any resemblance to actual persons, living or dead,
is purely coincidental.

Book design by State of the Art

Library of Congress Cataloging-in-Publication Data

Dibdin, Michael.
  Cabal / by Michael Dibdin.
    p.   cm.
  "A Perfect Crime book."
  I. Title.
PR6054.I26C3   1993
823'.914—dc20   92-30698
                                              CIP

ISBN 0-385-46806-7
Copyright © 1993 by Michael Dibdin
March 1993
First Edition in the United States of America

1   3   5   7   9   10   8   6   4   2

TO JOHN SHERINGHAM

I, on the other hand, believe that the whole affair, today as yesterday, was bound up with games of make-believe in which every role was itself playing a double role, of false information taken to be true and true information taken to be false: in short, with the sort of atrocious nonsense of which we Italians have had so many examples in these past few years.

Leonardo Sciascia

ONE

"... quia peccavi nimis cogitatione, verbo, opere et omissione: mea culpa, mea culpa, mea maxima culpa."

Amplified both by the loudspeaker system and the sonorous acoustics of the great basilica, the celebrant's voice reverberated with suprahuman authority, seemingly unrelated to the diminutive figure beating his breast like a hammy tenor in some provincial opera house. The fifty or so worshipers who had turned out on this bleak late November evening were all elderly and predominantly female. The apse and the chapel of the *cattedra,* itself a space larger than many churches, had been cordoned off for the service by uniformed attendants, but in other regions of St. Peter's basilica tourists and pilgrims continued to promenade, singly or in groups, dazed by the sheer scale of the sacred and secular claims being made on every side, numbly savoring the bitter taste of their individual insignificance.

For some, the tinkling of the bell, the strains of the organ, and the procession of red-clad priest and ministers had come as a welcome relief from these oppressive grandeurs, rather as though afternoon mass were a dramatic spectacle laid on by the authorities in an attempt to bring this chilly monstrosity to life, a *son et lumière* event evoking the religious function it had originally had. Curious as children, they crowded behind the ropes dividing off the apse, gawking at Bernini's shamelessly showy sunburst and the great papal tombs to either side. For a time the rhythmic cadences of the Latin liturgy held their attention, but during the reading from the Apocalypse of St. John many drifted away. Those who remained were fidgety and restless, whispering to each other or rustling through their guidebooks.

One man, standing slightly apart on one side of the crowd, was ostentatiously paying no attention at all to the service. He was wearing a suede jacket and a flowery print shirt opened at the neck to display the thick gold chain that nestled in the lush hairs on his chest. His big arms were crossed, one jacket sleeve riding up to reveal the gold Rolex Oyster watch on his left wrist, and his large, round, slightly concave face was tilted upward like a satellite dish tracking some celestial object high above, in the vast dark recess of the unlighted cupola. Not far away, at the base of one of the massive whorled columns supporting the fantastic canopy of the bronze baldachin over the papal altar, a woman was also absorbed by the spectacle above. With her gray tweed coat, black tailored wool jacket, calf-length velvet skirt, and the white silk scarf over her head, she looked like a designer version of the aged crones who constituted the majority of the congregation. But her lipstick, a blare of brilliant red only partially qualified by her cold blue eyes, sent a very different message.

The homily that followed the reading sounded less like a learned discourse than a spontaneous outburst of sour grapes on the part of the priest, nettled by the poor turnout. Once upon a time, he complained, the church had been the center of the community, a privileged place where the people gathered to experience the presence of God. Now what did we see? The shops, discotheques, night clubs, beer bars, and fast-food outlets were all turning people away, while the churches had never been so empty. The touristic passing trade had by this time largely dispersed, but this line of argument appeared to risk alienating even the core of the congregation, reminding them painfully of their status as a marginalized and anachronistic minority, representatives of an outmoded way of thinking. Coughing, shuffling, and inattention became endemic.

A brief diversion was provided by the arrival of a buck-toothed, bespectacled nun, breathless and flurried, clutching a large bouquet of flowers. She apologized to the attendants, who shrugged and waved her through the ropes. Depositing the bouquet on the balustrade surrounding the colossal statue of St. Veronica, the nun took her place on a bench near the back of the congregation as the priest began reciting the Creed. A plainclothes security man who had been looking on from the fringes of the crowd walked over, picked up the flowers, and inspected them suspiciously, as though they might explode.

"Et iterum venturus est cum gloria, judicare vivos et mortuos . . ."

At first the noise sounded like electronic feedback transmitted via the loudspeakers, then the screech of a low-flying aircraft. One or two departing tourists glanced up toward the looming obscurity of the dome, as the man with the suede jacket and gold chain and the woman in the tweed coat and white scarf had been doing all along. That certainly seemed to be the source of the eerie sound, somewhere between a whine and a growl, that billowed down to fill the basilica like colored dye in a tank of water. Then someone caught sight of the apparition high above, and screamed. The priest faltered, and even the congregation twisted around to see what was happening. In utter silence all watched the black shape tumbling through the dim expanses toward them.

The sight was an inkblot test for everyone's secret fears and fantasies. An arthritic seamstress who lived above an automobile body shop in the Borgo Pio saw the long-desired angel swooping down to release her from the torments of the flesh. A retired chemist from Potenza, on the other hand, visiting the capital for only the second time in his life, recalled the earthquake that had recently devastated his own city and saw a chunk of the dome plummeting down, first token of a general collapse. Others thought confusedly of spiders or bats, superhero stunts or circus turns. Only one observer knew precisely what was happening, having seen it all before. Giovanni Grimaldi let go of the nun's bouquet of flowers, which scattered on the marble floor, and reached for his two-way radio.

Subsequent calculations demonstrated that the period of time elapsing between the initial sighting and terminal impact cannot have exceeded four seconds, but to those watching in disbelief and growing horror it was a period without duration, time free. The figure might have been falling through a medium infinitely more viscous than air, so slowly did it appear to descend, revolving languidly about its own axis, the long sustained keening wrapped around it like winding robes, the limbs and trunk executing a leisurely saraband that ended as the body smashed head first into the marble paving at something approaching seventy miles per hour.

No one moved. The glistening heap of blood and tissue subsided gently into itself with a soft farting sound. Priest and congregation, tourists and attendants, stood as silent and still as figures in a plaster Nativity. In distant nooks and crannies of the vast enclosure, the final echoes of that long scream died away. Then, as strident as trumpets, first one, then many voices took up the strain, shrieking hysterically, howling, sobbing, and gasping.

Giovanni Grimaldi started toward the body. It seemed to take forever, as in a bad dream, the crowd perpetually closing up right in front of him, denying him passage. Then he was through the inner circle, beyond which no one was prepared to go, and promptly slipped and fell, his radio dropping with a loud clatter. Instinctively the crowd drew back, terrified by this renewed proof of the malignant power possessed by this killing floor. The screaming redoubled in volume as those at the back were toppled and trodden underfoot. As attendants ran to try and contain the crowd, Grimaldi stood up, his blue suit stained with the blood on which he had slipped. It was almost invisible on the marble slabs, a light spattering that blended perfectly with the scarlet veins beneath the highly polished surface of the stone.

He retrieved his radio and pressed the call-up button. While Control took their sweet time about answering, as usual, Grimaldi looked around to try and find the man in the suede jacket and the woman in the tweed coat, but they were no longer there.

"Well?" a crackly voice demanded crossly in his ear.

"This is Grimaldi. We have a jumper in the basilica."

"In progress or complete?"

"Complete."

He switched off the radio. There was no need to say more. Suicides were a regular occurrence in St. Peter's. This was partly due to the vertiginous attraction of high places in general, but still more to a popular belief that those who died on the Apostle's tomb went straight to heaven, bypassing the normal red tape and entry quotas. The Church had preached repeatedly and at length against this primitive superstition, but in vain. The part of the inner gallery beneath the dome that was open to the public had been fitted with a two-meter-high wire-mesh security fence, but if folk want to kill themselves badly enough, it's impossible to prevent their doing so.

Nevertheless, this particular jump was unique, at least in Grimaldi's experience. As far as he knew, no one had ever managed to commit suicide while Mass was being said, for at such times there was no access to the dome.

Grimaldi's message set in motion a well-established routine. The first step was to clear the basilica. Those witnesses suffering from shock were led across the piazza to the Vatican's first-aid post, pausing briefly to allow the passage of an ambulance from the nearby Santo Spirito hospital. When there was a life to be saved, as when Papa Wojtyla had been shot, the Church preferred the high standards of its own Policlinico Gemelli, but when it came to carting away corpses the institutions of the Italian state were good enough.

The ambulance slowed at the gate beneath the Arch of the Bells where the Swiss guards, who had been advised of the situation, waved it through to the succession of small, dark courtyards flanking the east side of St. Peter's. Just beyond the enormous bulge of the transept a uniformed member of the Vigilanza, the Vatican Security Force, waved the vehicle to a halt. The ambulance men got out, opened the rear doors, and lifted out a stretcher. Then they followed the security guard through a door into a bare sloping passage tunneled into the massive lower walls of the basilica. They passed through two small antechambers, then through a doorway concealed beneath the beckoning skeletons of Bernini's funeral monument to Alexander VII, and thence into the basilica itself.

In the open space between the apse and the papal altar, a team of cleaners in blue overalls waited with their mops and buckets, ready to remove every physical trace of the outrage once the body had been removed. A bishop would then be summoned to perform the spiritual equivalent, a rite of reconsecration. The ambulance men set down their stretcher and began unwrapping the green plastic sheeting used to wrap the remains. At this point Giovanni Grimaldi turned aside, his stomach thrashing like a live trout in a net. It was precisely to avoid having to witness things like this that he had come to work for the Vatican in the first place.

The son of a fisherman from Otranto, Grimaldi had started his career in the Carabinieri, and as a brighter than average recruit was rapidly promoted to investigative work. He had stuck it for four years, struggling heroically with a squeamishness he knew would master him in the end. Every time he had to go to the scene of a violent crime his guts tightened up, his breath choked like an asthmatic's, his skin became filmy with perspiration, and his heart went wild. For days afterward he couldn't sleep properly, and when he did, the dreams were so horrible that he wished he hadn't.

His colleagues seemed to think nothing of spending the morning poking around a burned-out car containing the remains of four local mobsters and then tucking into a nice charred roast at lunch, but Grimaldi lacked this ability to separate his professional and private lives. The experience had even marked him physically. His body was hunched, his head lowered, face averted, and his eyes peered up with the guarded, wary look of abused children. His hair had started falling out at an alarming rate, while deep wrinkles corrugated his face until by now he looked older than his own father—who still put to sea each night with his crew of illegal Algerian immigrants and didn't give a fuck about anything.

The usual fate of ex-Carabinieri is to join one of the many armies of private bank guards, but thanks to a local politician who had a word with a bishop who mentioned the matter to a monsignor in the Curia who had the ear of a certain archbishop in the Palazzo del Governatorato, Giovanni Grimaldi moved to Rome and became a member of the Vigilanza. Because of his experience and abilities, he was soon transferred to a select detective unit responsible directly to the cardinal secretary of state. In addition to investigating such minor crime as occurred within the Vatican—mostly petty theft—this group allegedly carried out a variety of covert operations that were the subject of considerable gossip among employees of the Curia. His children only visited him in the holidays now, and his wife in his dreams, for she had contracted cancer the year after he settled in the capital. The children now lived in Bari with Grimaldi's sister, while he himself eked out a solitary life in a Church property near the Vatican, trying to make ends meet for his absentee family, and to put a little aside for the future.

Despite himself, Grimaldi glanced over as the ambulance men transferred the corpse to the plastic sheeting. He noted with impersonal curiosity, as though watching a film, that the gray lounge suit in which the shattered body was clad was of the highest quality, and that one of the black brogues was missing. He looked again at the material of the suit. It looked oddly familiar. His breath started to come in heaves and gasps. No, he thought, not that. Please not that.

The ambulance men had already started to parcel up the body.

"Just a minute," Grimaldi told them. "We need to know who he was."

"That's all done at the hospital," one of the men replied dismissively, not even looking up.

"The victim must be identified before the body is released to the representatives of the Italian authorities," Grimaldi recited pedantically.

The ambulance man looked up wearily, as though dealing with a half-wit.

"All the paperwork's done back at the morgue, chum. We've got a strict turnaround time."

Grimaldi planted his foot on the plastic sheeting just inches from the ambulance man's hand.

"Listen, *chum,* this may be just another bit of Trastevere to you, but when you drove through the archway out there, past our Swiss friends in their fancy dress, you left Italy and went abroad. Just like any other foreign country, this one has its own rules and regulations, and in the present case they stipulate that before this cadaver can be released to the representatives of the Italian state—that's you—it must be identified to the satisfaction of an official of the Vatican City State—which in this case means me. So let's get busy. Pass me the contents of his pockets."

The ambulance man heaved a profound sigh, indicating helpless acquiescence in the face of might rather than right, and started to go through the dead man's clothing. The trouser pockets and the outer ones of the jacket were empty, but a zipped pocket inside the left breast of the jacket yielded a large metal key, seemingly new, and a worn leather wallet containing an identity card and driver's license. The security man scanned these documents, then brusquely turned his back on everyone and switched on his radio again.

"This is Grimaldi," he said, his voice hoarse with excitement. "Tell the chief to get over here immediately! And you'd better notify His Excellency."

Aurelio Zen, on the other hand, was to remember that particular Friday as the night the lights went out.

His first thought was that it was a personal darkness, like the one that had descended without warning a few months earlier on poor Romizi. "Come on, Carlo, at least try and *look* like you're working!" one of the other officials had jeered at the sight of the Umbrian frozen at his desk, a gray, sweating statue of flesh. Romizi had always been a laughingstock in the Criminalpol squad. Only that very morning Giorgio De Angelis had recited yet another apocryphal story about their hapless colleague. "Romizi is detailed off to attend a conference in Paris. He rings the travel agent. 'Excuse me, could you tell me how long it takes to get to Paris?' 'Just one moment,' says the travel agent, reaching for his timetable. 'Thanks very much,' says Carlo, and hangs up."

But Romizi's fate hadn't been funny at all. "A clot on the brain," the doctor had explained when Zen looked in at the San Giovanni hospital. When asked what the prognosis was, he simply shook his head and sighed. Giovanna, Romizi's wife, and his sister Francesca were looking after him. Zen recognized Giovanna Romizi from the photograph of her as a young mother that Carlo had kept on his desk, their twin baby boys on her lap. Now those fresh, plumpish features had been rendered down to reveal the bedrock Mediterranean female beneath, grim, dauntless, enduring. Zen said his piece and left as soon as he could, fearful and depressed at this reminder of the primitive, messy plumbing on which all their lives ultimately depended. It didn't seem remotely surprising that it should break down without warning. On the contrary, the miracle was that it ever functioned in the first place. In growing panic he listened to the thudding of his heart, felt the blood coursing about the system, imagined the organs going about their mysterious, secretive business. It was like being trapped aboard an airplane piloted by an on-board computer. All you could do was sit there until the fuel ran out, or one of the incomprehensibly complex and delicate systems on which your life depended suddenly failed.

Which is what he thought had happened when the darkness abruptly enveloped him. He was on foot at the time, heading for an address in the heart of the old city. The same raw November evening that had culled the congregation in St. Peter's kept people indoors. The streets were lined with small Fiats parked nose to tail like giant cockroaches, but there was no one about except a few youths on scooters. Zen made his way through the maze of the ancient center by following a succession of personalized landmarks, a painted window here, a patch of damaged plasterwork there, that rusty iron rib to stop men peeing in the corner. He had just caught sight of the great bulk of the Chiesa Nuova when it, and everything else, abruptly disappeared.

In different circumstances the wails, groans, and curses that erupted from the darkness on every side might have been distinctly unnerving, but in the present case they were a welcome token that whatever had happened, Zen was not the only one affected. It was not a stroke, then, but a more general power failure, the umpteenth to strike the city this year. And the voices he could hear were not those of the restless dead, seeping like moisture out of the ancient structures all around to claim the stricken Zen as their own, but simply the indignant residents of the neighborhood, who had been cooking or watching television or reading when the lights went out.

By the time he realized this, the darkness was already punctuated by glints and glimmers. In a basement workshop, a furniture restorer appeared, crouched over the candle he had just lit, one hand cupped around the infant flame. The vaulted portico of a Renaissance palace was illumined by a bowlegged figure clutching an oil lamp that cast grotesque shadow images across the whitewashed walls and ceiling. From a window above Zen's head a torch beam shone down, slicing through the darkness like a blade.

"Mario?" queried a woman's voice.

"I'm not Mario," Zen called back.

"So much the better for you!"

Like a vessel navigating an unfamiliar coast by night, Zen made his way from one light to another, trying to reconstruct his mental chart of the district. Reaching a corner, he got out his cigarette lighter. Its feeble flame revealed a stone tablet mounted on the wall high above, but not the name of the street incised in it. Zen made his way along the houses, pausing every so often to hold his lighter up to the numbers. The flame eventually wilted, its fuel used up, but by its dying flickers he read a name off the list printed next to the button of an entry phone. He pushed one of the buttons, but there was no response, the power being dead. The next moment his lighter went out, and his attempts to relight it produced only a display of sparks.

He got out his key-holder and felt the differing shapes and positions of the keys. When he had identified the one he was looking for, he reached out both hands and palpated the surface of the door like a blind man until he discovered the keyhole. He fit the key into it and turned, opening the invisible door into a new kind of darkness, still and dense with a dank, mildewy odor. He started groping his way up the stairs, hanging on to the handrail and feeling with his foot for each step. In the darkness the house seemed larger than he remembered, like the family home in Venice in his childhood memories. As he made his way up the steep flight of steps to the top floor, he heard a male voice droning on, just below the threshold of comprehension. Zen cautiously traversed the open spaces of the landing, located the door by touch, knocked. The voice inside did not falter. He knocked again, more loudly.

"Yes?" a woman called.

"It's me."

After a moment, the door opened to reveal a tall, slim figure silhouetted against a panel of candle gleam.

"Hello, sweetheart!"

They fell into each other's arms.

"How did you get in? I didn't hear the buzzer."

"It's not working. But luckily someone had left the door open."

He didn't want her to know that he had keys to the house and the flat.

"*. . . from the gallery inside the dome. According to the Vatican Press Office, the tragedy occurred shortly after five-fifteen this evening, while Holy Mass was being celebrated in the . . .*"

Tania covered Zen's face with light, rapid, birdlike kisses, then drew him inside. The living room looked and smelled like a chapel. Fat marbled candles flooded the lower regions of the room with their unctuous luminosity and churchy aroma while the pent-roof ceiling retreated into a virtual obscurity loftier than its real height.

". . . *where he had been a virtual prisoner since a magistrate in Milan issued a warrant for his arrest in connection with* . . ."

Tania broke free of his embrace long enough to switch off her small battery-operated radio. Zen sniffed deeply.

"Beeswax."

"There's an ecclesiastical wholesaler in the next street."

She slipped her hands inside his overcoat and hugged him. Her kisses were firmer now, and moister. He broke away to stroke her temples and cheeks, gently follow the delicate molding of her ear, and gaze into the depths of her warm brown eyes. Disengaging himself slightly, he ran his fingers over the extraordinary garment she was wearing, a tightly clinging sheath of what felt like velvet or suede and looked like an explosion in a paint factory.

"I haven't seen this before."

"It's new," she said lightly. "A Falco."

"A what?"

"Falco, the hot young designer. Haven't you heard of him?"

Zen shrugged.

"What I know about fashion you could fit on a postcard."

"And still have room for 'Wish you were here' and the address," laughed Tania.

Zen joined in her laughter. Nevertheless, there's one thing I do know, he thought—any jacket sporting the lapel of a "hot young designer" is going to cost. Where did she get the money for such things? Or *was* it her money? Perhaps the garment was a present. Pushing aside the implications of this thought, he produced a small plastic bag from his pocket, removed the neatly wrapped package inside, and handed it to her.

"Oh, Aurelio!"

"It's only perfume."

While she unwrapped the little flask, he added with a trace of maliciousness, "I wouldn't dare buy you clothes."

She did not react.

"I'd better not wear it tonight," she said.

"Why not?"

"It'll come off on your clothes and *she*'ll know you've been unfaithful."

They smiled at each other. "She" was Zen's mother.

"I could always take them off," he said.

"Mmm, that's an idea."

They had been together for almost a year now, and Zen still hadn't quite taken the measure of the situation. Certainly it was something very different from what he had imagined, back in his early days at the Ministry of the Interior, when Tania Biacis had been the safely inaccessible object of his fantasies, reminding him of the great madonna in the apse of the cathedral on the island of Torcello, but transformed from a figure of sorrow to one of gleeful rebellion, a nun on the run.

His fantasy had been more accurate than he could have known, for the breakup of her marriage to Mauro Bevilacqua, a moody bank clerk from the deep south, had transformed Tania Biacis into someone quite different from the chatty, conventional, rather superficial woman with whom Zen, very much against his better judgment, had fallen in love. Having married in haste and repented at leisure, Tania was now, at thirty-something, having the youthful fling she had missed the first time around. She had taken to smoking and even drinking, habits which Zen deplored in women. She never cooked him a meal, still less sewed on a button or ironed a shirt, as though consciously rejecting the ploys by which proto-mamas lure their prey. They went out to restaurants and bars, took in films and concerts, walked the streets and piazzas at all hours, and then went home to bed.

Things notoriously turned out differently from what one had expected, of course, but Zen was so used to them turning out worse, or at any rate *less,* that he found himself continually disconcerted by what had actually happened. Tania loved him, for a start. That was something he had certainly never expected. He had grown accustomed to thinking of himself as essentially unlovable, and he was finding it difficult—almost painful—to abandon the idea. He was comfortable with it, as with a well-worn pair of shoes. It would no longer do, though. Tania loved him, and that was all there was to it.

She loved him, but she didn't want to live with him. This fact was equally as real as the first, yet to Zen they were incompatible. How could you love someone with that passionate intensity, yet still insist on keeping your distance? It didn't make any sense, particularly for a woman. But there it was. He had invited Tania to move in with him and she had refused. "I've spent the last eight years of my life living with a man, Aurelio. I married young. I've never known anything else. Now I'm finally free, I don't just want to lock myself up again, even with you." And that was that, a fact as unexpected and irreducible as her love, handed him to take or leave.

He'd taken it, of course. More than that, he'd schemed and grafted to grant her the independence she wanted, and then conceal from her that it was all a sham, subsidized by him. If Italian divorce rates were still relatively low, this was due less to the waning influence of the Church than to the harsh facts of the property market. Accommodations were just too expensive for most single people to afford. When Zen and his wife broke up, they had been forced to go on living together for almost a year until one of Luisella's cousins found room to take her in. Tania's clerical job at the Ministry of the Interior had been a nice little perk for the Bevilacqua household, but it was quite inadequate to support Tania in the independent single state to which she aspired.

So Zen had stepped into the breach. The first place he'd come up with had been a room in a hotel near the station that had been retained by the police for use in a drug surveillance operation. In fact, the subject of the investigation had been killed in a shoot-out with a rival gang several months earlier, but the officer in charge had neglected to report this and had been subletting the room to Brazilian transvestite prostitutes. As illegal immigrants, the *viados* were in no position to complain. Neither was Zen's informant, a former colleague from the Questura, since the officer in question was one of his superiors, but Zen was under no such constraints. He sought the man out, and by a mixture of veiled threats and an appeal to masculine complicity, had got him to agree to let Zen's "friend" have the use of the room for a few months.

It was only when they met at the hotel to exchange keys that Zen realized what he'd gotten himself into. Quite apart from the transvestites and the pushers, the room was filthy, noisy, and stank. It was unthinkable for him ever to suggest that Tania move in there, still less to visit her, surrounded by the sounds and smells of commercial sex. Unfortunately, they had already celebrated the good news, so he had had to find an alternative, and quickly.

The solution came through an expatriate acquaintance of Ellen, Zen's former lover, who had been renting a flat right in the old center of the city. The property had been let as an office, to get around the *equa canone* fair-rent laws, and the landlord took advantage of this to impose a 20 percent increase after the first year. The American quickly found an apartment he liked even better, but in order to cause his ex-landlord as much grief as possible, he suggested that Tania come and live in the original flat as his "guest," thus forcing the owner to go through a lengthy and costly procedure to obtain a court order for his eviction. The rent still had to be paid, however, and since Zen had boasted of his cleverness in getting Tania a place for nothing—he told her that the American was away for some months and wanted someone to keep an eye on the flat—he had to foot the bill.

In the bedroom, Tania removed her clothes with an unself-conscious ease that always astonished Zen. Most women he'd known preferred to undress in private, or in the intimacy of an embrace. But Tania pulled off her jeans, tights, and panties like a child going swimming, revealing her long-legged beauty, and then pulled back the covers of the bed and lay down half-covered while Zen was still taking off his jacket. Her straightforwardness made it easy for him, too. His doubts and anxieties dropped away with his clothes. As he slipped between the cool sheets and grasped Tania's warm, silky-smooth flesh, he reflected that there was a lot to be said for the human body, despite everything.

"What's that?" Tania asked some time later, raising her head above the covers.

Zen raised his head and listened. The silent dimness of the bedroom had been infiltrated by an electronic tone, muffled but just audible, coming in regular, incessant bursts.

"Sounds like an alarm."

Tania raised herself up on one elbow.

"Mine's one of the old ones, with a bell."

They lay side by side, the hairs on their forearms just touching. The noise continued relentlessly. Eventually Tania sat up like a cat, flexing her back, and crawled to the end of the bed.

"It seems to be coming from your jacket, Aurelio."

Zen pulled the covers over his head and gave vent to a loud series of blasphemies in Venetian dialect.

"Your position here is essentially—indeed, necessarily—anomalous. You are required to serve two masters, an undertaking not only fraught with perils and contradictions of all kinds, but one that is, as you may perhaps recall, explicitly condemned by the Scriptures."

Juan Ramòn Sànchez-Valdès, archbishop *in partibus infidelium* and deputy to the Cardinal Secretary of State, favored Aurelio Zen with an arch smile.

"One might equally well argue, however," he continued, "that the case is exactly the opposite, and that so far from serving two masters, you are in fact serving neither. As a functionary of the Italian Republic, you have no *locus standi* beyond the frontiers of that state. Neither, clearly, are you formally empowered to act as an agent of either the Vatican City State or the Holy See."

Zen raised his hand to his mouth, resting his chin on the curved thumb. He sniffed his fingers, still redolent of Tania's vagina.

"Yet here I am."

"Here you are," the archbishop agreed. "Despite all indications to the contrary."

And just my luck, too, thought Zen sourly. Like every other Criminalpol official, he had to take his turn on the night-duty roster, on call if the need should arise. In Zen's case it never had, which is why he hadn't at first recognized the electronic pager that had sounded while he and Tania were in bed. He shifted in his elegant but uncomfortable seat. The dull ache of unachieved coition made his testicles ache, a common enough sensation in his adolescence but lately only a memory. Tania had said she'd wait up for him, but it remained to be seen when— or even whether—he would be able to return to the flat.

On phoning in, he'd been told to report to the Polizia dello Stato command post in St. Peter's Square. The telephonist he spoke to was reading a dictated message and could not elaborate. The taxi had dropped him at the edge of the square, and he walked around the curve of Bernini's great colonnade to the P.S. post. As part of the Vatican City State, St. Peter's Square is theoretically off-limits to the Italian police, but in practice their help in patrolling it is appreciated by the overstretched Vigilanza. But this is strictly the small change of police work, concerned above all with the pickpockets and the "scourers," men who infiltrate themselves into the crowds attending papal appearances with the aim of touching up as many distracted females as possible. Contacts between the Vatican security force and the police's antiterrorist DIGOS squad, set up in the wake of the shooting of Pope John Paul II, were conducted at a quite different level.

The patrolman on duty called a number in the Vatican and announced Zen's arrival. He then waited a few minutes for a return call, before escorting Zen to an enormous pair of bronze doors nearby, where two Swiss Guards in ceremonial uniforms stood clutching halberds. Between them stood a thin man with a face like a hatchet, wearing a black cassock and steel-rimmed glasses, who introduced himself as Monsignor Enrico Lamboglia. He inspected Zen's identification, dismissed the patrolman, and led his visitor along a seemingly interminable corridor, up a set of stairs leading off to the right, and through a sequence of galleried corridors to a conference room on the third floor of the Apostolic Palace, where he was ushered into the presence of Archbishop Juan Ramòn Sànchez-Valdès.

The deputy cardinal secretary of state was short and stout, with a face that seemed too large to fit his skull, and had thus spilled over at the edges in an abundance of domed forehead, drooping jowls, and double chins. His dull green eyes, exposed by the flight of flesh toward the periphery of the face, were large and prominent, giving him an air of slightly scandalized astonishment. He was wearing cheap gray slacks, a dark green pullover with leather patches on the elbows, and an open-necked shirt. This casual dress, however, did not detract from the formidable air of authority and competence he radiated as he reclined in a red velvet armchair, his right arm resting on an antique table whose highly polished surface was bare except for a white telephone. The hatchet-faced cleric who had escorted Zen stood slightly behind and to one side of the archbishop's chair, his head lowered and his hands interlocked on his chest as though in prayer. On the other side of the Oriental rug, which covered the center of the lustrous marble floor, Zen sat on a long sofa flanking one wall. Three dark canvases depicting miracles and martyrdoms hung opposite. At the end of the room was a floor-length window, covered by lace curtaining and framed by heavy red velvet drapes.

"However, let us leave the vexed issue of your precise status, and move on to the matter in hand."

Several decades in the Curia had erased almost all traces of Sànchez-Valdès's Latin American Spanish. He fixed Zen with his glaucous, hypnotic gaze.

"As you may have gathered, there was a suicide in St. Peter's this afternoon. Someone threw himself off the gallery inside the dome. Such incidents are quite common, and do not normally require the attention of this department. In the present instance, however, the deceased was not some jilted maidservant or ruined shopkeeper, but Prince Ludovico Ruspanti."

The archbishop looked significantly at Zen, who raised one eyebrow.

"Of course, the Ruspantis are no longer the power they were a few hundred years ago," Sànchez-Valdès continued, "or for that matter when the old prince, Filippo, was alive. Nevertheless, the name still counts for something, and no family, much less an eminent one, likes having a *felo de se* among its members. The remaining members of the clan can therefore be expected to throw their not inconsiderable weight into a concerted effort to discredit the suicide verdict. They have already issued a statement claiming that Ruspanti suffered from vertigo, and that even if he had decided to end his life, it is therefore inconceivable that he should have chosen to do so in such a way."

The middle finger of Sànchez-Valdès's right hand, adorned by a heavy silver ring, tapped the tabletop emphatically.

"To make matters worse, Ruspanti's name has of course been in the news recently as a result of these allegations of currency fraud. To be perfectly honest, I never really managed to master the ins and outs of the affair, but I know enough about the way the press operates to anticipate the kind of malicious allegations to which this is certain to give rise. We may confidently expect suggestions, more or less explicit, to the effect that from the point of view of certain people, who must of course remain nameless, Ruspanti's death could hardly have been more convenient or better timed, et cetera, et cetera. Do you see?"

Zen nodded. Sànchez-Valdès shook his head and sighed.

"The fact is, Dottore, that for a variety of reasons that we have no time to analyze now, this little city-state, whose sole object is to facilitate the spiritual work of the Holy Father, is the object of an inordinate degree of morbid fascination on the part of the general public. People seem to believe that we are a medieval relic that has survived intact into the twentieth century, rife with secrecy, skulduggery, and intrigue, at once sinister and colorful. Since such a Vatican doesn't in fact exist, they invent it. You saw the results when poor Luciani died after only thirty days as Pope. Admittedly, the announcement was badly handled. Everyone was shocked by what had happened, and there were inevitably delays and conflicting stories. As a result, we are still plagued by the most appalling and offensive rumors, to the effect that John Paul I was poisoned or suffocated by members of his household, and the crime covered up.

"Now a prince is not a pope, and Ludovico Ruspanti no Albino Luciani. Nevertheless, we have learned our lesson the hard way. This time we're determined to leave nothing to chance. That is why you've been invited to give us the benefit of your expert opinion, Dottore. Since Ruspanti died on Vatican soil, we are under no *legal* obligation to consult anyone whatsoever. In the circumstances, however, and so as to leave no room for doubt in anyone's mind, we have voluntarily decided to ask an independent investigator to review the facts and confirm that there were no suspicious circumstances surrounding this tragic event."

Zen glanced at his watch.

"There's no need for that, Your Excellency."

Sànchez-Valdès frowned.

"I beg your pardon?"

Zen leaned forward confidentially.

"I'm from Venice, just like Papa Luciani. If the Church says that this man committed suicide, that's good enough for me."

The archbishop glanced up at Monsignor Lamboglia. He laughed uneasily.

"Well!"

Zen beamed a reassuring smile.

"Tell the press anything you like. I'll back you up."

The archbishop laughed again.

"This is good to hear, my son. Very good indeed. If only there were more like you! But these days, alas, the Church is surrounded by enemies. We cannot be too careful. So although I applaud your attitude of unquestioning obedience, I fear that we need more than just a rubber-stamped *nihil obstat.*"

Sànchez-Valdès rose to his feet and walked over to stand in front of Zen.

"I shall introduce you to one of our security officers," he continued quietly. "He was at the scene and will be able to tell you anything you wish to know. After that you are on your own. Inspect, investigate, interrogate, take whatever action you may consider necessary. There is no need for you to consult me or my colleagues."

He stared intently at Zen.

"In fact, it is imperative that you do not do so."

Zen looked him in the eye.

"So as to preserve my independent status, you mean?"

The archbishop smiled and nodded.

"Precisely. Any suspicion of collusion between us would vitiate the very effect we are trying to produce. Do whatever you need to do, whatever must be done to achieve the desired result. I have been assured by your superiors that you are an extremely capable and experienced operative."

He turned to Monsignor Lamboglia.

"Fetch Grimaldi in."

On the wall of the antechamber in which Giovanni Grimaldi had been kept waiting for the best part of two hours hung a large, murky canvas. It depicted a number of armed figures doing something extremely unpleasant to a male nude in the foreground, while a group of oldsters with halos looked on with expressions of complacent detachment from the safety of a passing cloud. Closer inspection revealed that the prospective martyr was being torn apart by teams of yoked buffalos. Grimaldi winced sympathetically. He knew exactly how the poor bastard felt.

His initial reaction to what had happened was one of straightforward panic. He had been entrusted with a job whose delicacy and importance had been repeatedly stressed. It was a chance to prove himself once and for all, to make his mark as a responsible and trustworthy operative. And he had blown it. If only he hadn't allowed himself to be distracted by that man with the gold chain, the flashy watch, and the nasal accent who had apparently become detached from the *Comunione e Liberazione* sight-seeing group that had passed through a few minutes earlier. The man had approached Grimaldi as he stood at the rail of the external balcony at the very top of St. Peter's, apparently absorbed in the stupendous view, and fired off an endless series of questions about where the Spanish Steps were and which hill was the Aventine and whether you could see the Coliseum from there. Grimaldi had known he had better things to do than play the tourist guide, but his pride in knowing Rome so well, being able to identify each of its significant monuments, had been too great. It was such a thrill to point out the principal attractions of the Eternal City with languid, confident gestures, as though he were the hereditary landlord!

Besides, his quarry was in plain view, standing by the railing a little farther along the balcony, chatting up that classy number with the white silk head scarf who had been all alone on the balcony when they arrived. Grimaldi didn't blame him! He might have had a go himself if he hadn't been on duty. Not that he'd have stood a chance. It looked like she might well go for the prince, though. They were standing very close together, and their conversation looked unusually animated for two people who had only just met. Meanwhile, he was stuck with this northerner and his dumb questions. "And is that the Quirinale Palace?" he whined, pointing out the Castel Sant'Angelo.

The next time Grimaldi had looked across to the other side of the balcony, the prince and his pickup had disappeared. Abandoning the inquisitive tourist in midsentence, he clattered down the steel ladder leading to the precipitous stairway, crazily slanted and curved like a passage in a nightmare, which led down to the roof of the basilica. The cupola was riddled with such corridors and stairs, but most had been sealed off, and those open to the public were clearly signposted so as to send the flood of visitors on their way with the minimum of delay or confusion. There was nowhere to get lost, nowhere to hide. Minutes after leaving the lantern, Grimaldi was down in the nave of St. Peter's, and knew that he had lost the man he had been given strict orders to keep in view at all costs.

It was clear what had happened. The whole thing had been carefully set up. While the Vigilanza man's attention was distracted by the supposed *Comunione e Liberazione* truant, Ruspanti had been whisked away by his female companion. They could be anywhere by now. Grimaldi wandered disconsolately around the basilica, where preparations for the evening Mass were in progress. He was merely postponing the moment when he would have to report back to headquarters and reveal his failure. Then he caught sight of the woman in the gray tweed coat and white silk head scarf, and began to feel that everything might turn out all right after all. When the man in the suede jacket turned up a few minutes later, he felt sure of it. The two did not look at each other, but they were aware of each other's presence. They were a unit, a team. Only Ruspanti was still missing, but Grimaldi now had no doubt that the prince would also reappear in due course.

And indeed he *had,* although not in quite the manner the Vigilanza man had imagined. It certainly wasn't the perfect outcome, from his point of view, but on the other hand it could certainly have been worse. Rather than going on bended knees to Luigi Scarpione, his boss, and admitting he had fallen for a trick that shouldn't have fooled an untrained rookie, he had found himself summoned to the Secretariat of State, no less, in the Apostolic Palace itself, next door to the pope's private quarters, a *sanctum sanctorum* guarded by a handpicked elite of the Swiss Guards, where the riffraff of the Vigilanza were not normally permitted to set foot. Not only had he set foot there, he'd actually met the legendary Sànchez-Valdès face to face.

Normally, the special security unit to which Grimaldi belonged liaised with the Curia through the archbishop's secretary, Lamboglia, a cold and charmless man who received minions in his anonymous office in an obscure building off Via del Belvedere, in the Sant'Anna district. The clergy might need the likes of Grimaldi to do their dirty business, but that didn't give him entry to a society which had almost as little time for laymen as for women. However, the implications of Ruspanti's death were so dramatic that this caste system had been temporarily suspended, and on this occasion Grimaldi was received not just by Lamboglia but by Juan Ramòn Sànchez-Valdès himself. By all accounts, it was this Latin American who more or less ran the domestic side of the Holy See's affairs, leaving His Eminence the Cardinal Secretary of State at liberty to devote himself to the complexities of foreign policy.

Unfortunately, Grimaldi was unable to savor this exceptional honor as fully as it deserved, since he was preoccupied with the delicate question of deciding exactly how much of the truth to reveal. The aim was no longer simply to disguise his own incompetence. There was more at stake than that. Once the initial shock of the horror he had witnessed had worn off, Grimaldi had dimly begun to perceive possibilities of personal advantage, which took precedence even over his innate desire to impress his superiors. He wasn't quite sure whether he was going to exploit them, never mind how, but in the meantime he wanted to keep all his options open, and that meant not giving too much away.

In the event, his performance seemed to have gone down quite well. Sànchez-Valdès had accepted that Grimaldi's inability to keep track of Ruspanti's movements had been due to circumstances beyond his control, namely the press of tourists in the dome of St. Peter's that day. No attempt had been made to reprimand or punish him. Grimaldi was just congratulating himself on his success, when he was called back from the antechamber where he had been sent to kick his heels and introduced to a newcomer, a man he had never seen before. Slightly taller even than Lamboglia, he had fine, slightly wavy hair and a face stretched as tautly over its bones as a drum. His angular nose and square, protuberant chin might have looked strong, but the mouth was weak and indecisive, as were the opaque gray eyes. Or so Grimaldi thought, until they turned toward him. It only lasted a moment, but he felt as though he had never been looked at before.

"This is Dottor Aurelio Zen, a specialist investigator dispatched by the Italian authorities in response to an urgent request conveyed by the Apostolic Nuncio," Sànchez-Valdès announced. "He is lending us the benefit of his experience and expertise to ensure that no possible doubt remains concerning this tragic event. You are to accompany him wherever he wishes to go and to see that he is accorded total cooperation in carrying out his duties."

Zen shook hands with Sànchez-Valdès, and was accompanied to the door accompanied by Monsignor Lamboglia. Grimaldi was about to follow when the archbishop called him back.

"You need say nothing about the other business," he murmured *sotto voce*.

"The surveillance?"

Sànchez-Valdès nodded.

"Or the whereabouts of the deceased prior to today's events. As far as our guest is concerned, Ruspanti appeared from nowhere to obliterate himself on the floor of St. Peter's. *Descendit de caelis,* as you might say."

Grimaldi blushed, shocked by the levity of the reference. The archbishop flapped his right hand rapidly, urging him to join the others.

Lamboglia led Zen and Grimaldi from the Apostolic Palace by a circuitous route that brought them out directly in St. Peter's. In the nave, workmen were shifting benches into position in readiness for Saturday's papal Mass, but the area beyond the crossing was still sealed off by plastic tape and patrolled by two uniformed Vigilanza officials.

"I look forward to hearing from you," Lamboglia told Zen, and strode off. After a brief word with the uniformed guards, Grimaldi led Zen over the tape and around the baldachin. The body had been covered in a tarpaulin borrowed from the *sampietrini,* the workers responsible for maintaining the fabric of St. Peter's. Once the identity of the illustrious corpse had been established, the ambulance men from Santo Spirito hospital and the cleaning crew had been hurriedly dismissed until further notice. No one was to approach the body and nothing was to be removed or otherwise disturbed without an explicit order to that effect from the office of the Cardinal Secretary of State.

Grimaldi looked away as Zen lifted the tarpaulin to view the tangle of broken bone, unsupported flesh, and extruded innards that constituted the remains of Prince Ludovico Ruspanti. *He* certainly didn't appear to be bothered by such things, Grimaldi noted, risking a quick glimpse. Indeed, he seemed almost indecently unimpressed, this hotshot from the Interior Ministry, squatting over the corpse like a child over a box of hand-me-down toys, lifting the odd item that looked as though it might be of interest, bending down to sniff the blood-drenched clothing and inspect the victim's shoes.

"Looks like he thought about slashing his wrists first," Zen murmured, indicating the thin red weals on the victim's wrists. Deliberately unfocusing his eyes, Grimaldi turned his head toward the horror.

"Preliminary cuts," Zen explained. "But he didn't have the nerve to go through with it, so he decided to jump instead."

Grimaldi nodded, though he could see nothing but a merciful blur.

"We're going to have to do something about these shoes," added Zen.

The offending items, cheap brown suede slip-ons with an elastic vent, stood side by side on the marble flooring. Both were spotlessly clean, as was the stocking covering the victim's left foot. The other sock was covered in rust-red bloodstains.

Grimaldi was on the point of saying something, but then he remembered that the shoes had been Scarpione's idea. The Vigilanza boss had appeared at the scene before any of the clerics could get there. "Save trouble all around," he'd said, giving the necessary orders. Apparently he'd been wrong, but Grimaldi knew better than to get involved.

"What about them?" he asked.

Zen looked at him sharply, then shrugged.

"Very well, I'll raise it with Monsignor Lamboglia."

The lift had been shut down for the night, so they had to walk all the way up to the roof of the basilica. They climbed the shallow steps of the spiral staircase in silence. Zen had no small talk, and Grimaldi had decided to volunteer no information. This hotshot from the Interior Ministry, despite his lethargic manner, might not be as easy to fool as Archbishop Sànchez-Valdès.

They found Antonio Cecchi, chief of the *sampietrini* maintenance men, in one of a cluster of sheds and workshops perched on the undulating roof of the basilica like a lost corner of old Rome. Cecchi was a compact, muscular man of about fifty with the face of a gargoyle: thin, splayed ears protruding prominently from a bulbous skull topped by a shock of short wavy hair like white flames. Grimaldi explained the situation. With a sigh, Cecchi picked up a torch and led them up a short flight of steps on the outside of the dome. As they waited for Cecchi to find the right key on the huge bunch he produced from the pouch of his blue overalls, Zen studied a large crack in the wall. A number of marble strips had been bridged across it to keep track of its progress, the earliest being dated August 1835. He was not reassured to note that all the telltales were broken.

Inside the door, a ramp led up to a door opening onto the internal gallery at the base of the drum. The roof outside gave such a strong illusion of being at ground level, with its alleys and piazzas, its washing lines and open casements, that it was a shock to realize just how high up they were. Zen peered through the safety fence at the patterned marble floor over a hundred and fifty feet below. The fence ran inside the original railings, all the way from the floor to a point higher than Zen's head, closing off the half of the gallery that was open to the public.

"This is supposed to stop jumpers," Cecchi explained, shaking the mesh with his powerful fingers.

"This one went off the other side," put in Grimaldi.

He pointed across the circular abyss to a door set in the wall of the drum opposite, giving onto a section of the gallery that was not open to the public, and hence was protected only by the original railings.

"The stairs leading down from the top of the dome pass by that door," Grimaldi explained. "The door's kept locked, but he somehow got hold of a key."

Zen frowned.

"But he would have been seen by anyone standing over here."

"The dome was closed by then. This part of the gallery would have been shut and locked. Only the exit was still open."

Zen nodded.

"Sounds all right. Let's have a look around the other side."

Cecchi led the way along a corridor that ran around the circumference of the dome in a series of curved ramps. When they reached the doorway corresponding to the one by which they had left the gallery on the other side, the building superintendent again produced his keys and unlocked the door. Zen pushed past him and stepped out onto the open section of the gallery. The finger he wiped along the top of the railing came away covered in dust.

"They don't bother cleaning here," Cecchi remarked. "No call for it."

Halfway between the gallery and the floor, the roof of the baldachin rose up toward them, surmounted by a massive gold cross. Bernini had not envisaged his showpiece being seen from this angle, and it had an awkward, clumsy look, like an actress glimpsed backstage without her costume or makeup. Immediately underneath the gallery ran a wide

strip of gold, like an enormous hatband, with a legend in blue capitals:
TV ES PETRVS ET SVPER HANC PETRAM AEDIFICABO ECCLESIAM MEAM. The air
was filled with a sonorous squealing as the staff, far below in the body of
the nave, maneuvered the heavy wooden benches into place for the
papal Mass. It reminded Zen of the sirens of fog-bound shipping in the
Venetian lagoons.

Telling Cecchi and Grimaldi to wait, he walked around this semicircular section of the gallery, inspecting the railing and floor carefully.
He sighed heavily and consulted his watch. Then he leaned over the
railing, looking up at the sixteen frescoed segments into which the
interior of the dome was divided. Beneath each segment was a huge
rectangular window consisting of thirty enormous panes, like a mon-
strous enlargement of an ordinary casement. The glass was dark and
glossy, reflecting back the glare of the floodlights that Cecchi had
turned on as they entered the dome. Each pair of windows was separated by a double pilaster whose cornices supported a ledge topped with
what looked like railings.

Zen walked back to the waiting Vatican employees.

"Is there another gallery up there?" he asked.

Cecchi nodded.

"It's locked, though."

"So was this one."

"He had a *key* to this one," said Grimaldi, as though explaining
the obvious to a child.

Zen nodded.

"I'd like to have a look at the upper gallery, if that's possible."

Cecchi sighed heavily.

"It's possible, but what's the point? There's nothing to see."

"That's what I want to make sure of," Zen replied.

On the landing outside, two doorways faced one another. The one
on the right was the lighted public way leading down from the lantern.
Cecchi turned to the other, a locked wooden door. After searching
through his keys for some time, he opened it, revealing yet another
ramp curving upward into darkness. He switched on his torch and
strode away, Grimaldi and Zen following as best they could through the
dank, airless darkness. The ramp ended at a narrow spiral staircase bored
through the stonework between the gargantuan windows. At the top,

another door gave access to another gallery in the floodlit interior of the dome, sixty feet above the lower one.

Zen looked over the railing at the vertiginous prospect below. From here, the tarpaulin was a mere scrap of blue. Again he told Grimaldi and Cecchi to wait while he walked slowly around the ledge, running his finger along the top of the railing and examining the floor. He had gone about a quarter of the way around when abruptly he stopped dead. He glanced back at the other two men. They were standing near the door, chatting quietly together. Zen bent down beside the object that had caught his attention. It was a black brogue shoe, resting on its side between two of the metal stanchions supporting the railing. The toe, its polish badly scuffed, protruded several inches over the void.

A moment later he noticed the twine. Thin, colorless, almost invisible, it was tied to one of the stanchions against which the shoe rested. The other end dangled over the edge of the gallery. Zen pulled it in. There were several yards of it. He got out his lighter and burned through the twine near the knot securing it to the metal post. Straightening up again, he stuffed the twine into his pocket with the plastic bag in which the perfume had been wrapped.

Looking over the railing, he studied the scene below. The workmen were still shifting benches farther down the nave, but the area below was deserted. With a gentle kick, Zen eased the black shoe off the edge of the gallery and watched it tumble end over end until he could make it out no longer. Whatever sound it made as it hit the floor of the basilica was lost in the squealing and honking of the benches. Rubbing his hands briskly together, Zen completed his circuit of the gallery, returning to the spot by the door where Grimaldi and Cecchi were in conversation.

"Quite right," he told the building superintendent. "There's nothing to see."

Cecchi sniffed a "told you so." Zen tapped Grimaldi's two-way radio.

"Does this thing work up here?"

"Of course."

"Then get hold of Lamboglia and tell him to meet me by the body in ten minutes."

He glanced at his watch again.

"And then call a taxi to the Porta Sant'Anna," he added.

When Zen and Grimaldi emerged into the amplitude of the basilica, like wood lice creeping out of the skirting of a ballroom, Monsignor Lamboglia was waiting for them. Zen regretted not having paid much attention to Sànchez-Valdès's secretary earlier, since it meant dealing with an unknown quantity at this crucial juncture. If he played it smart, he could be back in bed with Tania in half an hour. He therefore studied the cleric as he approached, trying to gather clues as to how best to handle him. Lamboglia's gaunt, craggy face, a mask of gloomy disapproval that looked as though it had been rough-hewn from granite, gave nothing away. But the rapid tapping of his fingers and the darting, censorious eyes betrayed the testy perfectionist who loved catching inferiors out and taxing them with inconsequential faults. It was this that gave Zen his opening.

"Well?" demanded Lamboglia brusquely, having dismissed Grimaldi with a curt wave of the hand.

Zen shrugged.

"More or less, yes. Apart from the business of the shoes, of course."

Lamboglia's lips twisted in disapproval and his eyes narrowed.

"Shoes? What do you mean?"

Zen pulled the edge of the tarpaulin back, exposing the victim's feet and the brown suede slip-ons.

"The archbishop said you people had learned a thing or two from the way Papa Luciani's death was handled," he remarked contemptuously. "You wouldn't know, judging by this sort of thing."

By now Lamboglia looked apoplectic. For an instant, Zen caught a glimpse of the little boy, desperate to please, yet finding himself unjustly accused, fighting to restrain the tears, the panicky sense that the universe made no sense. The boy was long gone, but the strategies he had worked out in his misery still determined the behavior of the man.

"If you have noticed anything amiss," the cleric snapped, "then kindly inform me what it is without further prevarication."

Zen handed him one of the shoes.

"For a start, these shoes have only ever been worn by a corpse. Moreover they are mass produced items totally out of keeping with the quality of the victim's other garments. On top of that, they're *brown*. A man like this wouldn't be seen dead—to coin a phrase—wearing brown shoes with a blue suit. And finally, the stocking on the right foot is stained with blood all the way down to the toe, and must therefore have been uncovered when the body struck the ground."

After inspecting the shoe carefully, Monsignor Lamboglia nodded. His panic was subsiding, converting itself to a cold anger that would eventually be discharged on the appropriate target.

"And what conclusion do you draw from these observations?" he demanded challengingly.

Zen shrugged.

"You'd need to interrogate your staff to find out exactly what happened. My guess is that when the body was discovered, one of the shoes was missing. Some bright spark realized that this might look suspicious, and since they couldn't find the missing shoe, a different pair was substituted. But people are superstitious about letting their shoes be worn by a dead man, so they used a new pair. Result, an amateurish botch job calculated to arouse exactly the sort of suspicions it was meant to allay."

Lamboglia measured Zen with a cold glare. It was one thing for *him* to criticize his underlings—and whoever was responsible for this was going to wish he had never been conceived—but that did not mean that he was prepared to condone gratuitous insults from outsiders.

"Nevertheless," he pointed out, "the problem remains that no one's going to be prepared to believe that Ruspanti walked up to the dome with one shoe off and one shoe on."

Zen nodded slowly, as if recalling something.

"Ah yes, the shoe."

Walking over to the benches of pews lined up in the north transept, he walked along them until he saw the missing black brogue. He picked it up and walked back to Lamboglia.

"Here you are."

Lamboglia turned the shoe over as though it were a property in a magic trick.

"What was it doing there?" he demanded.

"It must have gotten pulled off as Ruspanti clambered over the railings. Perhaps he changed his mind at the last minute and tried to climb back."

Lamboglia thought about this for a moment.

"I suppose so," he said.

"There are no further problems as far as I can see," Zen told him briskly. "But you can of course contact me through the ministry, should the need arise."

Lamboglia glared at him. Although the man's behavior couldn't be faulted professionally, his breezy, offhand manner left a lot to be desired. Lamboglia would dearly have loved to take him down a peg or two, to make him sweat. But as things stood there was nothing he could do except give him the sour look his subordinates so dreaded.

"Are you in a hurry, Dottore?" he snapped.

"I have a taxi waiting."

Lamboglia's glare intensified.

"Another appointment? You're a busy man."

Zen looked at the cleric, and smiled.

"No, I'm just in a hurry to get to bed."

TWO

On the face of it, the scene at the Ministry of the Interior the
following Tuesday morning was calculated to gladden the hearts
of all those who despaired of the grotesque overmanning and
underachievement of the government bureaucracy, a number
roughly equal to those who had failed to secure a cushy *statale* post of
their own. Not only were a significant minority of the staff at their
desks, but the atmosphere was one of intense and animated activity. The
only snag was that little or none of this activity had anything to do with
the duties of the ministry.

In the ministerial suite on the top floor, where the present incum-
bent and his coterie of undersecretaries presided, the imminent collapse
of the present government coalition had prompted a frantic round of
consultations, negotiations, threats, and promises as potential contenders
jockeyed for position. On the lower floors, unruffled by this *aria di crisi,*
it was business as usual. The range of services on offer included a fax
bureau, an agency for Filippino maids, two competing protection rackets, a Kawasaki motorcycle franchise, a video rental club, a travel agent,
and a citywide courier service, to say nothing of Madam Beta, medium,
astrologer, sorcerer, cards, and palms read, the evil eye averted, talismans
and amulets prepared. One of the most flourishing of these enterprises
was situated in the Administration section on the ground floor, where

Tania Biacis ran an agency that supplied specialty food items from her native Friuli region.

Tania had got the idea from one of her cousins, who had returned from a honeymoon trip to London with the news that Italian food was now as much in demand in the English capital as Italian fashion, "only nothing from our poor Friuli, as usual!" At the time this had struck Tania as little more than the usual provincial whining, all too characteristic of a border region acutely aware of its distance from the twin centers of power in Rome and Milan. It had been the energies released by the breakup of her marriage that had finally driven her to do something about it. Claiming some of the leave due to her, she had traveled to London with a suitcase full of samples rounded up by Aldo, the husband of her cousin Bettina, whose job with the post office at Cividale gave him ample opportunity for getting out and about and meeting local farmers.

Posing as a representative, Tania had visited the major British wholesalers and tried to convince them of the virtues of Friuli ham, wine, honey, jam, and grappa. Rather to her surprise, several had placed orders, in one case so large that Aldo had the greatest difficulty in meeting it. Since then, the business had grown by leaps and bounds. Aldo and Bettina looked after the supply side, while Tania handled the orders and paperwork, using the Ministry's telephones and fax facilities to keep in contact with the major European cities, as well as New York and Tokyo. One of Agrofrul's greatest successes was a line of jams originally made by Bettina's aunt; this had now been expanded into a cottage industry involving several hundred women. Genuine Friuli grappa, made in small copper stills, had also done well, while the company's air-cured hams were rapidly displacing their too famous rivals from Parma as the ultimate designer charcuterie.

Tania had told Aurelio nothing of all this. Her nominal reason for reticence was that he was a senior Ministry official, and although everyone knew perfectly well what went on in the way of moonlighting, scams, and general private enterprise, she didn't want to compromise her lover by making him a party to activities that were theoretically punishable by instant dismissal, loss of pension rights, and even a prison sentence. Tania was pretty sure that no one would throw the book at *her.* The rules were never enforced on principle, only as a result of someone's personal schemes for advancement or revenge, and she simply wasn't important enough to attract that kind of negative compliment. Moreover, as a result of her six years' service in the Administration section, she was now privy to most of her colleagues' dirty little secrets, which in itself would make any potential whistle-blower think twice.

Aurelio's situation was quite different. By nature a loner, his reputation damaged by a mistaken fit of zealousness at the time of the Moro affair, he was promoted to the Ministry's elite Criminalpol squad as a result of an unsavory deal during his comeback case in Perugia, and had subsequently been connected with a heavily compromised political party at the time of the Burolo affair. As a result, Zen was surrounded by enemies who would like nothing better than to implicate him in a case involving misuse of bureaucratic resources and conspiracy to defraud the state, not to mention a little matter of undeclared taxes amounting to several billion lire.

The fact that they were lovers would just make the whole scandal even more juicy, but it also explained Tania's unadmitted reason for not telling Aurelio about the success of Agrofrul. She was well aware that the story he had told her about the flat was not true. It supposedly belonged to an American who was out of the country on business for a few months and was happy to have someone looking after the place, but this was clearly nonsense. Where were this American's belongings? Why did he never get any mail? Above all, why had he handed it over free of charge to the friend of a friend, a person he'd never even met, when he could have sublet it for a small fortune? Flats as gorgeous as that, in such a sought after district, didn't just fall into your lap free of charge. Someone was paying for it, and in the present case that someone could only be Aurelio Zen.

This put Tania in an awkward position. Eight years of marriage to Mauro Bevilacqua had left her with no illusions about the fragility of the male ego, or the destructive passions that can be unleashed without the slightest warning when it feels slighted. She knew that Zen had already been hurt by her refusal to move in with him, and she guessed his belief that he was supporting her financially might well be the necessary salve for this wound. He could accept Tania's independence as long as he was secretly subsidizing it, as long as he believed that she was only *playing* at being free. But how would he react if he learned that his mistress was in fact the senior partner in a business with a turnover that already exceeded his salary by a considerable amount? She had no wish to lose him, this strange, moody individual who could be so passionately there one moment, so transparently distant the next, who seemed to float through life as though he had nothing to hope or fear from it. She wanted to know him, if anyone could, and to be known in return. But not possessed. No one would ever own her again, about that she was quite adamant.

She pulled the phone over, got an outside line, and dialed a restaurant in Stockholm's business district where a brambly *refosco* made by a relative of Aldo's sister had become a cult wine. The distributor who had been importing Agrofrul's produce had recently gone bankrupt and the restaurant now wanted to know if they could obtain supplies direct. Using her limited but serviceable English, Tania ascertained that the proprietor had not yet arrived but would call back. She lit a cigarette and turned her attention to the newspaper open on the desk in front of her, which was making great play with allegations of a cover-up in the death of a Roman nobleman in the Vatican.

Tania turned the page impatiently. She had no appetite for such things any more, the grand scandals that ran and ran for years, as though manipulated by a master storyteller who was always ready with some fresh "revelation" whenever the public interest started to wane. The one thing you could be sure of, the only absolute certainty on offer, was that you would never, ever, know the truth. Whatever you did know was therefore by definition not the truth. Like children playing "pass the parcel," the commentators and analysts tried to guess the nature of the mystery by examining the size, shape, and weight of the package in which it had been concealed. But the adult game was even more futile, for once the wrappings had all been removed the parcel usually proved to be empty.

The shrilling of the phone interrupted her thoughts. Pulling over the rough jotting of proposals she had prepared for the Swedish restaurateur, Tania lifted the receiver.

"Good morning," she said in her best English.

"Who the hell is this?"

The speaker was male, Italian, and very angry. Tania immediately depressed the rest with her finger, breaking the connection. A moment later the phone rang again. She let it go on for some time before lifting her finger and snarling "Yes?" in her best bureaucratic manner, bored and truculent.

"Is that Biacis?" demanded the same male voice.

"Who do you think, the Virgin Mary?"

There was a furious spluttering.

"Don't you dare talk like that to me!"

"And how am I supposed to know how I should talk when you haven't told me who you are?" Tania snapped back.

In fact she knew perfectly well who it was, even before the caller angrily identified himself as Lorenzo Moscati, head of the Criminalpol division. Within the caste system of the Ministry, Moscati was a person of considerable stature, whose relation to a mere Grade II administrative assistant such as Tania was roughly that of one of the figures in the higher reaches of a baroque ceiling-piece, almost invisible in the refulgence of his glory, to one of the extras supporting clouds or propping up sunbeams in the bottom left-hand corner. But Tania didn't give a damn. As a successful independent businesswoman, she had no reason to be impressed by some shit-for-brains with the right party card and an influential clique behind him. Even the Russians were finally having second thoughts about the virtues of such a system. Only the Italian state apparatus remained utterly immune to the effects of *glasnost*.

"Zen, Aurelio!" Moscati shouted.

"What about him?"

"Where is he?"

"How should I know? This isn't Personnel."

Moscati's voice modulated to a tone of unctuous viciousness.

"I am aware of that, my dear, but all Ciliani can tell me is that he's off sick. So I called his home number and asked if I could speak to the invalid, only to find that his mother hasn't seen him since yesterday and seems to think he's gone to Florence for work."

"So? What have I to do with it?"

Moscati gave a nasty chuckle.

"To be perfectly honest, I thought he might be holed up at your little love nest in fashionable Parione."

Tania gasped involuntarily. Moscati chuckled again, more confidently now.

"No wonder he needs a day off to recover, poor fellow," he continued in the tone of silken brutality he used with female underlings. "All that night service, and at his age, too. Anyway, that's another matter. The fact is that our Aurelio is deep in the shit, wherever he may be. Have you seen the papers? These allegations are extremely serious, even alarming, but as his colleague I naturally feel a certain solidarity. That's why I'm giving him one last chance to put things right. Have him call me, now."

He hung up. Tania stubbed out her cigarette, which had burned down to the filter, and dialed a Rome number. It rang for some time before a sleepy voice answered.

"Yes?"

"Did I wake you, sweetheart?" she asked gently.

A pleased grunt.

"Not exactly. I've been lying here beside you. The pillow is still shaped by your head, and the sheets smell of you. There's really quite a lot of you still here."

"More than there is here, believe me. Look, I'm sorry to have to be the one to break this to you, but Moscati has been on to me. He's after your blood for some reason."

There was a brief silence.

"Why did he call you?" Zen asked.

He sounded wide awake now.

"He knows, Aurelio."

"He can't!"

The exclamation was as involuntary as a cry of pain.

"I'm afraid he does," said Tania. "And about the flat, too."

A silence. Zen sighed.

"I'm sorry," he muttered almost inaudibly.

"It doesn't make any difference. Not to me, at any rate. You'd better phone him, Aurelio. It sounded urgent."

Another sigh.

"Any other messages?"

Tania leafed through the mail for the Criminalpol department, which she planned to deliver when the pressures of business permitted.

"Just a telegram."

"Let's have it."

Tania tore open the envelope and read the brief typed message.

"It sounds like some loony," she told him.

"What does it say?"

" 'If you wish to get these deaths in the proper perspective, apply at the green gates in the piazza at the end of Via Santa Sabina.' "

He grunted.

"No name?"

"Nothing. Don't go, Aurelio. It could be a nutter."

She sounded nervous, memories of Vasco Spadola's deadly vendetta still fresh in her mind.

"When was it sent?"

"Just after five yesterday afternoon, from Piazza San Silvestro."

He yawned.

"All right. I'd better ring Moscati now."

"What's it all about, Aurelio? He said it was in the papers."

"Well, well. Fame at last."

Tania said nothing.

"I'll ring you later about tonight," he told her. "And don't worry. It's just work, not life and death."

The letters had been faxed from the Vatican City State to the Rome offices of five national newspapers about ten o'clock on Monday evening. The time had been well chosen. The following day's editions were about to "go to bed," while most people in the Vatican had already done so. There was thus no time to follow up the startling allegations the letter contained, still less to get an official reaction from the Vatican Press Office, notoriously reticent and dilatory at the best of times.

The anonymous writer had thoughtfully included a list of the publications to whom he had sent copies of the document. The editors phoned each other. Yes, they'd seen the thing. Well, they were undecided, really. They weren't in the habit of printing unsubstantiated accusations, although these did seem to have a certain ring of authenticity, and if by any chance they were true then of course. . . . Nevertheless, in the end all five agreed it would be wiser to hold back until the whole thing could be properly investigated. Chuckling with glee at their craftiness in securing this exclusive scoop, each then phoned the newsroom to hold the front page. Here was a story that had everything: a colorful and notorious central character, a background rife with financial and political skulduggery, and—best of all—the Vatican connection.

Aurelio Zen read the reports as his taxi crawled through the dense traffic, making so little progress that at times he had the impression they were being carried backward, like a boat with the tide against it. He had bought *La Stampa,* his usual paper, as well as *La Repubblica, Il Corriere della Sera,* and, for a no-holds-barred view, the radical *Il Manifesto.* Each served up the rich and spicy raw materials with varying degrees of emphasis and presentation, but all began with a resume of the affair so far, which inevitably centered on the enigmatic figure of Prince Ludovico Ruspanti, an inveterate gambler and playboy but also a pillar of the establishment and a prominent member of the Knights of Malta. Unlike the vast majority of the Italian aristocracy—most notoriously the so-called "Counts of Ciampino" created by Vittorio Emanuele III before his departure into exile from that airport in 1944—the Ruspantis were no parvenus. The family dated back to the fifteenth century, and had at one time or another counted among its members a score of cardinals, a long succession of Papal Knights, a siege hero flayed alive by the Turks, the victim of a street fray with the Orsini clan, and a particularly gory uxoricide.

After unification and the collapse of the Papal States, one junior member of the Ruspantis had sensed which way the wind was blowing, moved to the newly emergent power center in Milan, and married into the Falcone family of textile magnates. The others remained in Rome, slowly stagnating. Ludovico's father, Filippo, had succumbed to the febrile intoxications of fascism, which had seemed for a time to restore some of the energy and purpose that had been drained from their lives. But this drunken spree was the Ruspantis' final fling. Filippo survived the war and its immediate aftermath, despite his alleged participation in war crimes during the Ethiopian campaign, but the peace slowly destroyed him. The abolition of papal pomp and ritual in the wake of the

Second Vatican Council was the last straw. Prince Filippo took to his bed in the family palazzo on Lungotevere opposite the Villa Farnesina, where he died anathemizing the "anti-Pope," John XXIII, who had delivered the Church into the hands of the Socialists and freemasons. Lorenzo, the elder of Filippo's two sons, had been groomed since birth for the day when he would become prince, but in the event he survived his father by less than a year before his Alfa Romeo was crushed between an overtaking truck and the wall of a motorway tunnel. And thus it was that Ludovico, to whose education and character no one had given a second thought, found himself head of the family at the age of twenty-three.

The young prince appeared at first a reassuring clone of his late brother, doing and saying all the right things. As well as joining such exclusive secular associations as the Chess Club and the Hunting Club, he also put himself forward for admission to the Sovereign Military Order of Malta, like every senior Ruspanti for the previous four hundred years. He hunted hard, gambled often, and busied himself with running the family's agricultural *tenuta* near Palestrina. His political and social opinions were reassuringly predictable, and he expressed no views on the controversial reforms instituted by John XXIII, or indeed on anything else apart from hunting, gambling, and running the aforementioned country estate. The only thing that caused a raised eyebrow among certain ultras was his reconciliation with the family's mercantile relatives in Milan. This event, which most people considered long overdue, unfortunately came too late for the Falcone parents, who had paid the price of their high industrial and financial profile by falling victim to the Red Brigades, but Ludovico went out of his way to cultivate his cousins Raimondo and Ariana—to such an extent, indeed, that malicious tongues accused him of having conceived an unhealthy passion for the latter, a striking girl who had never fully recovered from her parents' death. These improprieties, however, even if such they were, occurred a world away, in the desolate, misty plains of Lombardy. Where it mattered, in the salons of aristocratic Rome, Ludovico's behavior seemed absolutely unexceptionable.

Nevertheless, as the years went by, the family's financial situation gradually began to slide out of control. First, sections of the country estate were sold off, then the whole thing. Palazzo Ruspanti was next to go, although Ludovico managed to retain the *piano nobile* for the use of himself and his mother until she died, when he sold up and moved to rented rooms in the unfashionable Prenestino district. Friends and relations were heard to suggest that marriage to some suitably endowed young lady might prove the answer to these problems. Such things might be a good deal rarer than they had been a hundred years earlier, when a noble title counted for more and people were less bashful about buying into one, but they were by no means unheard of.

Ludovico, though, showed no interest in any of the potential partners who were more or less overtly paraded before him. This indifference naturally added fuel to the rumors concerning his love for Ariana Falcone, whose brother Raimondo had recently and quite unexpectedly achieved fame as a fashion designer. Other versions had it that Ruspanti was gay, or impotent, or had joined that inner circle of the Order of Malta, the thirty "professed" Knights who are sworn to chastity, obedience, and poverty—cynics joked that Ludovico would have no difficulty with the final item, at any rate. Then there was the question of where all the money had gone. Some people said it had been swallowed by the prince's cocaine habit, some that he had paid kidnappers a huge ransom for the return of his and Ariana's love child, while others held that the family fortune had gone to finance an abortive monarchist coup d'état. Even those who repeated the most likely story—that Ludovico's inveterate love of gambling had extended itself to playing the stock market, and that his portfolio had been wiped out when Wall Street collapsed on "Black Monday"—were careful to avoid the charge of credulous banality by suggesting that this was merely a cover for the *real* drama, which involved a doomsday scenario of global dimensions, involving the CIA, Opus Dei, and Gelli's P2, and using the Knights of Malta as a cover.

Thus, when word spread that Ruspanti had taken refuge with the latter organization following his disappearance from circulation about a month earlier, the story was widely credited. The official line was that Ruspanti was wanted for questioning by a magistrate investigating a currency fraud involving businessmen in Milan, but few people were prepared to believe that. Far larger issues were clearly at stake, involving the future of prominent members of the government. This explained why the prince had chosen a hiding place that was beyond the jurisdiction of the Italian authorities. The Sovereign Military Order of Malta had long lost the extensive territories that once made it, together with the Knights Templar, the richest and most powerful medieval order of chivalry, but it is still recognized as an independent state by over forty nations, including Italy. Thus Palazzo Malta, opposite Gucci's in elegant Via Condotti, and the Palace of Rhodes on the Aventine hill, headquarters of the local Grand Priory and chancery of the Order's diplomatic mission to the Holy See, enjoy exactly the same extraterritorial status as any foreign embassy. If the fugitive had taken refuge within the walls of either property, he was as safe from the power of the Italian state as he would have been in Switzerland or Paraguay. Whatever the truth about this, Ruspanti had not been seen again until his dramatic reappearance the previous Friday in the basilica of St. Peter's.

This event initially appeared to render the question of the prince's whereabouts in the interim somewhat academic, but the letter to the newspapers changed all that with its dramatic suggestion that his death might not be quite what it seemed—or rather, what the Vatican authorities had allegedly been at considerable pains to *make* it seem. According to the anonymous correspondent, in short, Ludovico Ruspanti—like Roberto Calvi, Michele Sindona, and so many others illustrious corpses —had been the subject of "an assisted suicide."

The letter made three principal charges. The first confirmed the rumors about Ruspanti having been harbored by the Order of Malta, but added that following his expulsion, which took place after a personal intervention by the Grand Master, the prince had been leading a clandestine existence in the Vatican City State with the full connivance of the Holy See. Moreover, the writer claimed, Ruspanti's movements and contacts during this period had been the subject of a surveillance operation, and the Vatican authorities were thus aware that on the afternoon of his death the prince had met the representatives of an organization referred to as "the Cabal." But the item of most interest to Zen was the last, which stated categorically that the senior Italian police official called in by the Holy See, a certain Dottor Aurelio Zeno, had deliberately falsified the results of his investigation in line with the preconceived verdict of suicide.

Almost the most significant feature of the letter was that no more was said. The implication was that it was addressed not to the general public but to those in the know, the select few who were aware of the existence and nature of "the Cabal." They would grasp not only how and why Ruspanti had met his death, but also the reasons why this information was now being leaked to the press. "In short," *Il Manifesto* concluded, "we once again find ourselves enveloped by sinister and suggestive mysteries, face to face with one of those convenient deaths signed by a designer whose name remains unknown but whose crafts-manship everyone recognizes as bearing the label 'Made in Italy.' "

"This one?"

The taxi had drawn up opposite an unpainted wooden door set in an otherwise blank wall. There was no number, and for a moment Zen hesitated. Then he saw the black Fiat saloon with SCV numberplates parked on the other side of the street, right under a sign reading PARKING STRICTLY FORBIDDEN. It could sit there for the rest of the year without getting a ticket, Zen reflected as he paid off the taxi. Any vehicle bearing *Sacra Città del Vaticano* plates was invisible to the traffic cops.

A metal handle dangled from a chain in a small niche beside the door. Zen gave it a yank. A dull bell clattered briefly, somewhere remote. Nothing happened. He pulled the chain again, then got out a cigarette and put it in his mouth without lighting it. A small metal grille set in the door slid back.

"Yes?" demanded a female voice.

"Signor Bianchi."

Keys jingled, locks turned, bolts were drawn, and the door opened a crack.

"Come in!"

Zen stepped into the soft, musty dimness inside. He just had time to glimpse the speaker, a dumpy nun "of canonical age," to use the Church's euphemism, before the door was slammed shut and locked behind him.

"Follow me."

The nun waddled off along a bare tiled corridor that unexpectedly emerged in a well-tended garden surrounded on three sides by a cloister whose tiled, sloping roof was supported by an arcade of beautifully proportioned arches. Zen's guide opened one of the doors facing the garden.

"Please wait here."

She scuttled off. Zen stepped over the well-scrubbed threshold. The room was long and narrow, with a freakishly high ceiling and a floor of smooth scrubbed stone slabs. It smelled like a disused larder. The one window, small and barred, set in the upper expanses of a bare whitewashed wall, emphasized the sense of enclosure. The furnishings consisted of a trestle table flanked by wooden benches and an acrylic painting showing a young woman reclining in a supine posture while a bleeding heart hovered in the air above her, emitting rays of light that pierced her outstretched palms.

Zen sat heavily on one of the benches. The tabletop was a thick oak board burnished to a sullen gleam. He took the cigarette from his lips and twiddled it between two fingers. It seemed inconceivable that only half an hour earlier he had been lying in a position not unlike that of the female stigmatic in the painting, wondering if it was worth bothering to get out of bed at all given that Tania would be back shortly after two. For no particular reason, he had decided to treat himself to a couple of days sick leave. Like all state employees, Zen regularly availed himself of this perk. A doctor's certificate was only required for more than three days' absence, and as long as you didn't abuse the system too exaggeratedly, everyone turned a blind eye. That was how Zen had known that something was seriously wrong when Tania told him about Moscati checking up on him. When he phoned in, Lorenzo Moscati had left him in no doubt whatever that the shit had hit the fan.

"I don't know how you do it, Zen, I really don't. You take a simple courtesy call, a bit of window dressing, and manage to turn it into a diplomatic incident."

"But I . . ."

"The Apostolic Nuncio has intervened in the very strongest terms, demanding an explanation, and to make matters worse, half the blue-bloods at the Farnesina were fucking *related* to Ruspanti. Result, the Minister finds himself in the hot seat just as the entire government is about to go into the blender and he had his eye on some nice fat portfolio like Finance."

"But I . . ."

"The media are screaming for you to be put on parade, which is all we need. We're saying you're in bed, not with la Biacis but a fever, something nasty and infectious. We've sent Marcelli along to handle the press conference. All you need to do is fiddle a doctor's certificate and then keep out of sight for a day or two. But first get along to Via dell'Annunciata in Trastevere, number 14, and make your peace with the priests. You'd better turn on the charm, Zen—or Bianchi, as they want you to call yourself. Remember how the Inquisition worked? The Church graciously pardoned the erring sinners, and then turned them over to the secular authorities to be burned alive. And that's what's going to happen to you, Zen, unless you can talk your way out of this one."

The implications of this threat could hardly have been more serious. If the Vatican lodged a formal complaint, the Ministry would have no option but to institute a full internal inquiry. The verdict was almost irrelevant, since the severity of the eventual disciplinary proceedings was as nothing compared to the long, slow torment of the inquiry itself, dragging on for month after month, while the subject was ostracized by colleagues wary of being contaminated by contact with a potential pariah.

So gloomy were these speculations that even the arrival of Monsignor Lamboglia was a distinct relief. The cleric was wearing a plain, dark overcoat, a gray scarf, and a homburg hat and carrying a black leather briefcase, and his sharp-featured face looked even grimmer than usual.

"Will that be all?" murmured the elderly nun from the doorway.

Lamboglia scanned the room slowly through his steel-rimmed glasses. He might have been alone for all the sign he gave of having noted Zen's existence. Without turning, he nodded once. The nun backed out, closing the door behind her.

The cleric took off his overcoat, folded it carefully, and laid it beside his hat and briefcase on the table. He opened his briefcase and removed a portable tape recorder, then looked at Zen for the first time since entering the room.

"You may smoke."

Zen twirled the unlit cigarette between his lips.

"Do I get a blindfold as well?"

Lamboglia regarded him like an entomologist confronted by an unfamiliar insect whose characteristics had nothing much to recommend them from a personal point of view, but which would have to be cataloged just the same. He sat down opposite Zen, set the tape recorder on the table midway between them, and pressed the red "record" button.

"Did you send that letter to the papers?" he asked.

Zen gazed at him in shock, then growing anger. He nodded.

"There hasn't been enough aggravation in my life recently. I'd been wondering what to do about it."

It was Lamboglia's turn to get angry.

"So you find this funny, do you?"

"Not at all. I find it *stupid.*"

He fixed Lamboglia with a steady glare.

"Look, if I were crazy enough to risk my career by pointing out irregularities in the conduct of an investigation for which I was responsible, I'd at least have done it properly!"

He tapped the pile of newspapers lying at his elbow.

"This letter is all bluff, a farrago of vague, unsubstantiated generalities. Now I don't know anything about this secret society Ruspanti was apparently involved with, but as far as the manner of his death is concerned there is absolutely no doubt in my mind. I know what happened, and when, and how."

Impressed despite himself by Zen's confident, decisive manner, Lamboglia nodded.

"So there's no truth in these allegations?"

"What allegations?"

Lamboglia tapped the table impatiently.

"That Ruspanti was murdered!"

Zen frowned.

"But of *course* he was murdered!"

The two men gazed at each other in silence for some time.

"You mean you didn't know?" Zen asked incredulously.

Behind the twin disks of glass, Lamboglia's eyes narrowed dangerously.

"What made you think we did?"

"Well, according to the letter, Ruspanti was living in the Vatican and you were keeping him under surveillance."

"But you didn't know that on Friday!"

"It's true, then?" Zen asked quickly.

Lamboglia turned off the tape recorder, rewound the cassette briefly, and pressed "play."

"*. . . keeping him under surveillance.*"

The cleric looked at Zen.

"You were quite right, dottore—your career *is* at risk. Don't try and catch me out again. Just answer my questions."

He pressed the "record" button.

"It is your professional conduct on Friday that is the subject of this inquiry, Dottore. At that time, you had no reason to assume—rightly or wrongly—that we had any idea Ruspanti might have been murdered. The word was never even mentioned in the course of your interview with Archbishop Sànchez-Valdès."

At last, Zen lit his cigarette, then looked around in vain for an ashtray. Irritated by this delay, Lamboglia waved dismissively.

"Use the floor. The nuns will clean it up. That's what nuns are for."

Zen released a breath of fragrant smoke.

"It was precisely the fact that no one mentioned the possibility of murder that I found so significant," he said.

Lamboglia gave a sneering laugh.

"That's absurd."

"On the contrary. I wasn't asked to investigate Ruspanti's death but to confirm that he had committed suicide. When I offered to do so without more ado, as a good Catholic, the archbishop made it quite clear that he wanted more than that. 'Do whatever you need to do,' he told me, 'whatever must be done to achieve the desired result.' "

"Exactly!" cried Lamboglia. "To determine the truth!"

Zen shrugged.

"No one mentioned that word either."

"Because it was taken for *granted!*"

Zen tapped his cigarette, dislodging a length of ash that tumbled through the air to disintegrate on the smooth flagstones.

"Then the members of the Curia are a great deal less subtle than they have been given credit for," he replied.

Lamboglia rapped the table authoritatively.

"Don't be impertinent! You had no right to conceal anything from us."

"Excuse me, Monsignore, but Archbishop Sànchez-Valdès explicitly instructed me to take whatever action I considered necessary without consulting him or his colleagues."

"Yes, but only to avoid compromising your status as an independent observer. No one asked you to cover up a murder!"

Zen tossed the butt of his cigarette under the table and crushed it out.

"Of course not. It would have been impossible for me to do so if I'd been asked openly. That's why murder was never once mentioned, despite the fact that there was no sense in calling me in unless there was a real possibility that Ruspanti had been murdered. By the same token, I couldn't reveal the evidence I subsequently discovered without making it impossible for you to sustain the suicide verdict."

And for me to get home to Tania, he thought, for the decisive factor that evening had been his eagerness to return as soon as possible to the bed from which he'd been ejected by the electronic pager. Any hint of what he had discovered would have put paid to that for good.

"Let's be honest, Monsignore," he told Lamboglia. "You didn't want me coming to you and saying, 'Actually Ruspanti didn't fall from the gallery he had the key to but the one sixty feet above it.' You didn't want to know about it, did you? You just wanted the matter taken care of, neatly and discreetly. That's what I did, and if someone hadn't decided to give the game away, no one would be any the wiser."

Lamboglia stared at him across the table in silence. Several times he seemed about to speak, then changed his mind.

"That's impossible," he said at last. "The dome was closed when Ruspanti fell. The killer would have been trapped inside."

"The killers—there must have been at least two—left fifteen or twenty minutes earlier."

Lamboglia laughed again, a harsh, brittle sound.

"And what did Ruspanti do during that time, may I ask? Hover there in midair like an angel?"

"More or less."

"You forget that we have extensive professional experience of false miracles."

"This wasn't a miracle. They trussed the poor bastard up with a length of nylon fishing line and left him dangling over the edge of the gallery."

"Fishing line?"

Zen nodded.

"Thin, transparent, virtually invisible, but with a breaking strain of over a hundred kilos. I found several meters of the stuff tied to one of the railing supports on the upper gallery. I removed it, of course."

Lamboglia suddenly held out a hand for silence. He got up and walked quickly to the door, which he flung open dramatically. The elderly nun almost fell into the room, clutching a mop.

"Jesus, Mary, and Joseph! Forgive me, Monsignore, I didn't mean to startle you. I was just scrubbing the floor . . ."

"Cleanliness is indeed a great virtue," Lamboglia replied in a tone of icy irony, "and the fact that you have seen fit to undertake this menial labor yourself, rather than delegate it to one of your younger colleagues, indicates a commendable humility. If your discretion matches your other qualities—as is fervently to be hoped—then your eventual beatification can be only a question of time."

He glowered at the nun, who gazed back at her tormentor with an expression that, to Zen's eyes at least, appeared frankly erotic.

"Such a degree of sanctity no doubt makes any contact with the secular world both painful and problematic," Lamboglia continued remorselessly. "Nevertheless, I'm sure that someone as resourceful as yourself will find a way to procure us two coffees, easy on the milk but heavy on the foam, and a couple of pastries from a good bakery, none of that mass-produced rubbish."

Abandoning her mop, the nun scampered off. Lamboglia slammed the door shut and returned to the table. He rewound the tape to the beginning of the interruption and replaced the recorder in front of Zen.

"You say you found this twine attached to the upper gallery. But what made you look there in the first place?"

"I examined the lower gallery, the part that is closed to the public, overlooking the spot where Ruspanti fell. It was at once obvious that no one had thrown himself from there. There was an undisturbed layer of dust all along the top of the guardrail, and even on the floor. Besides, there was no sign of the missing shoe there. The upper gallery was the only other possibility."

Lamboglia frowned with the effort of keeping up with all this new information.

"But we found the shoe in the basilica, under one of the benches. You said it had fallen there separately from the body."

Zen nodded.

"Separately in space *and* time. Several hours later, in fact, while I was searching the gallery."

There was a timid knock at the door and the elderly nun appeared, carrying a tray covered with a spotless white cloth. She set it down on the table and removed the cloth like a conjuror to reveal two steaming bowls of coffee and an appetizing assortment of pastries. The cleric gave a curt nod and the nun slunk out.

"So none of this can now be proved?" Lamboglia asked.

Zen selected a pastry.

"Well, there were some marks on Ruspanti's wrists. I thought at first that they were preliminary cuts showing where he'd tried to slash his wrists, but in fact they must have been weals made by the pressure of the twine. A postmortem might reveal traces of the chloroform or whatever they used to keep him unconscious, but I don't suppose there's the faintest possibility of the family agreeing to allow one."

"But if the killers left before Ruspanti fell, how did they release the bonds that were holding him to the gallery?"

Zen washed down the pastry with a long gulp of the creamy coffee and got out his cigarettes.

"They didn't. *He* did."

Lamboglia merely stared.

"This is just a guess," Zen admitted as he lit up, "but they probably tied him up with a slippery hitch and looped the free end around his wrists. The family said that Ruspanti suffered from vertigo, so when he came around from the chloroform to find himself suspended two hundred feet above a sheer drop to the floor of the basilica, he would have panicked totally. The witnesses all talked about the terrible screams that seemed to start several seconds before the body appeared. During those seconds Ruspanti would have been desperately struggling to free his hands so that he could reach the railings and pull himself to safety. What he didn't realize was that by doing so, he was clearing the hitch securing him to the gallery."

Lamboglia stuck one finger between his teeth for a single moment, which revealed him to be a reformed nail-biter.

"You should have informed us."

Zen shrugged.

"The way I read it, you either knew or you didn't want to. Either way, it was none of my business to tell you."

Lamboglia stood up. He switched off the tape recorder and replaced it in his briefcase.

"Look, there's no problem," Zen told him, getting up too. "Just deny everything. I'll back you up. Without hard evidence, the media will soon drop the case."

Lamboglia buttoned up his coat and took his hat.

"There is also the question of the mole."

"You want me to tackle that?" offered Zen, eager to show willingness. "Someone must have supplied Ruspanti's killers with keys to the galleries. I could make a start there."

Lamboglia stared at the wall as though it were a teleprompter from which he was reading a prepared text.

"The question of the keys can be left to our own personnel. As far as the mole is concerned, we already have a suspect. The anonymous letter was faxed to the newspapers from a machine in the offices of Vatican Radio. At ten in the evening, there is only a skeleton staff on duty, and it was a fairly simple matter to eliminate them from suspicion. The only other person who had access to the building that evening was the duty security officer, Giovanni Grimaldi."

Zen let his cigarette fall to the floor and stepped on it carefully.

"The man who showed me around on Friday?"

Lamboglia inclined his head.

"He was at the scene when Ruspanti fell, wasn't he?" Zen demanded. "Was he already involved in the case in some way?"

The cleric looked at him blankly.

"That is neither here nor there. We are concerned to determine whether or not he sent that letter to the press, and if so to prevent it happening again. The problem is that Grimaldi is himself a member of the force that normally undertakes operations of this kind."

"*Quia custodet ipsis custodies,*" murmured Zen.

"*Quis custodiet ipsos custodes,* actually. But you've got the right idea.

Who is to investigate the investigators? We normally have every confidence in our staff, but in this case it is simply too much of a risk to expect Grimaldi's colleagues to act against him. It is essential that the mole not be tipped off before we can act."

He looked at Zen.

"Which is where you come in."

Zen returned his stare.

"You want me to . . . 'act'?"

Lamboglia placed his hands on the table, fingers splayed as though on the keyboard of an organ.

"A positive and decisive intervention on your part would contribute greatly toward bringing this unfortunate episode to a mutually satisfactory conclusion," he said.

Zen nodded.

"But this time, perhaps you'd better tell me exactly what you want done," he said. "Just to avoid the possibility of any further confusion."

"The first thing is to search Grimaldi's room. With any luck, you might find some incriminating material that we can use. He's on duty this afternoon, so you won't be disturbed."

He handed Zen a brown envelope.

"This contains his address and a telephone number on which you can call us this evening to relay your findings. Any further instructions will be conveyed to you at that stage."

He turned to go.

"Oh, there's just one more thing," Zen said.

The cleric turned, his glasses gleaming with reflected light like the enlarged pupils of a nocturnal predator.

"Yes?"

"Can you recommend a good doctor?"

He closed the door with great care, lifting it slightly on its hinges to prevent the telltale squeak, and stood listening. The sounds he could hear would have meant little to anyone else, but to Zen they provided an invaluable guide to the hazards he was going to have to negotiate.

At the end of the hallway, beyond the glass-paneled door to the living room, his mother was talking loudly in short bursts separated by long intervals of silence. Zen couldn't make out what she was saying,

but the singsong intonation and the buzzing of the Venetian "z" revealed that she was speaking in dialect rather than Italian. So unless she
was talking to herself—always a distinct possibility—she must be on the
phone, almost certainly to Rosalba Morosini, their former neighbor in
Venice, whom she called regularly to keep in touch with the news and
gossip in the only city that would ever be quite real for her.

Farther away, a mere background drone, came the sound of a
vacuum cleaner, indicating that Maria Grazia, the housekeeper, was at
work in one of the bedrooms at the far end of the apartment. Zen
moved cautiously forward along the darkened hallway. The room to his
left, overlooking the gloomy internal courtyard, was crammed with
boxes of papers and photographs, trunks full of his father's clothes, and
miscellaneous furniture that had been transferred wholesale to Rome
when his mother had finally been persuaded to abandon the family
home overlooking the Cannaregio canal. The thought of that emptied
space pervaded by the limpid, shifting Venetian light made Zen feel as
weightlessly replete as a child for a moment.

With extreme caution, he opened the door opposite. The elaborate plaster molding, picture rail, and ceiling rose revealed that this had
been intended to serve as the dining room, but following his mother's
arrival Zen had commandeered it as his bedroom. As far as he was
concerned, whatever it lacked in charm and intimacy was more than
compensated for by its proximity to the front door. High on the list of
problems caused by his mother's presence in the house was the fact that
every time she saw him putting on his coat Signora Zen wanted to
know where he was going and when he'd be back, while on his return
she expected a detailed account of where he'd been and what he'd been
doing. Exactly as though he were still ten years old, in short. It was, Zen
had concluded, the only way in which mothers could relate to their
sons, and therefore not something for which they were to be blamed,
still less which there was any point in trying to change. Nevertheless, it
got on his nerves, particularly since his relationship with Tania Biacis
had begun to make ever greater demands on his time.

Zen had been separated from his wife, Luisella, for over a decade,
but in the eyes of the Church and Zen's mother they were still married.
In his previous affair, with an American expatriate, Zen had used this as
a way of maintaining his distance. Ellen had ultimately returned to New

York, disappointed by Zen's unwillingness to commit himself to her more fully. Now the tables had been turned with a vengeance. Zen would have been more than happy to present Tania to his mother as his *fidanzata,* that usefully vague category somewhere between steady girl-friend and future wife. It was she who had refused, with a light laugh that, had he been less in love, might have seemed almost insulting.

"I'm sorry, Aurelio, but after eight years of Signora Bevilacqua I just can't face having to deal with another *mamma* just yet."

So it was back to the lies and deceptions that had characterized his affair with Ellen. If he felt less guilty about them, it was not only because his feelings for Tania had a self-justifying intensity, but also because his mother was no longer the pathetic figure she had been at that time. The change dated from the previous year, when the Zens' apartment had been broken into by Vasco Spadola, an ex-mobster bent on revenge. Signora Zen had been forced to go and stay with Gilberto and Rosella Nieddu, where she had proved to be such a hit with the Nieddu children that she now spent two afternoons a week looking after them.

The effect of this surrogate auntyhood—greatly appreciated by the Nieddus, whose relatives were all in their native Sardinia—had been to transform Signora Zen from a semicomatose recluse, parasiticly devoted to the imported soap operas doled out by Channel 5, into a sprightly, inquisitive old person with opinions and interests, still sharply critical of the city in which she lived like a foreigner, but also aware of its attractions and possibilities. Zen had had mixed feelings about this at first, since it meant revising a number of his own attitudes and habits, but he soon came to appreciate the fact that Signora Zen was out of the house more. It was easier in every sense to sneak off and spend time with Tania when he knew that his mother was happily occupied elsewhere.

He still needed to keep his stories straight, though, and in the present case that meant not being seen at home. He had been away from both home and work for the past two days, but as far as his mother was concerned his absence was not caused by illness but by an urgent mission to Florence. Alarmed by the effects of Moscati's call to the house, Zen had phoned her that morning from Tania's bed and repeated the story, so it would be difficult for him to explain his abrupt return just a few hours later. Hence the extreme caution with which he closed himself into his bedroom and walked across to the chest of drawers, making sure to avoid the creaky floorboard near the foot of the bed.

He eased the middle drawer open as gingerly as though it were filled with unstable high explosives, although at first sight it seemed to contain nothing but socks and underwear. Zen moved a pile of vests at the back of the drawer and pulled out a small scarlet plastic bag printed *Profumeria Nardi*. He opened the mouth of the bag and peered at the tangled plastic twine inside, the end melted to a blob by the flame of his lighter. The remaining portion would still be there, tied to the foot of the railing on the upper gallery of the dome of St. Peter's. It too would have a terminal blob of transparent plastic, slightly darkened by the flame.

He stuffed the bag into his coat pocket and went over to the wardrobe in the corner. Pulling up a rickety wooden chair that stood near the washbasin in the corner, Zen lifted down the small leather suitcase on top of the wardrobe. He snapped the catches quietly and opened the lid. The suitcase was almost full with packets, boxes, and papers. Zen removed a small flat wooden box, which must have been upside down, for the hinged lid opened and the contents clattered all over the floor.

His mother either didn't hear the noise or must have assumed that it came from outside, for she didn't stop talking. Zen knelt down and collected the tools and instruments. One had rolled right under the bed, and when Zen crawled in there to retrieve it, he caught sight of some writing on the wooden bedstead. With an effort, he could just make out the irregular lettering: *Zen, Anzolo Zuane, 28 March 1947*. The inscription blurred and he felt a terrible panic grip him. Seizing the metal instrument he had come in search of, he thrust himself out from under the dream-soaked structure of the bed, back into the light and the air of the room. The name written on the bedstead was his father's—Angelo Giovanni in Italian—but the writing was his own, and by 1947 the man named must have been long dead in some frozen swamp or Soviet prison camp. Only his son had continued to insist, secretly, magically, on his father's continuing presence in the house.

He stood up and dusted himself down, then tiptoed over to the door leading to the hallway. Pressing against the door to prevent the catch snapping against the edge of the mortise, he gripped the handle and turned. He put his ear to the crack and listened. To his dismay, the aural radar on which he depended had gone dead. The only sound was the continual murmur of traffic in the street outside. With a glance at his watch, he opened the door quickly. The hinges shrieked.

"Is that you?" called his mother.

"Eh?" shouted Maria Grazia from the bedroom.

"Was that you?"

There was a pause as the housekeeper interrupted her work and appeared in the doorway of the living room.

"What, Signora?"

"Was that you?"

"Was what me?"

"That noise."

"What noise?"

"It sounded like . . . like the front door opening."

His mother sounded anxious. Homes never feel the same after they've been violated by a break-in. Maria Grazia's bulky form suddenly appeared in outline on the glass-paneled door to the living room. Zen stepped back hastily.

"It's shut," the housekeeper reported, having presumably taken a look down the hall.

"Go and check!" Zen's mother insisted.

Zen tried to close the door, but it was too late.

"Mother of God!" cried Maria Grazia as she caught sight of him.

"What is it?" Signora Zen called from the living room. "What's happened?"

"I'm not here!" Zen whispered urgently to the housekeeper.

Maria Grazia put her hand on her abundant bosom and mimed relief.

"It's all right, Signora," she yelled. "I just banged my elbow."

She opened the front door and made energetic shooing gestures to Zen, who left his hiding place and slipped out onto the landing and down the stairs to freedom with a smile of gratitude.

His local café had seen much less of him since he regularly slept at Tania's, and when he asked the cashier for *gettoni* he received a qualified welcome hinting at both the promise of rehabilitation if he ceased to patronize rival establishments and the threat of being reduced to the status of a casual customer if he didn't. Zen went to the pay phone and called the doctor whose name he had extracted from Lamboglia. In a pinch he could probably have gotten a certificate from his own doctor, but the last thing he wanted was to drag someone he knew and respected into this murky affair. If the press got suspicious about his "illness," let them hound someone else.

The Vatican medico, a Doctor Carmagnola, said that he had heard from Monsignor Lamboglia, and would influenza or infectious gastroenteritis do or did he want to be quarantined? Zen said that there was no need to exaggerate, and Carmagnola told him he could collect the certificate from the reception of the Ospedale del Bambino Gesù. Zen picked up a taxi in Piazza Cavour and went first to the hospital on the Gianicolo, and then on to one of the more illustrious of Rome's hills. They drove along the Tiber as far as the Palatino bridge, then across the river and up a narrow, curving street. Following Zen's directions, the driver turned right and continued along a wealthy residential street past a public garden planted with orange trees. They were going slower now, and the driver was checking the number of the houses. They passed two churches on the right, then a consulate on the left. A police jeep was parked opposite, and the two bored patrolmen watched the taxi drive past and park in the small piazza enclosed by a high wall.

A stiff breeze hissed in the trees all around, and from a nursery school nearby came the sound of children at play. There was no other sound. Zen walked over to the pair of large green gates set in the wall at one side of the piazza. The letters SMOM were etched on a small brass plate above the bell. Zen pressed the button.

"Yes?" replied a crackly voice from the entry phone.

"This is Dottor Aurelio Zen. I understand there is a message for me."

"One moment."

There was a brief pause before the voice resumed.

"I regret that we have no knowledge of any such message."

Zen wasn't surprised. In his bones he'd known all along that the errand was a hoax set up by some prankster who had read his name in the newspaper reports of Ruspanti's death. He might even be here, watching the success of his stratagem. Zen glanced around, but there was no one to be seen except an elderly couple sitting on a bench at the other side of the piazza. He made one more attempt.

"Listen, I'm a police official! I received a message telling me to come to this address."

"We have no knowledge of this matter," the voice insisted with finality.

"Who's 'we'?" snapped Zen, but the entry phone had clicked off. He stood staring up at the tall green gates. The stone lintel above them was decorated with a cross whose arms grew broader toward their forked tips. A Maltese cross, thought Zen. SMOM: the Sovereign Military Order of Malta. These were the gates of the Palace of Rhodes, the Order's extraterritorial property where, according to rumor, Ludovico Ruspanti had taken refuge from the rigors of Italian justice.

Perhaps the message hadn't been a hoax, after all. But in that case what did it mean? "If you wish to get these deaths in the proper perspective, apply at the green gates in the piazza at the end of Via Santa Sabina." Zen focused his eyes with an effort. The gates were high and tightly closed. The only opening of any kind was an ornamental metal plate set close to the edge of the left-hand gate. The plate was of bronze, worked by hand in a complex elliptic pattern, with a plain circular keyhole in the center. Zen bent down and squinted through the keyhole.

He expected the hole to be covered at the other end, so it was a shock to find, on the contrary, a view arranged specifically to be seen from that point. It was still more of a shock to realize that what he was looking at—framed by an alley of tall evergreen shrubs and centered in the keyhole like the target in a gun sight—was the dome of St. Peter's. Despite the distance, he could count each of the ribs protruding through the leading of the roof and the tiny windows lighting the internal gallery from which Prince Ludovico Ruspanti had plunged to his death.

An hour later Zen was in a take-out pizzeria just outside the walls of the Vatican City. The other side of the street was lined with the boutiques that had recently sprung up in this area, once notorious as a haunt of thieves and prostitutes. One window was bisected by a huge poster reading FALCO, which Zen remembered as the name of the "hot young designer" whose creation Tania had been wearing the previous Friday. This must have been a mistake, however, for the window was that of a bookshop. Next door stood a doorway giving access to the residential floors where Giovanni Grimaldi lived.

Zen finished his square slab of sausage and mushroom *boscaiolo* pizza and wiped his hands on the paper napkin in which it had been wrapped. Time to go. He had not actually seen Grimaldi leave the building, but he must be at work by now. The only person who had gone either in or out, in fact, had been a young woman in a long tweed coat with a white scarf over her head who had appeared about ten minutes earlier. As for Grimaldi, he had probably opted for a lunch in the heavily subsidized Vatican canteen. Zen tossed the soiled napkin into a rubbish bin and walked out into the hazy sunshine.

Like a quarter of all the real estate in Rome, including the house in which Zen himself lived, the building opposite was owned by the Church, in this case an order of Carmelite nuns. This was not an investment property, however, but one of those set aside to provide cheap accommodation as part of the package the Vatican offered in an effort to attract and retain its low-paid employees, the other principal incentives being access to duty-free goods and exemption from Italian income tax. From Zen's point of view there were both pros and cons to the building's low-rent status. On the plus side, there was no caretaker to worry about. The problem was that there was no lift either, and Grimaldi lived on the top floor.

The stairwell was dark, and the timer controlling the lights had been adjusted for the agility of a buck chamois in rut rather than a middle-aged policeman going about his dubious business. Lamboglia had told Zen that "with any luck" he might "find some incriminating material we can use." There were various ways you could read that, quite apart from the literal meaning, which was in fact the only one Zen was prepared to discount entirely. The question was not whether or not Lamboglia had expected him to plant evidence in Grimaldi's room—that was taken for granted—but what that evidence was to prove. After due consideration, Zen had decided to go for broke and frame Grimaldi for the murder. The way things were going, the Vatican was going to need a scapegoat. Grimaldi would do nicely, particularly if, as Zen suspected, he had been part of a team carrying out surveillance on Ruspanti.

The top floor of the building differed from the others only in that the rectangular circuit of bleak barracklike corridors was lit by a succession of grimy skylights. The stench of carbolic cleanser was fighting a losing battle against a guerrilla force of odors associated with stale food, dirty clothes, clogged drains, and night sweats. The only sounds were the murmur of a distant radio and a steady hushing as of rain. Zen made his way along the corridor to a brown-painted door marked 4W, a loosened screw having allowed the 3 to flop over on its side.

There was no sound inside, but as a precaution Zen knocked gently before getting out the wooden box he had removed from the suitcase in his bedroom. The door was fitted with a Yale-type lock above the handle and a deadlock with a keyhole below. Zen bent down and squinted into the opening of the lower lock, but the key was in position. He frowned briefly, then shrugged. Presumably Grimaldi used only the Yale lock when he went out.

He opened the tool kit and selected a device like a pair of calipers, which he inserted into the upper lock. Zen had acquired the tools during the years he had spent in Naples. He had been directing a plan to bug the beachside villa of a prominent *camorra* boss when a burglar had broken into the property. He couldn't arrest the intruder without compromising the original operation, but the burglar didn't know that, and was delighted when Zen offered to drop all charges in return for the tool kit and a series of master classes in its use. It was some time since he had needed to put these skills to the test, but he was nevertheless surprised to find that the lock totally resisted all his efforts.

The lack of play in the lock was so marked that if the lower lock hadn't had the key in it, he might have thought that the catch was snibbed back. But it had, and an unoccupied room couldn't very well be locked from the inside. He stood listening to the hushing of the rain and staring at the stubborn door. Wrapping a handkerchief around the door handle, he shoved his shoulder hard against the edge, to see which lock gave. The next thing he knew, the door had swung effortlessly open, depositing him on his knees in the middle of the floor.

A dull prickle of apprehension ran over his scalp as he got up again. Surely Giovanni Grimaldi's work could not have left him with such a rosy view of human nature that he went off leaving his belongings in an unlocked room in an unguarded building? The only possible answer seemed to be that he didn't *have* any belongings, or at least none worth stealing. Apart from a few magazines, a small radio, a cheap alarm clock, some empty soft drink bottles, and the clothes hanging in the closet and laid out on the bed, the place looked as impersonal as a hotel room. The furniture must have been an eyesore even when new, which it hadn't been for a very long time.

Zen looked around for somewhere to hide the plastic twine. The obvious candidate was the chest of drawers, a hideous monstrosity with bandy metal legs and a synthetic wood-grain top. The drawers were slightly open and the contents in disarray. Of course, men who live alone tend to be either obsessionally tidy or total slobs, and it might simply be that Grimaldi was one of the latter. Nevertheless, Zen once again felt the warning prickle.

On top of the chest of drawers lay a leather wallet, a bunch of keys, a red plastic diary, some loose change, an open letter, and a framed photograph of a young woman holding two small children by the hand. A faded chrysanthemum lay on its side in front of the picture. Zen picked up the letter, from some relative in Bari, and skimmed through it. It was mostly about Grimaldi's children, who were apparently well and "as happy as can be expected," although they sometimes confused their mother's absence with their father's, thinking that he was in heaven and she in Rome. Zen put the letter down beside the flower of death. He stepped over to the window and looked down at the street below, sighing deeply as though gasping for breath. By the entrance to the pizzeria opposite a group of men were standing in the mild sunshine, arguing good-naturedly.

Zen whirled around as though someone had touched him. There was no one there. *There was no one there.* The unlocked door, the clothes laid out on the bed, the wallet and money and keys all ready, the drawers in disorder, the sound of rain while the sun shone. . . . As if sleepwalking, Zen crossed the room and opened the door. Along the floor of the corridor, a long mobile tongue of dark liquid was making its slow way, curling this way and that across the red tiles. Zen set off in the direction from which it was coming. At the end of the corridor, in the end wall, was a door painted glossy white, with no number and no lock, just a semicircular metal handle. The sound of falling water grew louder as Zen splashed his way toward it. Light streamed out of the cracks around the door on three sides, water on the fourth.

He rapped loudly on the white paneling. When there was no reply, he pulled and then pushed the door handle. The door rattled, but it was bolted on the inside. Zen stepped back, measuring his distance carefully. He bent his right leg and raised his foot to about the level of the internal bolt, then kicked out hard. The door burst inward, but held.

"Hey!"

A man had poked his head out of a doorway farther along the corridor. Zen ignored him. He brought his leg up again and smashed his foot viciously at the door. This time the bolt gave way and the door sagged in. A wave of water poured down the steps into the corridor, creating a series of miniature waterfalls.

"What the hell do you think you're doing?" the man demanded.

Zen didn't even look around. He was staring at the water running down the white porcelain tiles of the floor, at the drenched dressing gown that had for some time stemmed the flood under the door, at the eight-pointed cross roughly chalked on the wall, at the naked body slumped in the shower, blocking the drain, and at the face of Giovanni Grimaldi staring back at him, seemingly with an astonishment to match his own.

If the man had done as Zen had told him—phoned the police, and then waited outside for them to arrive—there would have been no problem. There was no phone in the building, so he had to go across the road to the pizzeria. That should have left plenty of time for Zen to subject Grimaldi's room to a thorough search. As it was, he had barely started when he heard voices on the stairs. He hastily stuffed the red plastic diary into his pocket and regained the corridor just before the neighbor returned with a Carabinieri patrolman whose 850cc Moto-Guzzi had been parked outside the pizzeria while its driver demolished a plank of ham-and-mushroom within.

Apart from forcing him to curtail his search, this coincidence meant that Zen was cast in the role of Material Witness in the ensuing investigation, which went on for the rest of the afternoon. Faced with a couple of subordinates from his own force, he could have made a brief statement and then buggered off, but the paramilitary Carabinieri saw no reason to stretch the rules to accommodate some big shot from their despised civilian rivals. On the contrary! The inquiry into Giovanni Grimaldi's death was handled strictly according to the letter of the law, with every *t* crossed, every *i* dotted, and every statement, submission, and report written up in triplicate and then signed by the witnesses and countersigned by the officials.

Not that there was the slightest doubt as to the cause of the tragedy. "I always said it was just a matter of time before something like this happened," the dead man's neighbor told the patrolman as they gazed in through the open doorway of the shower. Marco Duranti was one of those florid, irascible men who have the answer to all the world's problems. It's all so very simple! The solution is right here, at their fingertips! Only—and this is what drives them *mad*—no one thinks to ask them. Not only that, but when they offer the information, as a disinterested gesture of goodwill, people take no notice! They even turn away, muttering "Give it a rest, Marco, for Christ's sake!" That's what Grimaldi had done, the last time he'd warned him—purely out of the kindness of his own heart—about that damned shower. It was thus understandable that Duranti's grief was tempered by a certain satisfaction that his oft-repeated warnings of disaster had been proved right.

He drew the attention of the Carabinieri patrolman to the electric water heater supplying the shower. Taped to the wall nearby was a piece of paper in a plastic cover punched for use in a folder. A faded message in red felt-tip pen indicated that the heater should always be turned off before using the shower. Now, however, the switch was clearly set to "ON."

"It should have been replaced years ago," Duranti went on indignantly, "but you can imagine the chances of that happening. The Church has always got enough money to keep Wojtyla jetting about the world, but when it comes to looking after its own properties and the poor devils who live in them—eh, eh, that's another matter! This whole place is falling to pieces. Why, there was someone in only yesterday morning poking about in the drains. The next thing we know the floor will be running with shit, never mind water!"

By this time a small group of residents, neighbors, and hangers-on had gathered in the corridor. No one wanted to go into the bathroom while the water was still potentially lethal, so Duranti fetched a hook with a long handle that was used for opening the skylight windows, and after several abortive attempts the patrolman managed to flip the heater switch to the "off" position. Protected by the solid leather soles of his magnificent boots, he then ventured into the flooded cubicle and turned off the water just as the *maresciallo* arrived with three more patrolmen and a doctor. No one paid any attention to the design chalked on the wall, and by the time they all adjourned to the local Carabinieri station it had been rubbed by so many sleeves and shoulders that it was no longer recognizable.

For the next few hours, Zen, Duranti, and a selection of the other residents were questioned, severally and together. Zen told them that he had gone to the house while following up a lead in a drug case he was engaged on, details of which he could not disclose without authorization from his superiors. The lead had in fact been false—an address on the fifth floor of a building that only had four—but when he reached the top of the stairs he had noticed the water seeping along the corridor. Having traced the source to the shower, he attempted to communicate with the occupant, and when that failed he had kicked the door down.

It was this homely gesture that had finally won the Carabinieri over. They glanced at each other, nodding sympathetically. Confronted by an obstinately locked door and a stubborn silence on the other side of it, that was what you did, wasn't it? You kicked the fucking thing down. It might not do the door any good, but it would sure as hell make the next one think twice about messing you around. The *maresciallo* thanked Zen for his cooperation and told him he could go. Marco Duranti, on the other hand, was detained for a further forty minutes. Zen spent the time in a café across the road, making a number of phone calls. The first was to the contact number he had been given in the Vatican. This was engaged, so he phoned Tania.

"Hello?"

It was a man's voice, with a reedy timbre and clipped intonation.

"Sorry, I must have a wrong number."

He dialed again, but now this number was engaged as well, so he fed the two hundred lire piece back into the slot and called Paragon

Security Consultants. A secretary made him hold the line for some time before putting him through to the managing director.

"Gilberto Nieddu."

"This is the Ministry of Finance, Dottore. Following a raid by our officers on a leading firm of accountants, we have uncovered evidence suggesting that for the last five years your company has consistently failed to declare twenty-five percent of its profits."

There was silence at the other end.

"However, we have no time to concern ourselves with such small-time offenders," Zen continued, "so we'd be prepared to overlook the matter in return for the services of a discreet, qualified electrician."

This was greeted by a sharp intake of breath.

"Is that you, Aurelio?"

Zen chuckled.

"You sounded worried, Gilberto."

"You bastard! You really had me going there!"

"Oh come on, Gilberto! You don't expect me to believe that you're fiddling a quarter of your taxes, do you?"

"Of course not, but . . ."

"It must be a hell of a lot more than that."

Nieddu make a spluttering sound.

"Now about this electrician," Zen went on.

"Look, Aurelio, it may have escaped your attention, but I'm not running a community information service. You need an electrician, look in the Yellow Pages."

"I'm not talking about changing a plug, Gilberto."

"So what *are* you talking about?"

Zen told him. Nieddu gave a long sigh.

"Why do I let you drag me into these things, Aurelio? What's it got to do with me? What's it got to do with *you,* for that matter?"

He sighed again.

"Give me the address."

When they'd agreed on a rendezvous, Zen called Tania again. The same male voice answered.

"Who's that?" demanded Zen.

There was a brief interval of silence, then the receiver was replaced. Zen immediately redialed, but the phone rang and rang without any answer. He hung up, went to the bar, and ordered a double espresso, which he gulped down, searing his throat. He got out the red plastic-bound diary he had removed from Giovanni Grimaldi's room. It turned out to be dated the following year, a freebie given away with a recent issue of *L'Espresso*. He riffled through it, but the pages were blank except for a few numbers and letters scribbled in the Personal Data section. Replacing the diary in his pocket, Zen touched his packet of Nazionali cigarettes. He took one out and lit it, then returned to the phone. There was still no reply from Tania's number, so he tried the Vatican again. This time the number answered almost immediately.

"Yes?"

"This is Signor Bianchi."

"Yes?"

It was a voice Zen didn't recognize.

"I've just seen Signor Giallo."

He felt ridiculous, but Lamboglia's instructions had been quite clear: Even on this supposedly secure line, Zen was to refer to Grimaldi only by this code name.

"He's dead."

There was a brief silence.

"Is there anything else?" asked the voice.

"You mean any other deaths?" Zen shouted. "Why, how many are you expecting?"

He slammed the phone down. When he turned, the barman and all five customers were staring at him. He was about to say something when he saw Marco Duranti emerge from the Carabinieri station and set off along the street at a surprisingly brisk trot. Zen tossed a five-thousand-lire note in the general direction of the barman and ran after him.

"Excuse me!"

Duranti swung around with a wary, hostile expression. When he saw Zen he relaxed, but only slightly.

"It's about this maintenance man you saw in the building yesterday," Zen told him.

"Yes?"

Zen pointed along the street.

"Are you going home? We could walk together."

Duranti shrugged gracelessly.

"I was wondering if there might be a connection with this case I'm working on, you see," Zen told him as they set off together. "They could be using the sewers as a place to hide their drug cache. Where was he actually working?"

"I didn't look. All I know is he had the electric drill going for about half an hour just when I was trying to have my siesta. Of course they *would* have to pick the week I'm on night shift."

They were just passing the Porta Sant'Anna, the tradesman's entrance of the Vatican City State. A Swiss guard in the working uniform of blue tunic, sleeveless cloak, and beret set at a jaunty angle was gesturing with white-gloved hands to a driver who had just approached the security barrier. Meanwhile his colleague chatted to a girl on the pavement. A little farther up the street was a second checkpoint, manned by the Vigilanza. Their uniform, dark blue with red piping, badly cut and with too much gold braid, made a sad contrast with the efficient elegance of the Swiss. Revolver on his hip, radio on his shoulder, the guard held up his hand to stop the car, which had now been permitted through the first barrier, and swaggered over to give the driver a hard time.

"What did this man look like?" Zen asked.

Duranti shrugged.

"Stocky, muscular, average height, with a big round face. He wasn't Roman, I'll tell you that."

"How do you know?"

"The accent! All up here in the nose, like a real Northerner."

Zen nodded as though this confirmed his suspicions.

"That's very helpful. You make an excellent witness, Signore. If only everyone were as observant."

They had reached the corner of the street where Duranti lived. Zen thanked him and then waited until he had disappeared before following him down the street to the pizzeria where he'd had lunch.

Normality had already returned to the neighborhood. In an area where safety standards were rarely or never observed, domestic accidents were even more frequent than suicide attempts in St. Peter's. In the pizzeria, the owner and three cronies were discussing the recent and spectacular explosion of a butane gas cylinder that had blown a five-year-old girl clean through the window of the family's third-floor apartment. The child had landed on the roof of a car below, unhurt but orphaned, her father having been disemboweled by a jagged chunk of the cylinder while the mother succumbed to brain injury after part of the wall collapsed on her.

Zen elbowed his way through to the counter and ordered another slab of pizza to keep him going until, God willing, he finally got to eat a proper meal. The baker had just pushed a large tray filled with bubbling pizza through the serving hatch from the kitchen next door, and the *pizzaiolo* hacked out a large slice, which he folded in two and presented to Zen with a paper wrapper. He moved to the back of the shop and leaned against a stack of plastic crates filled with soft-drink bottles, munching the piping hot pizza and awaiting the arrival of Paragon Security's electrician.

A blowsy near-blonde of rather more than a certain age walked in and greeted the four men with the familiar manner of one who has seen the best and worst they could do and not been at all impressed. She ordered one of the ham and mozzarella turnovers called *calzoni*, "trousers." The men guffawed, and one remarked that that was all Bettina ever thought about. She replied that on the contrary, *calzoni* these days were usually a disappointment, "delicious looking from the outside, but with no filling worth a damn." The owner of the pizzeria protested that his "trousers," on the other hand, were crammed with all the good things God sends. Bettina remained unimpressed, claiming that while his father had known a thing or two about stuffing, the best the present proprietor could manage was a pathetic scrap of meat and a dribble of cheese.

Zen's left elbow turned to a burning knob of pain.

"Hi there."

The pain vanished as suddenly as it had begun. Zen looked around to find Gilberto Nieddu grinning puckishly at him.

"I didn't expect you to come personally," said Zen.

He still found it odd to see Nieddu's rotund, compact body dressed in a smart suit and tie. Gilberto had been running an independent security firm for years now, and very successfully too, but Zen still thought of him as the colleague he had once been, and was always vaguely taken aback to see him disguised as a businessman. Nieddu set down the small metal case he was carrying.

"You don't think I'd risk one of my lads getting involved with your crazy schemes?"

Zen waved at the counter.

"Want something?"

Nieddu shook his head.

"I've got a meal waiting for me at home, Aurelio. If I ever *get* home."

Zen finished his pizza and lit a Nazionale.

"Okay, this is the situation. Like I said on the phone, someone was killed in an accident this afternoon, only I don't think it was an accident. The victim lived in a run-down tenement where the wiring was installed around the time Caesar got mugged in the Forum. The water heater in particular is very dodgy, and tenants have been warned to switch it off before using the shower. It seems to me that all someone needed to do was fix the heater so that it became seriously dangerous, and then wait for the victim to trot along and electrocute himself. In short, the perfect murder."

"Give me a smoke, polenta-head," said Nieddu.

"I thought you'd given it up."

"I've given up *buying* them. Don't laugh. My doctor says it's a first step."

He lit up and exhaled mightily, then shook his head.

"It wouldn't work," he said. "They'd need to get out the element, for a start. That's a major job even with a new heater. If this one's as old as you say, the nuts will have rusted up. Anyway, the thing's bound to be checked, and it'll be clear that it's been tampered with. There's no chance of it being mistaken for an accident."

"So it can't be done?"

"Of course it can be done, but not like that. What you want to do is bypass the heater altogether. Where exactly is this run-down tenement?"

"Right across the road."

Gilberto glanced at his watch.

"Let's have a quick look. Then I really must go, or Rosella will think I'm having an affair."

The hallway was dark and dank, the only sound the brushing of Zen's sleeve on the plaster as he groped for the switch.

"No!" whispered Nieddu.

He opened the metal case and removed a small torch. A beam of light split the darkness, precise as a pointing finger, indicating walls and ceiling, doorways, steps, painting brief slashes and squiggles in the stairwell as they walked upstairs. On each floor they could hear the murmur of radios and televisions, but they saw no one. When they reached the top, Zen led the way along the corridor. Light showed under the door of Marco Duranti's room, but there was no sound inside. Zen tried the door to Giovanni Grimaldi's room, but it was now locked. The shower sported a brand-new hasp and a large padlock, as well as a sign reading "OUT OF ORDER."

Zen opened his burglary kit and got to work on the padlock. Despite its impressive appearance, it was a cheapie. He had barely started work before it snapped open. Nieddu gave a low whistle.

"When you finally get the boot, Aurelio, you give me a call. We can always use people with skills like yours."

He pushed the door open. The broken hinges protested loudly and the base scraped across the tiles like fingernails down a blackboard. Zen shoved him inside quickly and pushed the door closed just as someone came out of a room further along the corridor. Nieddu doused the torch and he and Zen stood side by side in the darkness. Footsteps approached, then retreated again. A door closed and feet receded down the stairs.

Nieddu switched on the torch. The beam bounced and skittered around the glazed white tiles, picking out the water heater resting on its wooden trestle near an oblong window high up in the whitewashed wall.

"Give me a leg up."

Zen locked his hands together to make a step. With the adroitness of an acrobat, the Sardinian hoisted himself up, gripping the trestle with one hand and resting his foot on the wall screening off the shower cubicle.

"Just as I thought," he said, his voice reverberating off the bare walls. "The threads are all corroded to hell. No one's touched this for years."

He dropped back to the floor and padded around the bathroom, shining the torch over the glossy tiles and mat white plaster. When he reached the partition wall beside the door, he grunted significantly.

"Ah."

"Found something?" queried Zen.

Nieddu eased the door open and stepped outside. He shone the torch into the angle of the wall. Inside, a thin pencil of light appeared in the darkness. Zen bent down and inspected the wall. A small hole had been drilled right through it. He went out to join Nieddu in the corridor. The torch beam was now pointing along the wall at an electric junction box a few yards away.

Outside in the street, a police car approached at high speed, siren howling. The walls and ceiling of the corridor pulsed with a revolving blue light. Down below, in the entrance hall of the building, an excitable voice, which Zen recognized as that of Marco Duranti yelled "This way!" The stairwell resounded to the sound of voices and clattering boots.

"Time to go?" asked Nieddu calmly.

Zen nodded. The Sardinian opened the metal case and removed something that looked like a large firework. He ran along the corridor to the head of the stairs, tossed it down, and came running back.

"Smoke bomb," he explained. "Should hold them for a while."

There was an acrid smell in the air, and the sounds below had turned to coughing and spluttering. They ran back to the bathroom, where Nieddu held his hands cupped while Zen hoisted himself clumsily up to the wooden trestle. Nieddu then passed up his case. Going into the shower, he gripped the metal piping and pulled himself up onto the wall around the cubicle. From there he leaped across to join Zen on the trestle, which creaked ominously under their combined weight. Nieddu clambered on top of the water heater.

"Fuck!"

"What's the matter?"

"I've snagged my jacket on a nail."

"Christ, is that all?"

"*All?* It's brand-new, from Ferre."

He leaned across to the window and pulled it open. Taking the metal case from Zen, he pushed it through the opening, then sprang after it and held his hands out to Zen, who had clambered up on top of the tank. He tried not to look down. The trestle was still groaning and the window looked a long way away.

"It's no good," he said suddenly. "I can't do it."

The Sardinian sat down facing the window, his feet braced on either side.

"Give me your hands."

Zen leaned forward across the gap and Nieddu gripped his wrists. In the corridor outside he could hear a stampede of approaching boots. He kicked off from the heater, scraping his shoes desperately on the wall, and somehow Nieddu dragged him through the opening and out onto the sloping tiled roof.

"Come on!" the Sardinian said urgently. "I've got some stun grenades, but you wouldn't want me to have to use those. They cost a fortune, and you already owe me for the suit."

They ran off together across the roofs toward the lights of the next street.

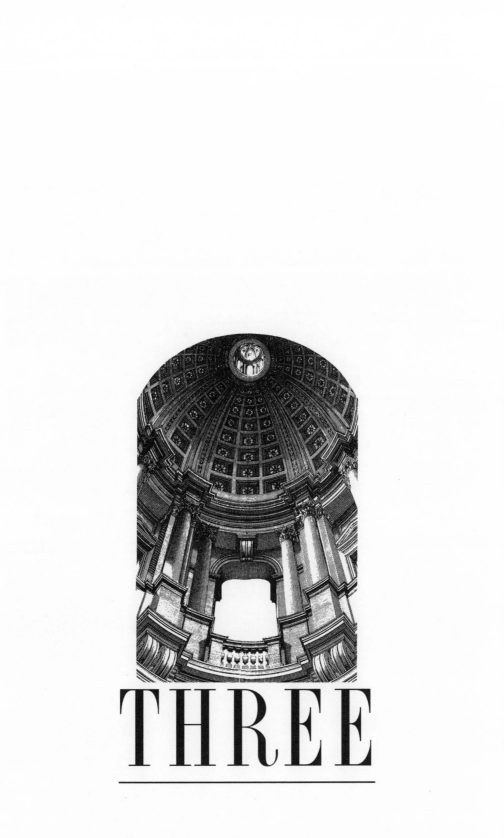

THREE

I f Zen had spent the night at home instead of at Tania's, he could
have walked to his first appointment the next morning. As it was
he ended up on foot anyway, the taxi he summoned having ground
to a halt in the traffic outside the Liceo Terenzio Mamiani, just
around the corner from Zen's apartment. Wednesday mornings were
always bad in the area near the Vatican, as the usual rush-hour jam was
supplemented by the influx of pilgrims heading for the weekly papal
audience. After sitting in the stationary taxi for almost five minutes, Zen
paid the driver and strode off past lines of honking, bleating vehicles
moving no faster than the cars parked along the curb, dead linden leaves
plastered to the paintwork with bird shit. Among the immobile mass of
traffic were tour buses whose utilitarian styling and robust construction
exuded a graceless charm that awakened nostalgic memories of the far
off, innocent 1950s in Zen's mind. From portholes wiped in their
misted-up windows, the Polish Pope's compatriots peered out at the
Eternal City, perhaps wondering if the last kilometer of their pilgrimage was going to take as long as the previous two thousand.

Zen crossed Piazza del Risorgimento and followed the towering
ramparts of the Vatican City State up the hill, passing women carrying
wicker baskets and plastic bags of fruit and vegetables home from the
Trionfale market. The bells of the local churches were in some disagree-

ment about the exact moment when nine o'clock arrived, but the Vatican itself opened its doors dead on time, as though to emphasize that although *in* Rome, it was by no means *of* Rome. The handful of tourists waiting for the museums to open began to file inside. Zen followed them up the curving ramp to the cash desk, where he plonked down his ten thousand lire note with the rest. Then, like someone doing Rome in two days, he hurried through the collections of classical antiquities, following the arrows marked "Raphael Stanze and Sistine Chapel Only."

A marble staircase brought him to a gallery receding as far as the eye could see. The walls were hung with tapestries and painted maps alternating with windows overlooking a large courtyard. Dust swarmed like a school of fish in the sunlight streaming in through the windows. He had already left the other early visitors far behind, and this part of the museums was deserted. At the end of the gallery, Zen turned left into a chamber hung with enormous battle scenes, then down a staircase to a suite of rooms on the lower floor overlooking a courtyard patroled by a Swiss Guard. Zen smiled wryly, thinking of the night before. Following their hasty exit from the house where Giovanni Grimaldi had been murdered, he and Gilberto Nieddu had climbed down a fire escape into the internal courtyard of a building in the next street and then sneaked past the lodge where the *portiere* was watching television.

"Never again, Aurelio!" Gilberto told him as they parted in the street. "Don't even bother phoning."

Back at Tania's, Zen had called his mother to tell her that his duties in Florence unfortunately required him to stay another night but he would be back for sure the following day.

"That's all right," his mother replied. "At least you ring up and let me know what's happening, not like some."

"What do you mean, Mama?"

"Oh, that Gilberto! It makes me furious, it really does! Rosella phoned here only half an hour ago, to ask if I knew where you were. Apparently Gilberto called her this afternoon and said he might be a bit late home this evening because he was meeting *you*, if you please! Can you believe the cheek of it? Poor Rosella! Of course, come nine o'clock there's no sign of him and the dinner's ruined, so she phones me to try and find out what's going on. Of course I didn't know any of this at first, so I just told her the truth, that you were in Florence. It's the old story, of course. I told her, I said, just look the other way. There's no point in making a fuss. You're not the first and you won't be the . . ."

"Listen, Mama, I'm running out of tokens. I'll see you tomorrow."

"Wait, Aurelio! There's a message for you. This gentleman called, he wouldn't leave his name, but he said it was about a Signor Giallo. He asked you to phone him immediately."

Zen dialed the number he had been given by Lamboglia. It was answered by a different voice, this time with a foreign intonation. But why not? The Vatican was the headquarters of an international organization.

"Your presence is required tomorrow morning," the man told him. "Come to the main entrance to the Vatican Museums, pay in the normal way, then follow these directions."

Zen noted them down.

"Now there's something I want *you* to do," he told the anonymous voice. "Contact whoever is responsible for the maintenance of the building where Signor Gialli lived and find out whether a workman was sent there yesterday to investigate the sewers."

He had hung up just as Tania walked in naked from the shower, looking rather like the gracefully etiolated females in the frescoes that covered the chamber where he now found himself. The subjects were nominally biblical, but the action had been transferred from the harsh realities of historical Palestine to a lush Italian landscape peopled by figures of an ideal renaissance beauty. On one wall, ships navigated under full sail and armies maneuvered for battle. Another showed a large chamber where men were disputing and orators pronouncing. The painted room was about the same size and shape as the one on whose wall it was depicted, and the artist had cleverly included a painted door at floor level, creating the illusion that one could simply turn the handle and step into that alternative reality. Zen was just admiring this amusing detail when the handle in fact turned and the door opened to reveal the stooping figure of Monsignor Lamboglia.

"Come!" he said, beckoning.

Inside, a spiral stone staircase burrowed upward through the masonry of the ancient palace. They climbed in silence. After some time, Lamboglia opened another door, which led into a magnificent enclosed loggia. The lofty ceiling was sumptuously carved and gilded, the rear wall adorned with antique painted maps representing a world in which North America figured only as a blank space marked *Terra Incognita*. The large windows opposite offered an extensive view over St. Peter's Square, now reduced to serving as a parking lot for those pilgrim buses that had managed to fight their way through the traffic.

Zen followed his guide through a door at the end of the loggia, beneath a stained-glass light marked "Secretariat of State" and into a vaulted antechamber. The walls and ceiling were covered in fantastic tracery, fake marble reliefs, and painted niches containing trompe l'oeil classical statues. Lamboglia pointed to one of the armless chairs uphol-stered in gray velvet that stood against the painted dado, alternating with carved wooden chests and semicircular tables supporting bronze angels.

"Wait here."

He disappeared through a door at the end of the corridor. Zen sat down in the designated chair, which proved to be as uncomfortable as it was no doubt intended to make the occupant feel. The windows on the opposite wall were covered in lace curtaining that strained the sunlight like honey through muslin. Zen closed his eyes and tried to concentrate on what he was going to say. Try as he would, though, his thoughts kept drifting away to the night before. Tania had lied to him, there was no doubt about that. Not just filtered the truth, as he would shortly do for the benefit of the Vatican authorities. No, Tania had lied.

"Were you out this afternoon?" he had asked casually as they lay in bed together.

"Out?"

He ran his fingertips lightly over her ribs and belly.

"Mmm. About six o'clock."

She pretended to think.

"Oh yes, that's right. I stepped out for a moment to do some shopping. Why?"

"I tried to phone. To tell you I'd be late."

He rolled up on his side, gazing down at her.

"A man answered."

A distant look entered her eyes, and he knew she was going to lie. The rest was routine, a matter of how hard he wanted to press, how much he could bully her into revealing.

"You must have gotten a wrong number," she said.

He looked away, embarrassed for her, regretting that he'd brought it up. Nevertheless, he couldn't help adding, "It happened twice. I dialed again."

She laughed lightly.

"Probably a crossed wire at the exchange. It's a pity the Vatican doesn't run a phone system as well as a postal service. They fly their mail out to Switzerland to be sorted, you know, yet it still arrives in half the time it takes the post office."

He accepted the diversion gratefully.

"That's because the post office sends it to *Palermo* for sorting. By boat."

She laughed again, with amusement and relief. Thinks she's gotten away with it, Zen thought to himself. Already he was getting used to the idea of her treachery. To be honest, once he'd recovered from the initial shock it was almost a relief to find that she was indeed deceiving him. The immense and unconditional gift Tania had made of her love still amazed him. Being worthy of it had been a bit of a responsibility. This discovery evened things up considerably. All in all, he told himself, it was probably the best thing that could have happened.

The door at the end of the corridor opened and Lamboglia reappeared. He extended his right hand, palm down, and waggled the fingers beckoningly. Zen rose and followed him into the office, where he had been received by the Cardinal Secretary of State's deputy the previous Friday. On this occasion, Juan Ramòn Sànchez-Valdès was in his full episcopal regalia, an ankle-length soutane with a magenta sash, piping, and buttons. The crown of his head was covered by a skullcap of the same color. The rim of an ecclesiastical collar was just visible beneath the soutane, while a plain silver cross hung from its chain at the base of the archbishop's chest.

As before, Zen was placed on the long red sofa while the archbishop sat in the high-backed armchair by the table. At his elbow,

beside the white telephone, lay a single sheet of paper with some lines
of typing. Lamboglia took up his earlier position, just behind the archbishop's shoulder, but Sànchez-Valdès waved him away.

"Sit down, Enrico! You make me nervous, hovering there like a
waiter."

Flinching as though he'd been struck, poor Lamboglia trotted off
across the elaborately patterned rug with the quick fluttering gait of a
woman, all stiff knees and loose ankles, and subsided into a chair on the
end wall.

"Enrico is from Genova," Sànchez-Valdès remarked to Zen. "On
the other hand I seem to recall that you, Dottore, are from Venice. The
two cities were of course fierce trading rivals at one time, and vied with
each other like two competing companies to supply us with transporta-
tion and logistics for the Crusades. I came across rather a good comment on the subject just the other day, in a dispatch from our nuncio at
Venice at the turn of the century—the thirteenth century, that is. He
advises the Holy Father to treat with the Doge, exorbitant though his
terms might seem, explaining that while both the Genoese and the
Venetians will gladly offer to sell you their mothers, the crucial difference is that the Venetians will *deliver*."

Although he was aware of being manipulated by a skilled operator,
Zen could not help smiling.

"I gather it was you who found poor Grimaldi's body," the archbishop went on without a pause.

Zen's smile faded.

"What a terrible tragedy!" sighed Sànchez-Valdès. "Those poor
children! First they lose their mother to illness, and now . . .' "

He broke off, seemingly overcome by emotion. Lamboglia was
rubbing his hands together furiously, as though to warm or wash them.

"I believe Enrico informed you that we had strong reason to suppose that Grimaldi was the author of that anonymous letter to the
press," Sànchez-Valdès continued. "Needless to say, that fact has now
become one more of the many embarrassments this case threatens to
cause us. If it became known, one can easily imagine the sort of vicious
insinuations and calumnies that would inevitably follow. No sooner is
the identity of the "Vatican mole" discovered than he is found dead in

the shower. How very convenient for those who wish to conceal the truth about the Ruspanti affair, et cetera, et cetera.

"That's why we've summoned you here this morning, Dottore. Enrico has explained to me your unfortunate misunderstanding of our intentions with regard to the death of Ludovico Ruspanti. On this occasion I want to leave you in no doubt as to our position. Fortunately it is very simple. With Grimaldi's death, this tragic sequence of events has reached its conclusion. Any mistakes or miscalculations that may have occurred are now a matter for future historians of Vatican affairs. As far as the present is concerned, we shall instruct the Apostolic Nuncio to convey our thanks to the Italian government for your, quote, discreet and invaluable intervention, unquote."

The archbishop lifted the sheet of paper from the table and scanned it briefly.

"Enrico!" he called.

Lamboglia sashayed back across the carpet to his master's side. Sànchez-Valdès handed him the paper.

"There is just one remaining formality," he told Zen, "which is for you to sign an undertaking not to disclose any information you may have come by in the course of your work for us."

Lamboglia carried the paper over to Zen, who read through the six lines of typing.

"I'm sorry," he said. "I can't sign this."

"What do you mean?" snapped Lamboglia, who was waiting to convey the signed document back to Sànchez-Valdès.

"To do so would risk placing me in an untenable position with regard to my official duties."

Sànchez-Valdès hitched up the hem of his soutane to reveal a pair of magenta socks.

"You didn't display such exaggerated scruples the last time we spoke," he said dryly.

"That was altogether different, Your Excellency. Ruspanti's death occurred in the Vatican City State, and was therefore not subject to investigation by the Italian authorities. When I acted for you in that affair, I did so as a free agent. If Grimaldi had also died within the walls of the Vatican, I would have been happy to sign this undertaking. But he didn't, he died in Rome. If I sign this, and Grimaldi's death is subsequently made the subject of a judicial investigation, I would be unable to avoid perjuring myself whether I spoke or remained silent."

Archbishop Sànchez-Valdès laughed urbanely.

"But there's no possibility of that happening! Grimaldi's death was an accident."

Zen nodded.

"Of course. Just like Ruspanti's was suicide."

The two clerics stared at him intently. The archbishop was the first to break the silence.

"Are you suggesting that Grimaldi did *not* die accidentally?" he asked quietly.

"That's absurd!" cried Lamboglia. "We've seen the Carabinieri report! There's no question that Grimaldi was electrocuted by a faulty shower."

Zen shook his head.

"He was electrocuted *in* the shower, not *by* the shower."

Sànchez-Valdès looked up at the ceiling, as though invoking divine assistance.

"There's no doubt about that?" he murmured.

"None at all."

The archbishop nodded.

"A pity."

"Indeed," agreed Zen. "Nevertheless, although I am unable to sign this undertaking, I can assure you that I will honor it in practice. Your secrets will go no further."

He smiled shyly.

"As I mentioned the first time Your Excellency honored me with an audience, whatever the Church decides is good enough for me."

Sànchez-Valdès looked at Zen with amusement.

"You're a great loss to the Curia, Dottore," he remarked, shaking his head. "A very great loss indeed! But then of course they already accuse us of creaming off the best administrators in the country."

He got to his feet, sighing.

"Thank you, Enrico, that will be all."

After a momentary hesitation, Lamboglia left sullenly. When the door had closed behind him, Sànchez-Valdès walked over to the window. He pulled aside the screen of net curtaining, allowing a beam of raw sunlight to enter.

"What a lovely morning."

He turned to Zen.

"I think we should take a walk, Dottore."

Zen stared at him blankly.

"A walk?"

"That's right. A walk in the woods."

"Have you heard the one about the whore and the Swiss Guard?" asked the archbishop.

Zen, who was lighting a cigarette, promptly choked on the smoke. When the fit of coughing had subsided somewhat, he shook his head.

"I don't think I have."

Sànchez-Valdès's face beamed with expectation.

"This new recruit has just arrived in Rome, fresh from the mountains. On his first evening off duty he decides to explore the city a little. He wanders out through the Sant'Anna gate and down into the Borgo, where he is accosted by a lady of the night."

He paused to inspect a flowering shrub in the rockery they were passing.

" 'It's just like my friends told me,' thinks Hans. 'These Roman women can't resist a blonde hunk of manhood like me.' When they reach Asphasia's business premises, she says, 'Before we go any further, let's just settle the little matter of the fee.' The Swiss smiles complacently. 'Out of the question! I wouldn't dream of accepting money from a woman.' "

Zen laughed politely.

"I heard that one from Scarpia, the head of the Vigilanza. His real name is Scarpione, but Paul VI always called him Scarpia, like the police chief in *Tosca*. No one was sure whether it was a mistake or a joke, and Montini wasn't the kind of person you could ask, but somehow the name stuck, perhaps precisely because anyone further removed from Puccini's villain would be hard to imagine. Poor Luigi is all home and family, mild and jovial to a fault. But you'll be able to judge for yourself."

They passed an elaborate fountain in the form of an artificial grotto from which a stream issued to pour over a series of miniature falls while two stone cherubs watched admiringly from the pool below. The path they were following led straight uphill through a coppice of beech trees. Except for a faint background murmur of traffic, they might have been deep in the country.

"Anyway," Sànchez-Valdès went on, "that joke sums up the way the Vigilanza regard their colleagues in the Cohors Helvetica—as Nordic yokels with a superiority complex, so stupid they think they're smart. The Swiss, for their part, look down on the security men as jumped-up traffic wardens. This conceit is perhaps understandable in a corps that not only enjoys an unbroken tradition of service stretching back almost five hundred years, but is charged with the glorious responsibility of guarding the person of the Holy Father. As for the Vigilanza, their duties are indeed fairly mundane for the most part, but there is a small elite unit within the force that undertakes more specialized and sensitive tasks. The existence of this unit is officially denied, and we never discuss its operations. If I've decided to make an exception in your case, it's because you already know too much. The Ruspanti affair has gotten completely out of control, and we must proceed as they do with forest fires, isolating the affected area and letting the flames burn themselves out."

Perhaps affected by this metaphor, Zen ground his spent cigarette out with exaggerated caution, creating an unsightly smudge of soiled paper and tobacco shreds.

"There's no filter," he explained awkwardly. "It'll wash away as soon as it rains."

He felt constrained to apologize by the extreme tidiness of the gardens. There was something not quite real about the Vatican, he was beginning to feel. It was like Rome devoid of Romans, peopled instead by a quiet, orderly, industrious race. There was no litter, no graffiti, no traffic. Cars were parked strictly within the painted boxes allotted for the purpose, and the few people about walked briskly along, intent on their business. The grass was not only neatly trimmed and innocent of used condoms and spent syringes, it was also a richer, more vibrant shade of green, as though it were part of the divine dispensation that the Holy City received more rain than the secular one without the walls. Trees and shrubs, hedges and flower beds, all appeared vibrant and vigorous, like illustrations from a theological textbook exemplifying the argument from design. In principle this was all extremely pleasant. In practice it gave Zen the creeps, like a replica everyone was conspiring to pass off as the real thing.

"Among the responsibilities of this special Vigilanza department," Sànchez-Valdès was saying, "is the covert surveillance of individuals living or working within the Vatican City State whose activities have for one reason or another attracted the attention of my department. Until last Friday, one of these was Prince Ludovico Ruspanti."

The archbishop broke off as they approached a team of gardeners at work resetting a rockery. He nodded at the men, who inclined their heads respectfully. Once they were out of earshot again, Sànchez-Valdès resumed.

"As you are no doubt aware, Ruspanti was under investigation by the Italian judiciary for his part in the illegal export of currency. What you probably do not know, since the matter was *sub judice,* is that his part in this alleged fraud consisted of recycling large sums through his account at the Institute for the Works of Religion. In short, the prince was accused of using the Vatican bank to break Italian law. After the scandals surrounding the collapse of the Banco Ambrosiano, we clearly could not be seen to be sheltering him from justice. But although we had our own reasons for allowing Ruspanti the temporary use of a grace-and-favor apartment while he sorted out his affairs, we weren't naive enough simply to leave him to his own devices."

Zen looked up at the crest of the hill above them, where the mighty bastion of the original fortifications was now crowned with the transmitting aerials of Vatican Radio.

"In that case . . ." he began, then broke off.

Sànchez-Valdès finished it for him.

"In that case, we should know who killed him, just as the anonymous letter to the papers claimed. Yes, we should. The problem is that the official assigned to Ruspanti on the day he died was . . ."

"Giovanni Grimaldi."

The archbishop gestured as though to say "There you are!" The alley they were following had reached a roundabout from which five others led off in various directions, each with its name inscribed on a travertine slab mounted in a metal stand. Sànchez-Valdès turned left along a straight gravel path running along the foot of a section of the original Vatican walls, towering up thirty meters or more to their machicolated battlements.

"Grimaldi was presumably debriefed before I arrived that Friday," Zen commented.

Sànchez-Valdès nodded.

"He said he had lost Ruspanti among the throng of tourists up on the dome of St. Peter's and was trying to find him again in the basilica when the body fell. At the time there seemed no reason not to believe this. The first thing to raise our suspicions was the disappearance of the transcript that had been made of Ruspanti's telephone conversations. Ah, there's Luigi!"

A plump man with carefully permed silvery hair and a benign expression stood by a pine tree beside the path, watching them approach. Zen felt a surge of revulsion. He suddenly couldn't wait to get out of this place, where even the chief of police looked like a parody of a kindly, absentminded village priest.

"We made the inquiries you requested," Scarpione told Sànchez-Valdès once the introductions had been performed. "The supervisor responsible for the Carmelites' holdings says that no repair work had been ordered in the house where Grimaldi lived."

The archbishop looked at Zen.

"Well, there's the answer to the question you put to us last night. What is its significance?"

"Grimaldi's neighbor, Marco Duranti, said that someone was working there on Monday afternoon with an electric drill, supposedly repairing the drains."

"And someone was there again last night," Scarpione broke in, proud of his scoop. "I've just had a call about it from the Carabinieri. They were called out by this Duranti, but unfortunately the intruders managed to escape by using some sort of smoke bomb."

Zen coughed loudly.

"They probably came back to search Grimaldi's room again."

The archbishop frowned.

"Again?"

"They tried once before, after they killed him."

Luigi Scarpione took a moment to react. Sànchez-Valdès turned to

Zen, indicating the Vigilanza chief's stunned and horrified expression as proof that the Vatican's hands were clean of Grimaldi's death. Zen held up his palms in token of the fact that he had never for a moment believed otherwise.

"But the Carabinieri . . ." Scarpione began.

"The Carabinieri don't know about Grimaldi's involvement in the Ruspanti case," Zen broke in. "In fact they don't even know there *is* a Ruspanti case. If they did, they might have concluded that two such deaths in five days was a bit too much of a coincidence, and taken the trouble to investigate the circumstances of Grimaldi's 'accident' a little more thoroughly, as I did. In which case, they would no doubt have discovered that the workman who came to the house on Monday afternoon had drilled a hole through the wall between the bathroom and the passage outside, enabling him to connect an electric cable to the water pipes feeding the shower. A woman was over at the house on Monday morning, talking to Grimaldi, and I saw her leave on Tuesday, just after he died. She would have waited for him to go into the shower, as he did every day before starting work, and then thrown the switch. The moment Grimaldi stepped under the water he was effectively plugged into the mains. Afterward the woman pulled the cable free and removed it, leaving an electrocuted body inside a bathroom bolted from the inside. Of *course* the Carabinieri thought it was an accident. What else were they supposed to think?"

Scarpione shuddered. Sànchez-Valdès patted him reassuringly on the shoulder and led the way along an alley leading past the helicopter landing pad from which the pope set off to his villa and swimming pool in the Alban hills, or on one of his frequent foreign trips.

"And what about you, Dottore?" he asked Zen. "What do *you* think?"

Zen shrugged.

"What had Grimaldi been working on this week, since Ruspanti's death?"

"A case involving the theft of documents from the Archives," said Scarpione. "Giovanni was patroling the building, posing as a researcher."

"Not the sort of thing people would kill for?"

"Good heavens, no! A minor trade in illegal antiquities, that's all."

"In that case, my guess is that he tried to put the squeeze on the men who murdered Ruspanti. That transcript that's gone missing probably contained some reference implicating them. Grimaldi put two and two together, stole the transcript, and offered to sell it for the right price. That would also explain why he sent the anonymous letter to the papers. He couldn't blackmail the killers without casting enough doubt on the suicide verdict to get the case reopened."

The three men passed through a gap in the battlemented walls, the truncated portion covered with a rich coat of ivy, and started downhill through the formally landscaped gardens, the dome of St. Peter's rising before them in all its splendor.

"Have you located the source of the keys Ruspanti's killers used?" Zen asked casually.

Sànchez-Valdès nodded.

"Yes indeed! Tell Dottor Zen about the progress we've been making this end, Luigi."

Scarpione glanced at the archbishop.

"All of it?"

"All, all!"

The Vigilanza chief cleared his throat and began.

"We thought at first it might be one of the *sampietrini.*"

He lowered his voice discreetly.

"There have been complaints on several occasions from some of the younger workers about the behavior of Antonio Cecchi, their boss."

"A little matter of attempted buggery, to be precise," Sànchez-Valdès explained cheerfully.

Scarpione coughed again.

"Yes, well . . ."

"Like many people," the archbishop went on, speaking to Zen, "Luigi makes the mistake of supposing that we priests are either ignorant of or embarrassed by the facts of life. If he had spent half as much time in a confessional as we have, he would realize that there is nothing likely to shock us very much. Carry on, Luigi!"

"Well, anyway, in the end one of the uniformed custodians who patrol the dome during the hours of public access admitted that he had been responsible. He said he was approached by a man who represented himself as a monsignore attached to the Curia. This person claimed that a party of notables from his native town were visiting the Vatican, and said he wanted to give them a private tour of the basilica. He would be so obliged if it would be possible for him to borrow the keys for an hour or two."

"All such requests are supposed to be submitted in writing," Sànchez-Valdès explained, "but no lay worker in the Vatican is going to refuse a favor to a member of the Curia."

Zen grunted.

"Only in this case, he wasn't."

"We have a description of the impostor," Scarpione assured him. "He was of average stature, quite young, with fair hair and fine features."

"Well, that rules out La Cicciolina."

"I'm sorry?"

"Dottor Zen is being ironic," Sànchez-Valdès explained heavily. "His implication is that, while the description you have given may effectively exclude the ex–porn queen and present Radical Party deputy from suspicion, it is imprecise enough to cover almost everyone else."

"I'm sure you did the best you could," Zen murmured, glancing at his watch.

They had reached a terrace overlooking a formal garden in the French style. In a cutting below, a diesel locomotive hooted and started to reverse around a freight train on the branch line linking the Vatican to the Italian state railway system.

"We mustn't detain you any longer, Dottore," Sànchez-Valdès told Zen. He turned to Scarpione. "How can we get him out of here without attracting attention, Luigi? The last thing we want is a front-page photograph of the man from the Ministry of the Interior leaving the Vatican after high-level consultations at the Secretariat of State when he's supposedly too ill to answer questions from the press."

"How did he get in?" asked Scarpione.

"Through the museum. But that'll be too risky at this time of day."

The Vigilanza man pondered for a moment.

"I suppose I could get one of my men to smuggle him out in a delivery van or something . . ."

Sànchez-Valdès shook his head.

"I don't want to subject their loyalty to any further tests just at present," he remarked acidly.

He snapped his fingers.

"I know! That train looks like it's about to leave. Go and have a word with the crew, Luigi, and ask them to drop our visitor off at the mainline station. It's only a short ride, and that way he's sure to be unobserved."

Scarpione hurried off, eager to prove that *his* loyalty, at any rate, was unimpeachable. As soon as he was out of earshot, Sànchez-Valdès turned to Zen.

"Despite what our detractors say, Dottore, I urge you to accept that the Vatican has no vested interest in obscurity or mystification, still less in such wickedness as these killings. Our only wish is to see the perpetrators brought to justice, and I can assure you that we will bend all our efforts to that end. On the basis of the information you have provided today, I shall make representations to the Carabinieri to re-open their investigation into Grimaldi's death . . ."

"Without mentioning my name," Zen insisted.

Sànchez-Valdès waved his beringed hand to indicate that this might be taken for granted. Outside the huge unused station building below, the diesel locomotive blew its horn. Luigi Scarpione stood on the platform nearby, beckoning frantically.

"It's about to leave," said Sànchez-Valdès.

Zen turned to him suddenly.

"What about the Cabal?"

A distant look entered the archbishop's eyes.

"What?"

"Grimaldi's letter to the newspapers claimed that on the day he died, Ruspanti had been going to meet the representatives of an organization called the Cabal. His other allegations have turned out to be true. What about that one?"

Sànchez-Valdès laughed lightly.

"Oh, *that!* No, no, that was just some nonsense Ruspanti dreamed up."

"Ruspanti?"

"Yes, he used it as bait, to tempt us into giving him sanctuary. It's rather embarrassing, to tell you the truth! He took us in completely with this cock-and-bull tale about some secret group within the Knights of Malta that supposedly . . ."

Zen stared.

"The Knights of Malta?"

"Absurd, isn't it? That bunch of old fogies and social climbers! Mind you, Ruspanti was one of them himself, which lent his claims a certain *prima facie* credibility. In return for our assistance, he promised to spill the beans on the various political conspiracies this group was supposedly planning. As soon as we examined his claims, of course, it was evident that there was nothing in them."

The diesel hooted again, longer this time.

"Hurry, Dottore, or they'll leave without you!" Sànchez-Valdès urged. "We don't want to create an international incident by preventing the departure of an Italian train, do we? Incidentally, you're probably the first person to leave the Vatican by train since Papa Roncalli went on a pilgrimage to Assisi back in the sixties. What about that, eh? Something to tell your grandchildren!"

"Deuce!"

"Thirty-forty, isn't it?"

"No, no, my friend. It was thirty-forty after you fluffed my last service return."

"All right, all right."

Rackets were raised once more, the fluffy yellow ball flew to and fro, the players pranced about the pink asphalt. The server sported a racy Sergio Tacchini outfit whose top, shorts, socks, shoes, and sweatbands were all elements in the same bold abstract pattern. His opponent had opted for a classic all-white image by Ellesse, but it was falling flat. Having just blown the opportunity to save the set, he looked plain rather than restrained, not timeless but out of date.

"Advantage!" called Sergio Tacchini confidently.

"It was out!" whined Ellesse.

"Says who?"

"I saw it cross the line! It was nowhere near!"

"Oh! Oh! Gino, don't try that stuff on with me!"

"I tell you . . ."

"All right, let's get a neutral opinion."

The server turned to the man who was looking on from the other side of the tall mesh netting that surrounded the court.

"Hey, you! You saw that shot? It was in, wasn't it?"

"Come off it, Rodolfo!" his opponent objected. "If they let the guy up here, he must work for you. Do you think he's going to tell his own Minister that his shot was too long?"

"On the contrary, everyone knows I'll be on my way once this reshuffle finally hits. I can't even get a cup of coffee sent up any more. In fact, he's going to give it *your* way, Gino, if he's got any sense. For all anyone knows, you could be his boss next week!"

He turned again to the onlooker, a gaunt, imposing figure with sharp, angular features and a gaze that hovered ambiguously between menace and mockery.

"Listen, er—what's your name?"

"Zen, Minister. Vice-Questore, Criminalpol. I'm afraid I didn't see the ball land."

Rodolfo returned to the baseline shaking his head.

"Fine, we'll play a let. I don't need flukes to beat you, Gino. I've got in-depth superiority."

He skied the ball and whacked it across the net with a grunt suggestive of a reluctant bowel movement. Zen clasped his hands behind his back and pretended to take an interest in the progress of the game. Fortunately there were other distractions. Despite being located on the least illustrious of Rome's seven hills, the roof of the Ministry of the Interior still afforded extensive views. To the right, Zen could admire the neighboring Quirinal and its palace, once the seat of popes and kings, now the official residence of the President of the Italian Republic. To the left, the ruined hulks of ancient Rome's most desirable residential quarter gave a rural appearance to the Palatine. In between, the densely populated sprawl of the city center, covered by a veil of smog, resembled the treacherous marshland it had once been. In the hazy distance below the hills on the far bank of the Tiber, the dome of St. Peter's hovered, seemingly weightless, like a baroque hot-air balloon.

The sun was hidden behind a skin of cloud that diffused its light evenly across the flat roof. The Ministry's complex system of transmitting and receiving aerials, towering above like ship's rigging, increased

Zen's sense of detachment from the mundane realities of life in the invisible streets far below. The train that had carried him back to Italy that morning consisted of four empty cars that had discharged their duty-free imports and one flatbed laden with the mosaics that were the Vatican's only material export. Zen had looked back from the cab of the superannuated green-and-brown diesel locomotive at the massive iron gates closing behind the train, just as all the Vatican gates still did at midnight, sealing off the one-hundred-acre city state from its encircling secular neighbor. The complexities of the relationship between the two were something Zen was only beginning to appreciate now that he found himself trapped at the interface, a speck of grit caught in the bearings of power.

Despite his promise to Sànchez-Valdès, he had every intention of filing a full report on the Ruspanti affair. The first rule of survival in any organization is "Cover thyself." No matter that Moscati had told Zen he was on his own, it was between him and the Vatican, the Ministry didn't want to know. None of that would save Zen if—or, as now seemed almost inevitable, when—the tortuous and murky ramifications of the Ruspanti affair turned into a major political scandal. If Zen failed to keep the Ministry fully briefed, this would either be ascribed to devious personal motives or to twitchings on the strings by which one of the interested parties controlled him. Either way, his position would be untenable. A man as sophisticated as Sànchez-Valdès must have known this, so Zen assumed that the real purpose of that "walk in the woods" had been to pass on information the Curia could not release officially, to smuggle a message out of the Vatican in much the same way as Zen himself. It was now up to Zen to make sure the message got through.

Under normal circumstances, his section chief would have been the person to go to, but after hearing Tania recount Moscati's gloating remarks about their relationship Zen didn't trust himself to handle the conversation with the necessary professional reserve. Then he recalled something Moscati had said when they spoke on the phone the previous morning. "Result, the Minister finds himself in the hot seat just as the entire government is about to go into the blender and he had his eye on some nice fat portfolio like Finance." So the Minister was not only aware of Zen's gaffe, but had been politically embarrassed by criticism from the "blue-bloods at the Farnesina," the Ministry of Foreign Affairs, who would have sustained the full wrath of the Apostolic Nuncio. By the time the Vatican freight train drew into the station of San Pietro F.S., Zen had decided this was a time for going straight to the top. That way, when the lies and obfuscations started, he would at least know their source. He would speak to the Minister personally, tell him what had happened and what Archbishop Sànchez-Valdès had said. Then, later, he would write up a full report of the incident (with an editorial slant favorable to him, naturally) to be filed in the Ministerial database as permanent proof, dated and signed, that he had fulfilled his duties.

Until recently, San Pietro had been a little-used suburban stop on an antediluvian branch line to Viterbo. All that had changed with the decision to upgrade part of the route as a link between Stazione Termini and the new high speed *direttissima* line to Florence. As a result, a tunnel under the Gianicolo hill had been reconstructed and the station remodeled in the latest color-coordinated Eurostyle. Local service hadn't improved, however, so Zen had walked out of the station and took the 62 bus across town, slipping into the Ministry through a side entrance to elude any reporters who might be around. Now, watching the tennis players swooping and reaching in the mild sunlight, that interlude seemed to him like a brief dip into the polluted and treacherous waters separating the verdant isle of the Vatican City State from this stately cruise liner where the Minister and his opponent were disporting themselves. Gino was an undersecretary in the Ministry of Health, which occupied the other half of the huge building on the Viminal hill. To satisfy the elaborate formulas of the *manuale Cencelli,* by which positions of power are distributed among the various political parties, this post had been allocated to a member of the moribund Liberal party, while Rodolfo was a well-known figure in the Andreotti wing of the Christian Democrats. But although they were nominally political rivals, the contest that the two men were currently engaged in was infinitely more keenly fought than any that was ever allowed to disrupt the stifling calm in which the country's *nomenclatura* basked and grew fat.

"Game, set, and match!" called the Minister as the ball scudded off the asphalt out of reach of Gino's racket.

"Lucky bounce, Rodolfo."

"Crap, my friend. You have just been outplayed physically and intellectually. My only surprise is that you still haven't learned to lose with grace. After all, it's all your party has been able to do for the last thirty years."

He strode over to Zen, his skin gleaming with perspiration and flushed with victory. The Minister's even, rounded features expressed an image of sensitivity and culture that was fatally undermined by the mouth, a cramped slot that might have been the result of plastic surgery.

"You wanted to see me?"

Zen assumed his most respectful demeanor.

"Yes, sir. I have a message for you."

The Minister laughed shortly.

"The problem of overmanning must be even more dire than I'd imagined if we're using senior Criminalpol officials as messengers."

He turned back to his opponent.

"Consolation prize, Gino! You get to have first go in the shower while I see what this fellow wants."

Rubbing his head vigorously with a towel, the Minister led the way down a short flight of stairs into his suite on the top floor of the building and threw himself down on a black leather sofa. Zen remained standing.

"It's about the Ruspanti case," he said hesitantly.

He expected some furious response, threats or insults, demands for apologies and explanations. The Minister merely stared up at him slightly more intently.

"I'm sorry if . . . I mean, I understand that there were some . . . That is to say . . ."

Zen broke off, disconcerted. He belatedly realized that he had allowed himself to be tricked into the elementary blunder of implying that what underlings like him did or failed to do could seriously effect anyone other than themselves. Moscati's phrase about the Minister find-ing himself "in the hot seat" as a result of Zen's mishandling of the Ruspanti affair was pure hyperbole. Politicians could no more be brought down by such things than a ship could be capsized by the actions of fish on the ocean bed. It was the weather on the surface, in the political world itself, that would determine the Minister's career prospects. Judging by his manner, the forecast was good.

"I don't want to rush you, er . . . what did you say your name was?" he grunted, getting to his feet, "but if you have a message for me, perhaps you could deliver it without too much further delay. I have to see the prefect of Bari in twenty minutes to discuss the Albanian refugee problem."

He stretched out full-length on the floor and started doing push-ups. Zen took a deep breath.

"Yes, sir. The fact is, I've just returned from the Vatican, where I had an audience of His Excellency Juan Ramòn Sànchez-Valdès, first deputy to the Cardinal Secretary of State. His Excellency gave me to understand that he was entirely satisfied with my, quote, discreet and invaluable intervention, unquote. An official communiqué to this effect will be forwarded by the Papal Nuncio in due course."

The Minister rolled over on to his back, hooked his toes under the base of the sofa, and started doing sit-ups.

"And you just wanted me to know that you're happy as a pig in shit?"

"No, sir. There's more."

"And better, I hope."

"Yes, sir. His Excellency Sànchez-Valdès confirmed that Prince Ludovico Ruspanti had been living in the Vatican City State for some weeks prior to his death. Not only that, but a special undercover unit of the Vigilanza Security Service was tapping Ruspanti's phone and maintaining surveillance on his movements. The implication is that some people at least knew from the beginning that Ruspanti had not committed suicide, and even knew the identity of his killers."

That made the Minister sit up, and not just for exercise.

"Go on," he said.

"One of those people was Giovanni Grimaldi, the Vigilanza official who was assigned to Ruspanti on Friday afternoon. He also had access to the transcript of the prince's phone calls, which subsequently disappeared. The Curia also has evidence that Grimaldi was the source of the anonymous letter sent to the newspapers on Monday evening."

"Bet you're glad you're not in his shoes, eh, Zeppo?"

"Zen, sir. Yes, sir. He's dead. It was disguised as an accident, but he was murdered, presumably by the people who killed Ruspanti. His Excellency Sànchez-Valdès mentioned that the Vatican was induced to give Ruspanti sanctuary by the promise of information about a secret political conspiracy within the Order of Malta, a group called the Cabal. Nothing more seems to be known about this organization, but the implication must be that it was their agents who faked Ruspanti's suicide and arranged for Grimaldi to have his fatal accident."

The door opened and Gino strode in, spick and span in a Valentino suit, reeking of cologne, his hair implant cockily bouffant.

"All yours, Rodolfo."

The Minister got up heavily. He looked older and moved stiffly.

"Just a moment, Gino. I won't be long."

Gino shrugged casually and left. It was he who looked the winner now. The Minister mechanically toweled away the sweat on his brow and face.

"Is that all?" he muttered.

"Almost," nodded Zen. "There's just one more thing. Yesterday I received an anonymous telegram saying that if I wanted to 'get these deaths in perspective,' I should go to a certain address on the Aventine. It turned out to be the Palace of Rhodes, the extraterritorial property of the Order of Malta."

The Minister grimaced contemptuously.

"So what? Someone saw your name in the paper and decided to have a bit of fun at your expense. Happens all the time."

"That's what I thought at first. But the message referred to 'deaths,' *plural*. At the time it was sent, only one person had died— Ludovico Ruspanti. But the people who sent the telegram already knew that Giovanni Grimaldi would be killed the following day. They'd spent Monday afternoon making the necessary arrangements. And on the wall of the room where Grimaldi was killed, they'd chalked an eight-pointed Maltese cross."

The Minister regarded Zen steadily for what seemed like a very long time. All his earlier facetiousness had deserted him.

"Thank you, Dottore," he said, finally. "You did right to keep me informed, and I look forward to receiving your written report in due course."

He flung his towel over his shoulder and padded off to the bathroom.

"Can you find your own way out?"

The lift was through the Minister's office, where Gino was studying a framed photograph of the Minister with Giulio Andreotti. He smiled cynically at Zen.

"Behold the secret of Rodolfo's success," he said in a stage whisper.

Zen paused and looked up at the large photograph, which hung in pride of place above the Minister's desk. Both politicians were in formal morning dress. Both looked smug, solid, utterly sure of themselves. Beneath their white bow ties, both wore embroidered bands from which hung a prominent gilt pendant incorporating the eight-pointed cross of the Sovereign Military Order of Malta.

"With Big Ears by his side," Gino explained, "he'll go all the way."

"And how far is that?" asked Zen.

Gino stabbed the outer fingers of his right hand at the photograph in the gesture used to ward off evil.

"All the way to hell!"

The lift seemed to have a mind of its own that day. Zen was sure he had pushed the right button, but when the doors slid apart the scene that greeted him was very different from what he had expected. Instead of the polished marble and elegant appointments of the Criminalpol offices on the third floor, he found himself in a cavernous hangar, ill lit and foul smelling. The oppressively low ceiling, like the squat rectangular pillars that supported it, was of bare concrete. The air was filled with a haze of black fumes and a continuous dull rumbling.

"What can I do for you, *dottò?*"

A dwarflike figure materialized at Zen's elbow. The empty right sleeve of his jacket, flattened and neatly folded, was pinned back to the shoulder. The face, shriveled and deeply lined, expressed a readiness to perform minor miracles and cut-price magic of all kinds.

"Oh, Salvatò!" Zen replied.

"Don't tell me. You couldn't get through on the phone."

Salvatore ejected an impressive gob of spittle, which landed on the concrete with a loud splat.

"I had your boss Moscati down here the other day. Salvatò, he says, I've been on the phone half an hour trying to get through, finally I decided it was quicker to come down in person."

He waved his hand expressively.

"But what can I do? All I've got is one phone. One phone for the whole Ministry to book rides, *dottò!* You need a switchboard down here, Moscati says to me. Don't even think about it, I tell him. Look at the switchboard upstairs. The girls are so busy selling cosmetics and junk jewelry on the side that you can't get through at all!"

They both laughed.

"Where to, *dottò?*" asked Salvatore, resuming his air of professional harassment.

Zen was about to confess his mistake, or rather the lift's, when an idea sprang fully formed into his mind.

"Any chance of a one-way to Fiumicino in about half an hour?"

Salvatore frowned, as he always did. Then an almost incredulous smile spread slowly across his face.

"You're in luck, *dottò!*"

He pointed across the garage toward the source of the rumbling noise. Now that his eyes had adjusted to the dimness, Zen could just make out a blue saloon with its hood up. A man in overalls was bent over the engine while another sat behind the wheel with his foot on the accelerator.

"We've been having a spot of trouble with that one," Salvatore explained, "but it's almost sorted out now. It's the grace of God, *dottò*. Normally I'd have been a bit pushed to come up with a vehicle at such short notice."

This was an understatement. The real point of the joke at which Salvatore and Zen had laughed a moment before was that the garage phone was largely tied up by the demands of the private limousine service Salvatore and his drivers had organized. Their rates were not the lowest in Rome, but they had the edge over the competition in being able to penetrate to any part of the city, including those officially closed to motor vehicles. For a special rate, they could even lay on a police motorcycle escort to clear a lane through the Roman traffic. This was a boon to the wealthy and self-important and was frequently used by businessmen wishing to impress clients from out of town, but it did have the effect of drastically restricting use of the pool by Ministry staff.

"The airport in half an hour?" beamed Salvatore. "No problem!"

"Not the airport," Zen corrected as he stepped back into the lift. "The *town* of Fiumicino."

In the Criminalpol suite on the third floor, Zen flipped through the items in his in-tray. It was the first time he had been into work since Friday, so there was quite a pile. Holding the stack of papers, envelopes, and folders in his left hand, he dealt them swiftly into three piles: those to throw away now; those to throw away later, after noting the single relevant fact, date, or time; and those to place in his out-tray, having ticked the box indicating that he had read the contents from cover to cover.

"Dominus vobiscum," a voice intoned fruitily.

Zen looked up from an internal memorandum reading "Please call 645 9866at lunchtime and ask for Simonelli." Giorgio De Angelis was looking around the edge of the cloth-covered screen that divided their respective working areas.

"According to the media, you're dangerously ill with a rare infectious virus," the Calabrian went on, "so I won't come any closer. This miraculous recovery is just one of the perks of working for the pope, I suppose. Pick up thy bed and walk and so on. How did you swing it, anyway? They say you can't even get a cleaning job in the Vatican these days unless you have Polish blood."

For some time after his transfer to Criminalpol, Zen had been slightly suspicious of De Angelis, fearing that his apparent bonhomie might be a strategy designed to elicit compromising admissions or disclosures. The promotion of Zen's enemy Vincenzo Fabri to the post of Questore of Ferrara, combined with Zen's coup in solving the Burolo affair to the satisfaction of the various political interests involved, had changed all that. With his position in the department no longer under direct threat, Zen was at last able to appreciate Giorgio De Angelis's jovial good-humor without scanning everything he said for hidden meanings.

The Calabrian produced a newspaper article that quoted Zen as "reaffirming that there were no suspicious circumstances surrounding the death of Ludovico Ruspanti" and dismissing the allegations in the anonymous letter as "mischievous and ill-informed."

"Impressive prose for a man with a high fever," he commented, running his fingers through the babyish fuzz that was all that now grew on the impressive expanses of his skull. "I particularly liked the homage to our own dear Marcelli."

Zen smiled wryly. The phrase "mischievous and ill-informed rumors" was a favorite of the ministerial undersecretary in question, who had almost certainly penned the statement.

"But seriously, Aurelio, what really happened? Is there any truth in these allegations that Ruspanti was murdered?"

Catching the eager glint in De Angelis's eyes, Zen realized he was going to have to come up with a story to peddle around the department. At least half the fun of working there was the conversational advantage it gave you with your relatives and friends. Whether you spoke or kept silent, it was assumed that you were in the know. As soon as his colleagues discovered that Zen was no longer "ill," they were all going to want him to fill them in on the Ruspanti affair.

"Who's to say it *was* Ruspanti?" he replied.

De Angelis goggled at him.

"You mean . . ."

Zen shrugged.

"I saw the body, Giorgio. It looked like it had been through a food processor. I'd be prepared to testify that it was human, and probably male, but I wouldn't go any further under oath."

"Can't they tell from the dental records?"

Zen nodded.

"Which may be why the body was handed over to the family before anyone had a chance. The funeral's being held this afternoon."

De Angelis gave a low whistle.

"But why?"

"Ruspanti was broke and had this currency fraud hanging over him. He needed time to organize his affairs and play his political cards. So he decided to fake his own death."

De Angelis nodded, wide-eyed at the sheer ingenuity of the thing.

"So who died in St. Peter's?" he asked.

"We'll never know. You'd need a personal intervention by Wojtyla to get an exhumation order now. It was probably someone you've never heard of."

De Angelis shook his head with knowing superiority.

"More likely a person of the very highest importance, someone they needed to get out of the way."

Zen gestured loosely, conceding that this, too, was possible.

"Let's talk about it over lunch," the Calabrian suggested eagerly.

"Sorry, Giorgio, not today. I've already got an appointment. Now if you'll excuse me, I have to make a phone call."

As his colleague left to circulate the true story behind the Ruspanti affair through the department, Zen pulled the phone over and dialed the number written on the message form.

"Hotel Torlonia Palace."

The calm, deep voice was in marked contrast to the usual Roman squawk that hovered as though by an effort of will on the brink of screaming hysteria. Zen had never heard of the Hotel Torlonia Palace, but he already knew that you wouldn't be able to get a room there for less than a quarter of a million lire a night.

"May I speak to Dottor Simonelli, please."

"One moment."

After a brief silence, a male voice with a distinct reedy timbre came on the line.

"Yes?"

"This is Vice-Questore Aurelio Zen, at the Interior Ministry. I received a message . . ."

"That is correct. I am Antonio Simonelli, investigating magistrate with the Procura of Milan. Am I right in thinking we've been in contact before?"

"Not as far as I know."

"Ah," the voice replied. "I must have confused you with someone else. Anyway, I was hoping it would be possible for us to meet. I have some questions I wish to ask you relative to my investigations. Could you call on me this afternoon?"

Although his heart sank, Zen knew that this was one more hurdle he was going to have to go through. They made an appointment to meet at four o'clock in the lobby of the hotel. Zen hung up with a massive sigh and hastened downstairs to find Tania. This damned case was a hydra! No sooner had he seen off the Vatican, the Minister, and an inquisitive colleague than up popped some judge from Milan.

Of all the offices in the building, those occupied by the Administration department most clearly betrayed the Ministry's Fascist birthright: a warren of identical hutches, each containing six identical desks disposed in the same symmetrical order. Tania shared her cubicle with three other women and two men, both of whom had unwittingly been auditioned by Zen for the part of her mysterious lover. But their voices didn't match the one he had heard on the phone, and besides, he doubted whether Tania would have gone for either the fat, balding father-of-three or his neighbor, the neurotic obsessive with bad breath. He doubted, but he couldn't be sure. You could never tell with women. She had gone for *him* after all. With taste like that, who could tell what she might stoop to next?

Tania was talking on the phone when he walked in. As soon as she caught sight of Zen, a furtive air came over her. Shielding her mouth with one hand, she spoke urgently into the phone as he strode toward her. All he could make out before she hung up was "I'll speak to you later," but it was enough. The form of the verb was familiar, her tone conspiratorial.

"Who was that?" he demanded.

"Oh, just a relative."

She actually blushed. Zen let it go, out of self-interest rather than magnanimity. What with the stresses and strains of the morning, and those that loomed later in the afternoon, he needed an interval of serenity. In a way it didn't even seem to matter that her love was all a fake. If she was making use of him, then he would make use of her. That way they were even.

He stared at the computer screen on the desk, which displayed a list of names and addresses, many of them in foreign countries. Surely they couldn't *all* be her lovers? Tania depressed a key and the screen reverted to the READY display.

"Shall we go?" she asked.

But Zen continued to gaze at the screen. After a moment he pressed one of the function keys, selecting the SEARCH option. SUBJECT?

queried the screen. Zen typed "Malta/Knights." The screen went into a brief coma before producing two lines of print: "SOVEREIGN MILITARY ORDER OF MALTA / KNIGHTS OF MALTA / KNIGHTS OF ST. JOHN OF JERUSALEM / KNIGHTS HOSPITALERS: I FILES(S); 583 INSTANCE(S)."

"What does that mean?" he asked Tania.

She surveyed the screen with the impatience of a professional aware of the value of her time.

"It means, first of all, that these people evidently can't make up their minds what to call themselves, so they are referred to under four different titles. The database holds one report specifically dedicated to this organization. There are also five hundred plus references in other files."

"What sort of references?"

Tania's swift, competent fingers rattled the keyboard with panache. "AUTHORIZATION?" appeared. ZEN, she typed. Again the screen faltered briefly, then filled with text, which proved to be an extract from the Ministry's file on a Turin businessman who had been convicted of involvement in a local government corruption scandal in the early eighties. The reference Zen had requested was picked out by the cursor: "Member of the Sovereign Military Order of Malta since 1964 with rank of Knight of Magisterial Grace."

That sort of thing was apparently all there was, at least in the open files. He got Tania to run him off a copy of the report on the Knights of Malta, even though he knew that anything really worth knowing would be held in the "closed" section of the database, accessible only with special authorization restricted to a handful of senior staff. The files stored there supposedly detailed the financial status, professional and political allegiances, family situation and sexual predilections of almost fourteen million Italian citizens. Like everyone else, Zen had often wondered what his own entry contained. Was his connection with Tania included by now? Presumably, judging by Moscati's mocking remarks. How much more did they know? Reading such an entry would be like seeing a copy of your own obituary, and just as difficult.

FOUR

They strolled along the quay, hand in hand, fingers entwined. It had rained while they were in the restaurant, briefly but hard. Now the sky had cleared again, every surface glistened, and the air was flooded with elusive, evocative scents.

The little town of Fiumicino, at the mouth of the narrower of the two channels into which the Tiber divided just before it met the sea, was a place to which Zen always returned with pleasure. The scale of the place, the narrow waterway and the low buildings flanking it, the sea tang, the bustle of a working port, all combined to remind him of the fishing villages of the Venetian lagoon. In addition, Fiumicino contained several restaurants capable of doing justice to the quality and freshness of the catches its boats brought in.

Replete with *crema di riso gratinato ai frutti di mare* and grilled sea bass with artichokes, he and Tania strolled along the stone quays like a pair of young lovers without a care in the world.

". . . the best artichokes in the world," she was saying. "My aunt cooks them and prepares the hearts, then they bottle them in oil, ten kilos at a time."

"You're making me hungry again."

"You must try them, Aurelio! I'll get Aldo to send an extra jar with the next batch of samples . . ."

She broke off.

"Batch of what?" Zen asked mechanically, so as not to reveal that he hadn't been listening, absorbed in the spectacle of a skinny cat stalking a butterfly across a pile of empty fish crates.

"The next time one of the family comes to Rome, I mean," said Tania.

"Look!"

Balanced on its hind legs like a performing monkey, the cat was frantically pawing at the air, trying in vain to seize the elusive, substanceless quiver of color.

"You'll never catch it, silly!" laughed Tania in a slightly tipsy voice. "And even if you do, there's nothing there to eat!"

Still intent on its prey, the cat stepped off the edge of the boxes. It twisted round in midair and landed on its feet, shooting a hostile glance at the couple who had witnessed its humiliation.

"Actually I may go myself, this weekend," Tania announced as they continued on their way.

"Go? Where?"

"Home to Udine, to see my cousins."

Zen freed his hand.

"Suppose I came too?"

Tania shot him a panicky glance.

"You? Well . . ."

She gave an embarrassed laugh.

"You see, Bettina and Aldo don't actually know about you."

A few minutes earlier, as they walked together along the quay, Zen had found himself thinking, "This, or something very like it, is happiness." That exaltation now looked like nothing more special than a side effect of the verdicchio they had drunk at lunch. Now the hangover had arrived.

"So who *do* they know about?" he demanded truculently.

Tania looked at him, a new hardness in her eyes.

"They know I'm no longer with Mauro, if that's what you mean."

He didn't say whether it was or not.

"So they think you're living alone."

"Well, aren't I?"

They faced each other for a moment over that. Then Tania broke into a smile and took his arm.

"Look, Bettina's my cousin, the second daughter of my father's younger brother. It's not an intimate relationship, but since my parents died and Nino emigrated to Australia it's the best I've got. Bettina doesn't burden me with her problems and I don't burden her with mine."

"I didn't realize I was a problem," he replied, snapping up the cheap shot on offer.

"I didn't mean that, Aurelio. I mean that we don't share our innermost preoccupations, good or bad. We keep our distance. That's the best way sometimes, particularly with relatives. Otherwise the whole thing can get out of control."

"And control is important to you, is it?"

He hated the snide way he said it. So did Tania, it soon became clear.

"And why not?" she snapped. "Damn it, I spent the first thirty years of my life asleep at the wheel. You saw the result. Now I've decided to try taking charge for a while and see how that goes. I mean, is that all right?"

Aware of the weakness of his position, Zen backed down.

"Of course. Go where you like. It looks like I might have to work, anyway."

The fishing boats, which had landed their catches early that morning, were now tied up two abreast on either side of the channel, stem to stern. Two crewmen were mending nets spread out over the quay, and Tania and Zen chose to go opposite ways around them. As they joined up again, she said, "What *is* this work you're doing, anyway?"

Partly out of fatigue with the truth, partly to get his own back for her own evasions, Zen decided to lie.

"They've got a problem with documents disappearing from the Secret Archives," he said, recalling the case Grimaldi had been working on at the time of his death. "They can't use their own security people because they think some of them may be involved."

"And you hang around like a store detective waiting for someone to lift a pair of tights?"

"More or less. It's a hell of a way to make a living, but if I crack the case I get a full plenary indulgence."

Tania laughed.

"Not that I really need one," he went on, eager to please. "I'm already owed over a hundred thousand years' remission from purgatory. In fact, I'm a bit worried that I might soon reach the stage where my spiritual credit exceeds any practical possibilities I have of sinning. Just think what a ruinous effect that would have on my moral fiber."

"How did you get to be so holy?"

"Oh, I used to be quite devout in my way. I loved the idea of collecting indulgences, like saving up coupons for a free gift. If I said three *Pater noster*s after confession, I got three hundred years remission from purgatory. That seemed an incredible bargain! I couldn't believe my luck. It takes maybe a minute or so, if you gabble, and for that you got off three hundred years of unspeakable torture! I couldn't understand why everyone wasn't taking advantage. Tommaso, my best friend, and I used to vie with each other. I had well over a hundred thousand years' worth stored up before I finally fell in love with Tommaso's sister. After that, the next world no longer seemed quite so important."

His words were drowned by the roar of a plane taking off from the international airport just a few kilometers to the north.

"Anyway," he concluded, "having attended Mass on the first Friday of each month for the nine months after my first communion, I'm assured of dying in a state of grace whatever happens."

To his surprise, Tania immediately reached out and touched the nearest metal—a mooring bollard—for good luck.

"Don't mention such things, Aurelio."

He took her in his arms, and she kissed him in that way she had, making him wish they were in bed.

"Sweetheart," she said.

He laughed, moved despite himself, despite his knowledge that she was cheating on him.

"I didn't know you were superstitious," he said as they walked on. "You've spent too long living with Southerners."

"Now, now! Don't start coming on like some regionalist redneck who thinks the Third World starts at the Apennines."

"Of course it doesn't! It starts at Mestre."

"Mauro may have been a creep, but . . ."

"*May?* Tania, you once described Mauro Bevilacqua as someone for whom strangling at birth would have been too good."

Perhaps that was who she was seeing on the side, he thought. Perhaps Mauro would have the last laugh after all, and Zen would suffer the ignominy of being cuckolded by his lover's husband.

". . . but not *all* Southerners are like that," Tania continued. "Mauro's elder brother, for example, is a charming man, scholarly and cultured, with a nice dry wit."

"Oh yes?" demanded Zen, his jealousy immediately locking onto this new target.

"In fact, you might see him while you're snooping around the Vatican Archives. He works for the region's cultural affairs department, and he spends a lot of time there researching material for exhibitions and so on."

"Maybe he's the one who's been stealing the stuff," Zen muttered moodily.

"From what Tullio says, I'm surprised the thefts were ever noticed. According to him the Vatican collections are so vast and so badly organized that you can spend days tracking down a single item. It's more like a place for hiding documents than for finding them, he says."

She broke off, frightened by the intensity with which he was staring at her.

"What's the matter, Aurelio? Did I say something wrong? You seem so strange today, so moody and unpredictable. Is there something you haven't told me?"

There was a deafening siren blast as a large orange ocean-going tug slipped her moorings on the other side of the river. Zen transferred his obsessively fixated gaze to the vessel as it proceeded slowly downstream toward the open sea.

"Do you ever see this . . . what's his name?"

Now it was Tania's turn to stare.

"Just exactly what is that supposed to mean?"

He looked at her and shrugged, ignoring her indignant tone.

"What it says."

They faced each other like enemies.

"Do I ever see Tullio Bevilacqua?" Tania recited with sarcastic emphasis. "No, I haven't seen him since Mauro and I broke up. Does that satisfy you?"

"But are you on good terms? Would he do you a favor?"

"What sort of favor?" Tania shouted, scaring away the sea gulls. "What the hell are you talking about, Aurelio?"

So he told her.

They returned by train. Tania got off at Trastevere and got a bus back to her flat, while Zen continued to the suburban Tiburtina station. The determined effort they both made to part on good terms was itself the clearest indication yet of the growing crisis in their relationship, and of their mutual sense that things were no longer quite what they seemed.

From the station Zen caught a taxi to the Hotel Torlonia Palace. On the way, he looked through the Ministry's file on the Knights of Malta. As he had expected, the document was entirely noncontroversial, amounting to little more than an outline of the organization's history, structure, and overt aims. Founded in 1070, the Sovereign Military Hospitaler Order of St. John of Jerusalem, of Rhodes, and of Malta was the third oldest religious order after the Benedictines and Augustans, and the first to consist entirely of laymen. The Order was originally formed to staff and run infirmaries during the Crusades, but soon took on a military role as well. At the end of the twelfth century the Knights retreated to Rhodes, from where they conducted covert operations all over the Middle East until their expulsion by the Turks in 1522. Thereafter they led a token existence in Malta until Napoleon's conquest of the island once again forced them into exile, in Rome.

The Knights had thus lost their original religious and political relevance by 1522, and the last fragment of their territorial power three centuries after that. Nevertheless, like an archaic law that has never been repealed, the Order still enjoyed the status and privileges of an independent nation state, with the power to mint coins, print stamps, license cars, operate a merchant fleet, and issue passports to its diplomats and other favored individuals. "Like Opus Dei [q.v.]," Zen read, "the Order is exempt from the jurisdiction of local bishops, being under the direct authority of the Pope, exercised through the Sacred Congregation for Religious and Secular Institutes. The contradiction between the obedience required by this relationship and the independence inherent in the

Order's sovereign temporal status has on occasion led to acrimonious conflicts."

Zen scanned the rest of the report, which sketched the structure of this very exclusive organization. At least sixteen quarterings of noble blood were required for membership, except in a special category—Knights of Magisterial Grace—created to accommodate prominent but plebian Catholics. At the core of the Order were the thirty "professed" knights, or Knights of Justice, who had taken a triple vow of poverty, chastity, and obedience. "Governed by His Most Eminent Highness the Prince and Grand Master with the help of a 'general chapter' which convenes regularly, the Order donates medicine and medical equipment to needy countries and performs humanitarian work throughout the Third World."

The text began to blur in front of Zen's eyes. It was clear what was involved: a snobbish club designed to give the impoverished remnants of the Catholic aristocracy access to serious money, while bestowing a flattering glow of religious and historical legitimacy over the ruthlessly acquired wealth of the nouveaux riches. Under cover of the Order's meritorious charitable work, its members could dress up in fancy red tunics, flowing capes, and plumed hats and indulge themselves to their heart's content in the spurious rituals and meaningless honors of a Ruritanian ministate. All very silly, no doubt, but no more so than most pastimes of the very rich. What was really silly was the idea that such an organization might be capable of plotting—never mind executing—the cold-blooded murders of Ludovico Ruspanti and Giovanni Grimaldi.

The taxi drew up in the courtyard of an *umbertino* monstrosity on a quiet street overlooking the gardens of the Villa Borghese. The uniformed doorman surveyed Zen without notable enthusiasm, but eventually let him pass. Zen identified himself at Reception, walked across the spacious lobby, and flopped down in a large armchair, wondering what he was going to say. He knew it wasn't going to be easy. Antonio Simonelli had a vested interest in establishing that Ruspanti's death was connected with the currency fraud he had been investigating. If it wasn't, his entire dossier on the affair, painstakingly compiled over many months of arduous work, would become so much wastepaper. Since Ruspanti had died in St. Peter's, which was technically foreign soil, Simonelli could not pursue his suspicions officially without the

cooperation of the Vatican, which was not forthcoming. Zen was therefore the magistrate's only hope.

What Simonelli wanted from him was some inside information,
some awkward fact or compromising discrepancy, which he could use
to bring pressure to bear on the Vatican authorities to permit a full
official investigation of Ruspanti's death to be carried out by him in
collaboration with one of the Vatican's own magistrates. The affair
would then drag on inconclusively for years, until it petered out, smoth-
ered beneath the sheer volume of contradictory and confusing evidence.
That would be of no concern to Simonelli, who would meanwhile have
established himself as one of the rising stars of the judiciary, a man to
watch. As for Zen, he would be used and abused without respite by all
sides in the affair, and would be lucky to keep his job. Unless he
scotched this thing now, he would never hear the end of it.

There was a buzz of voices behind him.

"I have nothing further to say!"

"According to Giorgio Bocca, your philosophy encapsulates the
shallow, ahistorical consumerism of the nineties. Do you accept that?"

Zen turned to find a strikingly attractive man in his midtwenties
standing at bay before a pack of reporters brandishing notebooks and
microphones. His sleek, feral look clashed intriguingly with his boyish
fair hair and the candor of his pale blue eyes. His movements were
almost feminine in their suppleness, yet the look of breathtaking insolence with which he confronted the journalists could hardly have been
more macho.

"Bocca can say what he likes. No one's listening anyway. As for
me, my clothes speak for me!"

They certainly did, a layered montage of overlapping textures and
colors, so cunningly contrived that one hardly noticed where one garment ended and another began. Especially in motion, the resulting
flurry of activity was so distracting that you hardly noticed the man
himself.

Another reporter waved a microphone in the man's face.

"Camilla Cederna has said, 'The one thing that is clear from this
book is that it was composed by a ghostwriter. Since the invented
personality the author describes is equally substanceless, the whole exercise amounts to one ghost writing about another.' Any comment?"

"If *La Cederna* is so out of touch with the rhythms of contemporary reality, perhaps she should restrict herself to a topic more suited to her talents, for example needlework."

This caused some laughter.

"Fortunately the thousands of people who read my book and wear my clothes have no such difficulties," the man continued. "They understand that what I am is what I made myself, using nothing but my own genius. I owe nothing to anyone or to anything! I am entirely my own creation! I am Falco!"

"Dottor Zen?"

A corpulent man had approached the chair where Zen was sitting and stood looking down at him with a complacent expression.

"I am Antonio Simonelli."

They're letting all sorts in these days, thought Zen as they shook hands. With his crumpled blue suit and hearty manner, Simonelli seemed more like a provincial tradesman than a magistrate. But this might well be a deliberate ploy designed to lull Zen into a false sense of security. And, indeed, Simonelli at once struck a confidential note.

"You know who that was, of course?"

The media star had swept out by now, surrounded by his entourage, and the lobby was quiet again.

"Some designer, isn't he? I don't really keep up with such things."

Simonelli subsided into a leather chair, which looked rather like an overdone soufflé.

"Falco, he calls himself," Simonelli explained in his Bergamask whine, like an ill-tuned oboe *d'amore*. "He's based in Milan, but he's down here promoting some book he's published, explaining his 'design philosophy' if you please. Of course he *would* have to choose the very hotel where I always stay. It's terrible. You can't move for reporters."

He signaled a waiter. Zen ordered an espresso, Simonelli a *caffè Hag*.

"It's my heart," he explained, unwrapping a panatela cigar with his big, blunt fingers. "One of my colleagues dropped dead just last month. He was fifteen years younger than me. Gave me a bit of a jolt, so I had a checkup, and it turns out I'm at risk myself."

Zen smiled politely.

"Anyway, I mustn't bore you with my problems," the magistrate went on. "Except for the Ruspanti case, that is. I don't know how much you know about the investigation I have been involved in . . ."

"Only what I've read in the newspapers."

"It's all water under the bridge now, of course," Simonelli sighed mournfully. "With my key witness dead, there's no case to be made. This is really only a private chat, just to satisfy my curiosity. Naturally whatever is said between us two will remain strictly off the record."

He broke off as the waiter brought their coffees. Simonelli emptied two packets of sugar into his cup and looked across the table at Zen as he stirred.

"So tell me, what really happened? Did he fall, or was he pushed?"

It had been perfectly done, thought Zen. The illusion of a personal rapport, the implied assumption that they were associates and equals, the casual request for information "just to satisfy my curiosity," the assurance that Zen could speak freely in the knowledge that what was said would go no further, even the facetious touch of the final question. If Zen hadn't been expecting something of the kind, he might well have fallen for it hook, line, and sinker—and then spent the next few years wriggling and thrashing as Simonelli reeled him in. As it was, the magistrate's adroitness merely reinforced Zen's determination to give nothing away. Reticence would be a mistaken tactic, however, merely confirming that there were significant secrets to be learned. The true art of concealment, Zen knew, lay not in silence but in garrulity, in rumor and innuendo. Best of all was to let the victim spin the web of deceit himself. That way, it was bound to conform perfectly to his fears and prejudices, forming a snug, cozy trap from which he had no desire to escape.

"I found no evidence to suggest that Ruspanti's death was anything other than it appeared to be," he declared firmly.

Simonelli gazed at him levelly.

"So you accept that he committed suicide."

"I see no reason not to."

The magistrate lit his cigar carefully, rotating the end above the flame of his lighter.

"Even in the light of this second fatality?"

Zen looked blank.

"I'm sorry?"

"The Vatican security man, Giovanni Grimaldi. You don't think his death was connected in any way to Ruspanti's?"

Zen downed his coffee in three swift gulps.

"How do you know about that?" he asked casually.

Simonelli sipped his coffee and puffed at his cigar, making Zen wait.

"Grimaldi was what the espionage profession calls a double agent," he explained at last. "In addition to his duties for the Vigilanza, he was also working for me as a paid informant."

Zen knew that this revelation was intended to encourage him to make one in return, but he was too intrigued not to follow it up.

"So you knew that Ruspanti had taken refuge in the Vatican?"

Simonelli nodded.

"After the Maltese kicked him out. Yes, I knew. But I couldn't prove it, and if I'd spoken out they'd have spirited him away before anyone could do anything. So I bided my time and used Grimaldi to keep track of what was happening. Until last week, he was providing me with regular, detailed reports of Ruspanti's movements, the people he met, the calls he made, and so on. Most of it was irrelevant, all about some organization Ruspanti was threatening to expose if they didn't help him. But the first thing I did when I heard of Ruspanti's death was to try and contact Grimaldi. He didn't return my calls, so I flew down here to look him up, only to find that he was dead."

Zen sat perfectly still, eyeing Simonelli. His racing pulse might have been due to the coffee he had just drunk.

"What was the name of this organization Ruspanti was threatening?" he asked.

Simonelli looked annoyed at this reference to something he had made clear was a side issue.

"I really don't remember."

"The anonymous letter to the papers spoke of a group calling itself the Cabal," said Zen.

"Yes, that's right. The Cabal. Why? Do you know any more about it?"

Zen shrugged.

"To be honest, I assumed it referred to this group of businessmen you've been investigating."

To his surprise, Simonelli reacted with a look of total panic. Then it was gone, and he laughed.

"Really?"

Zen said nothing. Simonelli broke a baton of ash off his cigar into the glass ashtray on the table.

"According to Grimaldi's reports, I'd rather gathered that it had some connection with the Knights of Malta," he said.

Zen raised his eyebrows.

"It's the first I've heard of it."

Simonelli gasped two deep breaths.

"Anyway, we've rather gotten away from my original question, which was whether you think Grimaldi's death could have been connected in any way to Ruspanti's."

Zen frowned like a dim schoolboy confronted by a concept too difficult for him to grasp.

"But Ruspanti committed suicide by jumping off the gallery in St. Peter's and Grimaldi was electrocuted in his shower by a faulty water heater. What connection could there be?"

"The two deaths occurring so close together was just a coincidence, then?"

"I can't see what else it could be."

In his heart he apologized to Ruspanti and Grimaldi for adding such insults to the fatal injuries they had sustained. But it was all very well for the dead, he thought to himself. They were well out of it.

"That anonymous letter to the press certainly was neither an accident nor a coincidence," Simonelli remarked with some asperity. "Someone wrote it, and for a reason. Do you have any ideas about that?"

Zen looked shiftily around the lobby, as though checking whether they could be overheard.

"One thing I did find out is that certain people in the Vatican are not satisfied with the official line on Ruspanti's death," he confided in an undertone. "The Vatican isn't a monolith, any more than the Communist party—or whatever it's calling itself these days. There are different currents, varying tendencies, opposing pressure groups. One of them might well have wished to try and throw doubt on the suicide verdict."

Simonelli plunged his cigar into the dregs of his coffee, where it expired with an almost inaudible hiss.

"An official leak, then."

Zen tipped his hand back and forth.

"Semiofficial disinformation."

"It must have been embarrassing for you," Simonelli suggested, "to have your professional integrity publicly attacked like that."

Zen shrugged.

"One has to live with these things."

Simonelli hitched up the sleeve of his jacket, revealing a chunky gold watch.

"Well, thank you for taking the trouble to come and satisfy my interest in this business," he said.

"Not at all. If that's all, I'd better be getting back to the Ministry."

Simonelli raised his eyebrows.

"Working?" he demanded coarsely. "At this hour?"

The magistrate's manner was so familiar that Zen almost winked at him.

"Thanks to this Vatican business, I've got a backlog of other work to catch up on," he confided. "I thought I might as well get paid overtime for doing it."

Simonelli laughed.

"Quite right, quite right!"

Just inside the hotel's revolving door, they shook hands again.

"Perhaps we'll meet again some time," Zen found himself saying.

Simonelli's eyes were enlivened by some expression he couldn't read at all.

"I shouldn't be at all surprised, Dottore. I shouldn't be at all surprised."

AUTHORIZATION?

Zen gazed at the band of green script, which stared back at him, as unwavering as a reptile's eye. Something had gone wrong, but he had no idea what. True, he was no longer as utterly innocent of computers as he had once been. He had no map to the computer's alien landscape, and wouldn't have been able to read it if he had, but he had laboriously learned to follow a number of paths that led to the places he wanted or needed to reach. As long as he stayed on them, and given time, he could usually reach his goal. But if by accident he pushed the wrong key, producing some unforeseen effect, there was nothing for it but to return to the beginning.

That was what must have happened now. He had intended to open a file in which to enter the outline details of the Ruspanti case, which he had passed on orally to the Minister earlier in the day. He wanted to do this now, while they were still fresh in his mind. Then, later in the week, he would call up the file and rewrite it as a proper report, which he would then save in the database as a "Read Only" item, imperishably enshrined in electronic form for any interested party to consult. Something had gone wrong, however. When he tried to open a file to jot down his notes, the computer had responded as though he had asked to read an already existing file, and demanded an authorization reference. With a sigh, Zen pressed the red "Break" button and began all over again.

The window beside the desk where the terminal was installed was steadily turning opaque as the winter dusk gathered outside. Down below in Piazza del Viminale the evening rush hour was at its height, the gridlocked vehicles bellowing like cattle in rut, but no sound penetrated the Ministry's heavy-duty reflective triple glazing, proof against everything from bullets to electronic surveillance. Zen gazed at that darkened expanse of glass where he had once caught sight of Tania, seemingly floating toward him in midair across the piazza outside. Searching his own personal database, he identified a day shortly before he went to Sardinia for the Burolo case, the day when Tania had come to lunch at his apartment. Although little more than a year earlier, that period already seemed to him like a state of prelapsarian innocence. What was Tania doing now, he wondered, and with whom? Concentrating his mind with an effort, he once again ran through the procedure for opening a file and pressed "Enter." As before, the screen responded with a demand for his security clearance. Infuriated, Zen typed "Go stuff your sister." AUTHORIZATION INVALID the computer returned priggishly.

It was not until the third time that he finally caught on. He had been scrupulously careful on this occasion, moving the cursor through

the menus line by line and double-checking every option before selecting it. When SUBJECT? appeared, he carefully typed "Cabal," the working title he was using for his notes. He was certain that he had observed
all the correct procedures, yet when he pressed the "Enter" key, the
computer once again flashed its demand for authorization like some
obsessive psychotic with a one-track mind. To dispel the urge to stick
his fist through the screen, he swiveled around in his chair and stood up
—and suddenly the solution came to him, huge and blindingly obvious.
The computer was not stupid or malicious, just infinitely literal-
minded. If it was treating his attempt to open a file named "Cabal" as a
"read" option, it could only be because *such a file already existed.*

He turned away from the screen as though it were a window from
which he was being watched. His skin was prickling, his scalp taut.
Grabbing the keyboard, he called up the directory. No such file was
listed. That meant it must be stored in the "closed" section of the
database, whose contents were not displayed in the directory.

Somewhere in the office behind him a phone was ringing. He
reached out blindly, picked up the extension by the computer terminal,
and switched the call through.

"Criminalpol."

He was sure it must be Tania. No one else would ring him at work
at that time. But to his disappointment, the voice was male.

"Good evening, Dottore. I'm calling from the Vatican."

Zen knew he had heard the voice already that day, although it
didn't sound like either Sànchez-Valdès or Lamboglia.

"How did you know I was here?" he asked inconsequentially.

"We tried your home number first and they said you were at work.
Listen, we need to see you this evening. It's a matter of great urgency."

"Who is this?"

"My identity is not important."

Zen reduced his voice to a charged whisper.

"I'm afraid that's not good enough. I have been assured on the
highest authority that my involvement with the Ruspanti affair is over. I
am currently preparing a report on the incident for my superiors. I'm
afraid I can't just drop everything and come running on the strength of
an anonymous phone call."

There was a momentary silence.

"This report you're writing," said the voice, "is it going to mention the Cabal?"

Zen raised his eyes to the glowing screen.

"What do you know about the Cabal?" he breathed.

"Everything."

Zen was silent.

"Come to St. Peter's at seven o'clock exactly," the voice told him. "In the north transept, where the light shows."

The phone went dead. Zen blindly replaced the receiver, still staring at the word AUTHORIZATION? and the box where the name of the official seeking access to the file would appear. As though of their own volition, his fingers tapped six times on the keyboard, and the box filled with the name ROMIZI. This was a perfectly harmless deception. If anybody bothered to check who had tried to read the closed file on the Cabal, it would at once be obvious that a false name had been used. Poor Carlo Romizi, helplessly comatose in the Ospedale di San Giovanni, clearly couldn't be responsible.

As he expected, though, the only response was AUTHORIZATION INVALID. Zen sat gazing at the screen until the words blurred into mere squiggles of light, but the message itself was so firmly imprinted on his eyeballs that it appeared on walls, floors, windows, and doors long after he had turned off the computer and left the building, imbuing every surrounding surface with a portentous, threatening shimmer.

When he got home, a familiar voice emanating from his living room was holding forth about the philosophy of fashion. Glancing at the television, Zen recognized the young man he had last seen delivering an impromptu press conference in the lobby of the Hotel Torlonia Palace. He was now perched on a leather and chrome stool, being interviewed by Raffaella Carrà about his book *You Are What You Wear.*

". . . not a question of dressing up, like draping clothes over a dummy, but of re-creating yourself. When you put on a Falco creation, you are reborn! The old self dies and a new one takes its place, instantly, in the twinkling of an eye . . ."

Zen crossed to the inner hallway.

"Hello? Anyone there?"

". . . if you're so insecure you need a label to hide behind, then by all means buy something by Giorgio or Gianni. I've got nothing against their stuff. It's very pretty. But I'm not interested in merely embellishing a preconceived entity, but in effecting a radical transformation of . . ."

He looked into the kitchen, the dining room, the bathroom, and his mother's bedroom. The flat was empty.

". . . clothes for people who don't want to look like someone else but to make themselves apparent, to create themselves freely and from zero, every instant of every day. People like me, who have nothing to hide, who are neither more nor less than what they seem to be . . ."

"And who *are* you?" Raffaella Carrà demanded. "Who *is* Falco?"

"What can I say? There's no mystery about me! What you see is what you get. I am nothing but this perpetual potential to become what I am, this constant celebration of our freedom to exorcise the demons of time and place, of who and what, where and why, and escape toward a goal that is defined by our approach to it. . . ."

As he reached to switch off the television, Zen saw the note in his mother's spidery handwriting on top of the set.

> *Welcome back Aurelio—Lucrezia from downstairs asked if I could keep an eye on her two boys while she collects her brother and his wife from Belgium—they were supposed to arrive yesterday evening but the plane was delayed—I'll be back in time for dinner—don't turn TV off as I am recording the last episode of "Twin Peaks"—Rosella and I have a bet on who did it but I think she has been told by Gilberto's brother in America where it was on last year—your loving mother.*

Zen put the note down with a sigh. They had had a video recorder for two years now, but his mother still refused to believe that it was possible to tape a television program successfully without the set being switched on and the volume turned up.

". . . refuse to recognize deterministic limitations on my right to be whoever I choose. No one has the right to tell me who I am, to chain me to the Procrustean bed of so-called 'objective reality.' *All* that counts is my fantasy, my genius, my flair, eternally fashioning and re-fashioning myself and the world around me . . ."

The voice vanished abruptly as Zen twisted the volume control. He took out his pen and scrawled a message at the bottom of his mother's note to the effect that he had got back safely from Florence and would see her for dinner. For some reason he found his mother's absence disturbing. It was good that she was out and about, of course, keeping herself busy. Nevertheless, there was something about the whole arrangement that jarred. He set the note down on top of the television, walked back down the hallway, and opened the last door on the right.

The pent-up odors of the past broke over him like a wave: camphor and mildew, patent medicines and obsolete toiletries, stiffened leather, smoky fur, ghostly perfumes, the whiff of sea fog. He pushed his way through the piles of overflowing trunks, chests, and boxes. Spiders and wood lice froze, then broke ranks and scattered in panic as the colossus approached. There it was, in the far corner, perched on a plinth of large cardboard boxes containing back numbers of *Famiglia Cristiana* from the early 1950s. The gaily painted wooden box had originally been stamped with the insignia of the State Railways and a warning about the detonators it had contained. Zen still vividly recalled his wonder at the transformation wrought by his father's paintbrush, which had magically turned this discarded relic into a toy box for little Aurelio.

Reaching over so far his stomach muscles protested, he pulled the box down and removed the lid. Then he sifted through the contents—windup train set, tin drum, lead soldiers and battleships—until he found the revolver that had been made specially for him by a machinist in the locomotive works at Mestre. The man had been an ardent Blackshirt, and although unfireable, the gun was an accurate replica of the 9mm Beretta he carried when he went out to raise hell with his fellow *squadristi*. Zen weighed it in his hand, tracing the words MUSSOLINI DUX incised in the solid barrel, remembering epic battles and cowboy showdowns in the back alleys of the Cannaregio. The pistol had been the envy of all his friends, but its connections with the leader whose adventurism had caused his father's death perhaps explained Zen's life-long reluctance to carry a firearm, or even learn to use one.

He squeezed his way back out of the storeroom with a sigh of relief, as though emerging from a prison cell. The past was always present in the Zen family. Nothing was ever thrown away, and even the dead remained unburied. That man Falco talked a load of pretentious rubbish, of course, but it was easy to see the attractions of his shallow, consumerist credo. Fascism no doubt seemed to offer similar raptures and consolations to the people of his father's generation.

It was ten to seven when he left the house, the replica pistol concealed in his overcoat pocket. The streets were crowded with shoppers and people going home from work or out on the town, and when he emerged into the vacant expanses of St. Peter's Square it was like stepping into another city. The throng of pilgrims and their tour buses had long since departed, and the only people to be seen were two Carabinieri on patrol. Zen climbed the shallow steps leading up to the facade of St. Peter's and passed under the portico.

Apart from a party of tourists who were just leaving, the basilica seemed as deserted as the piazza outside. Zen walked down the nave to the baldachin, then turned right into the north transept. Between each of the three chapels stood a curvaceous confessional of dully gleaming mahogany that reminded Zen of his mother's wardrobe. There were six in all, but only one showed a light indicating the presence of a confessor. The gold inscription above the entrance read EX ORDINE FRATRVM MINORVM. For a moment Zen hesitated, feeling both ridiculous and slightly irreverent. Then, with a shrug, he approached the recess and knelt down.

It was at least three decades since he had been to confession, but as he felt the wooden step beneath his knees and looked at the grilled opening before his face, the years slipped away and he once again felt that anxious sense of generalized guilt, assuaged by the confidence of possessing a system for dealing with it. So strong were these sensations that he was on the point of intoning "Forgive me, Father, for I have sinned" when a voice from the other side of the grille recalled him to the realities of his present situation.

"Can you hear me, Dottore?"

Zen cleared his throat.

"Only just."

"I prefer not to speak too loudly. Our enemies are everywhere."

It was the man who had phoned him earlier at the Ministry.

"You are probably wondering why you have been summoned at such short notice, and in this unusual fashion. I shall be frank. Many people think of the Curia as a monolith expressing a single, unified point of view. This is not surprising, since we spend a considerable amount of time and trouble cultivating just such an impression. Nevertheless, it is a fallacy. To take the present instance, considerable differences exist over the handling of the Ruspanti affair. There have been some heated exchanges. I represent a group who believe that the issues at stake here are too serious to be swept under the carpet. If our arguments had been rejected by the Holy Father, we should of course have submitted. We have in fact repeatedly urged that the matter be placed before him, but on each occasion we have been overruled. The decision to cover up the truth about the Ruspanti case has been made by a small number of senior officials acting on their own initiative."

Zen glanced at the grille, but the interior of the confessional was so dark he could not make out anything of the speaker.

"What have you been told about the Cabal?" the man asked abruptly.

Zen cleared his throat.

"That according to Ruspanti there was an inner group within the Order . . ."

"Speak up, please! I'm rather hard of hearing."

Zen raised his mouth to the grille.

"I was told that Ruspanti claimed there was an inner group within the Order of Malta known as the Cabal. These claims were investigated and found to be false."

"Nothing more?"

"*Is* there more?"

The response was a low chuckle that sent a shiver up Zen's spine.

"Both more and less. Some of what you've been told is true, but the manner of its telling has been deliberately designed to mislead you into discounting it and concentrating your efforts elsewhere. Certainly Ludovico Ruspanti approached us with allegations about a secret society within the Order of Malta, of whom he was himself of course a distinguished member, and with whom he had taken refuge before we gave him sanctuary. We had received similar information before, but this was the first emanating from an authoritative source and offering the possibility of verification. Ruspanti claimed to be able to provide names, dates, and full documentation. Relations between the Holy See and the Order of Malta have been strained for some time . . ."

The man's voice faded under a ululating howl that seemed to come from inside the confessional. It grew quickly louder until it was deafening, then gradually faded to nothing.

"What was *that?*" asked Zen.

"What?"

"That noise."

"I heard nothing. As I was saying, relations between the Holy See and the Order of Malta have been strained for some time, but our first reaction was indeed one of suspicion. To our dismay, however, our preliminary investigations substantiated every single claim Ruspanti had made. Far from finding his allegations baseless or false, we uncovered evidence of the most alarming kind. I hasten to add that these findings did not in any way implicate the Order of Malta as a whole, which is and has always been an admirable body, tireless in its charitable exertions and unwavering in its loyalty to the papacy. The Cabal is something quite different, a parasitic clique, a sinister inner coterie hidden within the ranks of a respectable organization, like Gelli's P2 within the Masonic Order."

The voice fell silent. For a moment, Zen thought he heard the rustling of paper.

"You may remember the Oliver North scandal in the United States," the man continued. "A small group of influential people in the Reagan administration decided there were actions that needed to be taken, actions the President would certainly approve, inasmuch as they were logical developments of his avowed policies, but whose existence and implementation he could not afford to know about. These men therefore decided to take matters into their own hands, since Reagan's were tied by his constitutional and legal obligations."

Hearing footsteps behind him, Zen looked around. One of the blue-jacketed attendants wearing the red leather badge of the basilica staff was passing on his rounds. He glanced briefly at the kneeling penitent, but with no more than the usual impersonal curiosity anyone might feel, wondering what secrets were being divulged in muttered undertones. Zen shifted his position slightly. His knees were beginning to ache.

"The idea behind the Cabal is very similar," the man went on. "In short, they believe they know what the Holy Father wants better than he does himself—or at any rate, better than he can afford to express openly. Like many of us, they are disturbed by the decline in church attendance and in the numbers presenting themselves for the priesthood, and by the rampant hedonism and materialism of society today. Wojtyla's early life was dominated by the struggle against a godless ideology, but he has come to feel that we now face an even more implacable foe than communism. The sufferings of the Church in Poland and elsewhere ultimately served to strengthen the faith of believers. But what the Communists failed to destroy with force and terror is now in danger of decaying through sheer apathy and neglect."

Zen emitted a grunt, of pain rather than agreement. Had some malicious cleric selected this rendezvous as a way of making him appreciate his place in the Vatican's scheme of things?

"In this situation, it is inevitable that some people should cast envious glances at the very different situation in the Muslim world. While our young people seem to think of nothing but the instant gratifications of a materialist society, theirs are gripped with a religious fervor of undeniable intensity, for which they are prepared both to die and to kill. While our cities are flooded with drugs and pornography, theirs are rigorously patroled by religious police with summary powers of arrest and punishment. And while the authority of our leaders, including the Holy Father himself, is challenged on all sides, a single pronouncement by one of theirs is enough to force a celebrated writer to go to ground like a Mafia informer. Can you doubt that there are those of us who are nostalgic for the days when our Church was also capable of compelling respect, by force if necessary? *Of course* there are!"

Once again the brief pause, the slight rustle of paper. Was the man reading a prepared text?

"But while some may idly regret an era that has passed forever, others are scheming to bring it back. These people have noted Wojtyla's effect on the cheering crowds who come to greet him by the hundreds of thousands during his tours of Africa and Latin America. Here is a man who has both the potential and the will to bring about a radical desecularization of society. Naturally the Holy Father cannot be seen to harbor any such ambitions, still less endorse the tactics of destabilization necessary to bring them to fruition. But by his sponsorship of such organizations as Opus Dei and *Comunione e Liberazione,* Wojtyla has made it quite clear in which direction he wishes the Church to move."

Zen tapped impatiently on the wall of the confessional. It resounded hollowly, like a stage property.

"This is all very interesting," he remarked in a tone that suggested just the opposite, "but I'm not a theologian."

"Neither are the members of the Cabal! Like the original Knights of Malta, from whom they draw their inspiration, they are men of action, men of violence, organized, capable, and ruthless. What happened to Ruspanti is proof of that."

"And what *did* happen?"

"Ruspanti made the mistake of trying to play a double game. On the one hand he was trading information for protection here in the Vatican, doling it out scrap by scrap, feeding us just enough to whet our appetite for what was still to come. He described the structure and aims of the Cabal in general terms, named a few of the minor players, and hinted that under the right circumstances he would be prepared to identify the leaders, including well-known figures in the political, industrial, financial, and military worlds. At the same time, he was also trying to put pressure on the Cabal itself, threatening to expose them if they didn't meet his terms. That was a mistake that proved to be fatal. Last Friday he was summoned to a meeting with two senior representatives of the Cabal, here in St. Peter's, and . . ."

Zen wasn't listening. He had just realized why his mother's absence from home had seemed so oddly disturbing. When this man had phoned him at the Ministry, he claimed to have tried Zen's home number and been told he was at work. That was a lie. There had been no one at home to answer the phone. The deception was trivial, but it altered Zen's whole attitude toward this faceless informant. No longer did he feel constrained or deferential. He felt rude and sassy. His knees were killing him, and he was going to get even.

". . . that the Cabal is everywhere, even within the Curia," the man was saying. "Any opposition to their aims, any threat to their secrecy, is punished by instant death."

"If they're so clever, why haven't they found the transcript of Ruspanti's phone calls?" demanded Zen.

There was silence in the confessional.

"Grimaldi had it, so they killed him. But they didn't find it."

"How do you know?"

"Because I did."

It was a shot in the dark, but he had nothing to lose. The urgent tremor in the speaker's voice revealed that it had gone home.

"You have the transcript?"

There was a vast explosion of sound, as though a bomb had gone off.

"Hello?" cried the voice. "Are you still there?"

Now the source of the noise was visible: a rack of spotlights being lowered from their position high above the south transept.

"Yes, I'm here," said Zen.

Why couldn't the man see him?

"Where is the transcript?"

"Where Grimaldi hid it. It was I who discovered his body, re-member, and I had time to search his room before the Carabinieri got there. Someone else had been there too, but they didn't know what to look for."

Beyond the grille, the confessional was as silent as the grave.

"Among Grimaldi's belongings was a red plastic diary," Zen con-tinued. "It was for the new year, so it was mostly empty, but he had noted down a series of letters and numbers that leads straight to the transcript, assuming you know where to look."

"And where's that?"

Zen laughed teasingly.

"Have you told anyone else where it is?" the man demanded.

"Not yet. It's hard to know who to tell, with so many conflicting interests involved."

There was a considerable silence.

"Naturally you want to do the right thing," the voice suggested more calmly.

"Naturally."

Again the man fell silent.

"This revelation changes everything," he said at last. "This is not the time or place to discuss it further, but I do urge you most strongly to take no further action of any kind until we contact you again."

"Wait a minute," Zen replied. "I don't even know who you are. Suppose you step out of there and let me see your face."

The sinister chuckle sounded again.

"I'm afraid that's not possible, Dottore."

Zen took the fake pistol from his pocket. He had been right to bring it after all.

"You're taking a big chance," he warned the man. "Supposing I decide to let someone else have the transcript instead?"

"But how would you know it *was* someone else? You know nothing about us."

One hand gripping the wooden railing, Zen raised himself painfully to a crouching position. Then he straightened up, gritting his teeth against the fierce aching of his knees. The revolver in one hand, he swept aside the heavy curtain covering the entrance to the confessional.

"I do now!" he cried.

He gazed wildly around. There was no one there. Then he heard the low chuckling once again. It was coming from a small two-way radio suspended from a nail that had been driven into the wall of the confessional, just below the grille.

"You know nothing about us," the voice repeated. "Nothing at all."

FIVE

E ver since his transfer to the capital from Naples, Aurelio Zen had traveled to and from work by bus. His removal from active duty at the Questura at the time of the Aldo Moro kidnapping had had no effect on this, since the Ministry of the Interior—where he had been allocated a menial desk job—was only a few blocks from police headquarters. Even the opening of the new underground railway line had not induced him to change his habits, despite the fact that the terminus at Ottaviano was only a few blocks from his house, and the Termini stop a short walk from the Ministry. Experience showed that twenty minutes in the tunnels of the Metropolitana A left Zen's day spavined before it had ever begun. The bus journey was by no means an unrelieved joy, but at least it took place in a real city rather than that phantasmagoric subterranean realm of dismal leaky caverns that might equally well be in London, or New York—or indeed the next century.

Tania Biacis had changed Zen's habits in this respect, as in so many others. They spent about three nights a week together, absences that Zen explained to his mother in terms of overtime or trips away from Rome. But whether Zen had slept at the flat or not, he and Tania traveled to work together by taxi every morning. It was yet another aspect of the new arrangement that was costing a small fortune, but it seemed worth it just to have that precious interval of time with Tania before they separated to go about their different jobs at the Ministry. He was perfectly willing to pay, Zen reflected as his taxi crossed Ponte Cavour on the way to Tania's that Thursday morning. The problem was his ability.

The simple fact was that he could no longer go on supporting two households in this kind of style, and what was the point in doing it if not in style? Mistresses were not something you could get on the cheap, any more than champagne or caviar. They were a luxury, a self-indulgence for the rich. If you couldn't afford them, you had to do without. Zen couldn't do without Tania, but it was becoming clear that he couldn't really afford her either—unless he found some way of making a large sum of money overnight. As the taxi turned right along the embankment of the Tiber, he found himself wondering idly how much the transcript of Ruspanti's phone calls would fetch, assuming that his intuition about its hiding place proved correct.

The idea was absurd, of course! He couldn't possibly contemplate making a personal profit from a piece of evidence that would presumably make it possible to bring the murderers of Ludovico Ruspanti and Grimaldi to justice. Of course, a cynic might argue that there was no chance of the murderers being brought to justice anyway, if the issues involved in the case were anywhere near as extensive as they appeared to be. Such a cynic—or a realist, as he would no doubt prefer to be called —might claim that in this particular case, as in so many others, justice was simply *not an option,* and to pretend otherwise was mere wishful thinking masquerading as idealism. In reality, there were only two possible outcomes. Zen could sell the transcript, thereby solving all his problems, or he could create a host of new problems for himself by setting in motion a major scandal with repercussions at every level of society. A rational man, the realist might well conclude, should be in no doubt which course to choose.

The taxi drew up in the narrow street, scarcely wider than an alley, where Tania lived. Almost at once the door opened and she appeared. It was a measure of what was happening to them that while Zen would once have been glad of a promptitude that allowed them a few extra minutes together, he now wondered whether she was anxious to prevent his seeing who was in the flat.

"I phoned Tullio," she said, slipping in beside him with a seemingly guileless kiss. "He sounded very keen. He'll see you this morning at his office in EUR."

"What time?"

"About ten, he said."

"Did you tell him who I was?"

"Of course not! As far as he knows, you're just a high-ranking colleague of mine at the Ministry who needs a favor done. Not that Tullio would care. He's made a pass or two at me himself, if it comes to that."

Zen inspected her.

"And did it?"

She sighed.

"Give me a break, Aurelio!"

It was a windless gray morning, humid and close. The taxi was now wedged into the flank of the phalanx of traffic on Corso Vittorio Emanuele. Zen patted her knee.

"Sorry."

She flashed him a smile.

"Shall we eat out tonight?"

He nodded.

"I'll be out till about eight," she said. "Perhaps we could try that Chinese place behind Piazza Navona."

Zen grunted unenthusiastically. Oriental cuisine, the latest Roman craze, left him cold. The food was excellent, but it seemed to him an exoticism as irrelevant to his life as Buddhism. The way he looked at it, you were either a Catholic or an atheist. There was no point in shopping around for odd doctrines, however original, nor in eating odd food, however delicious.

The taxi dropped Tania first, at the corner of Via Venezia and Via Palermo, then drove around to the other side of the Ministry, where Zen paid it off. Lorenzo Moscati's jibes had made it clear that their efforts to keep the affair secret had been a failure, but there was still a difference between accepting that people knew what was going on and flaunting it in their faces. The porter ticked Zen's name off in the ON TIME column of his massive ledger.

"Oh, Dottore! They want to see you up in Personnel."

Zen rode the lift up to the office on the fourth floor where Franco

Ciliani, a tiny balding tyrant given to Etna-like eruptions of temper, presided over the thankless task of trying to complete the jigsaw of staff allocation when over half the pieces were missing at any one time.

"What are you doing here?" he demanded as Zen appeared.

"Ciccillo said you wanted to see me."

"That's not what I mean! As far as I'm concerned, you're in Milan."

Zen gestured a comically excessive apology.

"Sorry, but I'm not, as you see."

Ciliani gave a brutal shrug.

"I don't give a damn where you are *in reality*. That's entirely your affair. I'm talking about what's down on the roster, and that tells me you're in Milan. So when I get a call yesterday asking why you haven't turned up, I naturally wonder what the hell."

"Who did you speak to?"

Ciliani made a half-hearted attempt to locate something in the chaos of papers on his desk.

"Shit. Sermonelli? Something like that."

"Simonelli?"

"That's it. Antonia Simonelli."

"Yesterday?" queried Zen, ignoring the little matter of Simonelli's gender.

"That's right. Real ball-breaker. You know what the Milanese are like."

"There must be some mistake. Simonelli's here in Rome. We met yesterday."

"I said you'd be there by tomorrow at the latest."

"But I just told you . . ."

"Told me?" demanded Ciliani. "You told me nothing. We aren't even having this conversation."

"What do you mean?"

Ciliani sighed deeply.

"Look, you're in Milan, right? I'm in Rome. So how can I be talking to you? It must be a hallucination. Probably the aftereffects of that fever you had."

Zen stared up at the fault line of a huge crack running from one end of the ceiling to the other.

"When did the original notification come through?"

Ciliani consulted his schedule.

"Monday."

"I was off sick on Monday."

He suddenly saw what must have happened. Simonelli had summoned Zen to Milan on Monday, then decided to come to Rome himself to investigate Grimaldi's continuing silence. He had then got in touch with Zen directly, but presumably his secretary in Milan—the officious woman Ciliani had spoken to—had not been informed of this, and was still trying to complete the earlier arrangement.

"Fine!" said Ciliani. "I'll give Milan a call and explain that your departure was unavoidably delayed due to medical complications, but you have since made a swift and complete recovery and will be with them tomorrow. Speaking of which, it's tough about Carlo, eh?"

"What?"

"Romizi, Carlo Romizi."

"Oh, you mean his stroke? Yes, it's . . ."

"Haven't you heard the news?"

"What news?"

Ciliani stuck his finger in his ear and extracted a gob of wax, which he scrutinized as though deciding whether to eat it.

"He went last night."

"Went? Went where?"

Ciliani looked at him queerly.

"Died."

"No!"

Such was the emotion in Zen's voice that Ciliani lowered his voice and said apologetically, "Excuse me, Dottore, I didn't know you were close."

We are now, thought Zen. As close as the driver he had read about in the paper that morning was to the two children his car had crushed to death as they walked home from school. He had never seen them before, and yet from this day on they would always be together. Those children would never leave him now.

Trembling with shock, Zen left Ciliani and joined the human tide that was now beginning to flow in the opposite direction, as those dedicated members of staff who had reported for duty on time rewarded their efficiency by popping out for a coffee and a bite to eat at one of the numerous bars that spring up in the vicinity of any government building like brothels near a port. Zen scandalized the barman by ordering a *caffè corretto,* espresso laced with grappa, a perfectly acceptable early morning drink in the Veneto but unheard of in Rome.

He stood sipping the heady mixture and gazing sightlessly at the season's fixture list for the Lazio football club. From time to time he took a stealthy peek at the idea that had leaped like a ghoul from the grave when Ciliani gave him the news of Carlo Romizi's death. It didn't go away. On the contrary, every time he glanced at it—surreptitiously, like a child in bed at the menacing shadows on the ceiling—it looked more substantial, more certain.

The pay phone in the bar was one of the old models that only accepted tokens. Zen bought two thousand lire's worth from the cashier and ensconced himself in the narrow passage between the toilet and a broken ice cream freezer. A selection of coverless, broken-spined telephone directories sprawled on top of the freezer. Zen looked up the number of the San Giovanni hospital. The first four times he dialed it was engaged, and when he finally did get through the number rang for almost five minutes and was then answered by a receptionist who had taken charm lessons from a pit bull terrier. But she was no match for a man with twenty-five years' experience as a professional bully, and Zen was speedily put through to the doctor he had spoken to the week before.

All went well until Zen mentioned Romizi's name, when the doctor suddenly lost his tone of polite detachment.

"Listen, I've had enough of this! Understand? Enough!"

"But I . . ."

"She's put you up to this, hasn't she?"

"I'm simply . . ."

"I refuse to be harried and persecuted in this fashion! If it continues, I shall take legal advice. The woman is mad!"

"Please understand that . . ."

"In a case of this kind, prognosis is always speculative, for the very good reason that a complete analysis is only possible postmortem. I naturally sympathize with the widow's grief, but to imply that the negligence of me or my staff in any way contributed to her husband's death is slanderous nonsense. There were no unusual developments in the case, and the outcome was perfectly consistent with the previous case history. If Signora Romizi proceeds with this campaign of harassment, she will find herself facing charges of criminal libel. Good day!"

There were two columns of Romizis in the phone book, so Zen got the number from the Ministry switchboard. Carlo's sister Francesca answered. Having conveyed his condolences, Zen asked if it would be possible to speak to Signora Romizi.

"Giovanna's just gone to sleep."

"It must have been a terrible shock for her."

"We've both found it very hard. They'd warned us that Carlo might not recover, but you never really think it will happen. He had seemed better in the last few . . ."

Her voice broke.

"I'm sorry to distress you further," Zen said. "It's just that I heard from someone at work that Signora Romizi felt the hospital hadn't done everything they might to save Carlo."

There was no reply.

"I was wondering if I could do anything to help."

"It's kind of you." Francesca's voice was bleak. "The problem is that Giovanna is finding it hard to accept what has happened, so she's taking it out on the hospital. And of course there's plenty to complain about. Carlo had a bed in a *corridor,* along with about thirty other patients, some of them gravely ill. There were vermin, cockroaches, and ants everywhere. The kitchen staff walked out last week after some junkie's relatives held them up at gunpoint, and the patients might have starved if the relatives hadn't got together and provided sandwiches and rolls. That's on top of taking all the sheets home to wash, of course. Meanwhile, when the politicians get ill, they go to the Villa Stuart clinic and get looked after by German nuns!"

"If it's not too painful, could you tell me what actually happened?"

Francesca sighed.

"We had been taking turns sitting up with Carlo around the clock, so that there would always be a familiar face there at his bedside if he regained consciousness. Last night it was Giovanna's turn to stay up. She says she dozed off in her chair and some time in the middle of the night a noise woke her. She sat up to find a doctor standing by the bed, someone she had never seen before. He seemed to be adjusting the controls of the life-support apparatus. When Giovanna asked him what he was doing, he left without . . ."

Francesca Romizi's quiet voice vanished as though the barman pointing his remote control unit at Zen had changed the channel of his life. From the huge television set mounted on a shelf at the entrance to the passage, the commentary and crowd noises of a football match that had taken place in Milan the previous evening boomed out to engulf the bar.

"Can you speak up?" Zen urged the receiver.

". . . grew light . . . cold and pale . . . nurse was . . . told her . . ."

High on the wall above the telephone was a black fuse box. Standing on tiptoe, Zen reached for the main cutoff. As abruptly as it had started, the clamor of the television ceased, to be replaced by the groans of the staff and clientele.

"Not again!"

"This is the tenth time this month!"

"I'm not paying my electricity bill! They can do what they like, send me to prison, anything! I'm not paying!"

"The government should step in!"

"Rubbish! The abuse of political patronage is the reason we don't have a viable infrastructure in the first place."

Zen covered one ear with his hand and pressed the other to the receiver.

"I'm sorry, I missed that."

"I said, Giovanna thinks the doctor who tampered with the electronic equipment was some intern, not properly trained. She's threatening to sue the hospital for negligence."

Zen struggled to keep his voice steady.

"Have you any evidence?"

"Well, they haven't been able to identify the doctor concerned so far. But Giovanna could have dreamed the whole thing, or even invented it to relieve her guilt at the fact that she had been sleeping while Carlo died. Such strong emotions are unleashed at these moments that really anything is possible."

Zen asked Francesca to convey his profoundest sympathy to Si-

gnora Romizi and offered to help in any way he could. As he replaced
the receiver with one hand, he reached for the main switch with the
other, and the bar sprang to rowdy life again.

Back at the counter, Zen consumed a second coffee, this time
without additives. Like Francesca Romizi, but for very different reasons,
he was skeptical about the idea of negligence on the part of the hospital
staff. Carlo's death had no more been an accident than Giovanni Grimaldi's. From the moment Zen used his name in an unsuccessful attempt to access the Ministry's "closed" file on the Cabal, Carlo Romizi
had been doomed. No wonder the hospital had been unable to trace the
mysterious doctor who had visited his bedside in the small hours of the
night. There was no doctor, only a killer in a white coat.

The demonstrable absurdity of this response merely guaranteed its
authenticity. The comatose Romizi, utterly dependent on a life-support
system, could not conceivably have been responsible for the electronic
prying carried out in his name at the Ministry the night before. His
death had been intended to serve as a message to Aurelio Zen. The
Cabal had of course seen through his feeble attempt at disguise, but they
had gone ahead and killed Romizi anyway, knowing that he had nothing whatever to do with it. It was a masterstroke of cynical cruelty,
calculated not only to strike terror into Zen's heart but also to cripple
him with remorse. For it was he who had condemned Carlo Romizi to
death. If Zen had chosen another name, or used his own, the Umbrian
would still be alive.

These reflections were much in Zen's mind as he arrived at the
ponderous block in Piazza dell'Indipendenza that housed the consulate
of a minor South American republic, three *pensioni* patronized largely by
American backpackers, a cut-price dental surgery, a beauty salon, and
the headquarters of Paragon Security Consultants. Zen was still too
shocked by the reality of what had happened to work out the long-term
implications, but of one thing he was absolutely determined. The file
that had cost Carlo Romizi his life was going to give up its secrets. If
that part of the database was "closed," then he would break in. Zen had
no idea how to do this, but he felt sure that Gilberto Nieddu would
know someone who did.

Gilberto at first seemed something less than enchanted to see his
friend.

"No!" he cried as Zen walked in. "No, no, no, no, no, no, no, no!"

"I haven't said anything yet."

"I don't care! Jesus, last time I agree to look at a faulty water heater for you, and what happens? Not only do I end up having to teargas the Carabinieri and then risk my neck escaping across the rooftops, but when I get home my wife assaults me with the pasta rolling pin, accusing me of having another woman on the side! Well that *was* the last time, Aurelio, the very last! From now on . . ."

Zen got out his cigarettes and offered them to Nieddu, who ignored the gesture.

"I'm really sorry about that, Gilberto. You see, I'd told my mother I was in Florence so that I could spend a few nights with a friend. We should all get together some time. You'd like her. She's called Tania and . . ."

"Oh I see! You sin and I pay the price."

"I'll explain to Rosella . . ."

"If she thinks I've buddy-buddied you into covering up for me, she'll kill us both."

"All right then, I'll get *Tania* to call her."

"She'd assume she was my mistress, pretending to be yours. Can you imagine what Rosella would do if she thought I'd tried to con her like that? Sardinian girls learn how to castrate pigs when they're five years old. And they don't forget."

Zen blew a cloud of smoke at the rows of box files and tape containers stacked on the shelves.

"She'll get over it, Gilberto. It might even be a good thing in the end. There's nothing like jealousy to liven up a marriage."

"Spare me the pearls of wisdom, Aurelio. I'm up to my eyes in work."

He bent ostentatiously over the blueprint of an office building that was spread out across his desk.

"I need to see some classified information held in a computer database," said Zen.

Nieddu unstoppered an orange highlight pen and marked a feature on the plan.

"I was wondering how you'd go about that," Zen went on.

"Who runs the computer?" asked Nieddu without looking up.

"The Ministry."

The Sardinian shot him a quick glance.

"But you have clearance for that."

"Not this part."

Nieddu shook his head and pored over the blueprint again.

"I know someone who can do it. It'll cost you, though."

"That's no problem. But it's urgent. I have to go up to Milan on the early train tomorrow, and I need to set it up before leaving. What's the address?"

"I'll run you out there before lunch."

"I don't want to put you to any more trouble, Gilberto."

Nieddu gave him a peculiar smile.

"You'd never find the place," he said. "And anyway, you don't just turn up. You have to be *presented.*"

The new metro was going to be wonderful when it was finished, but then Romans had been saying that about one grandiose and disruptive construction project or another ever since Nero set about rebuilding the city after the disastrous fire of July 64. The national pastime of *dietrologia,* "the facts behind the facts," was also well established by that time, and many people held that the blaze had been started deliberately so as to facilitate the Emperor's redevelopment scheme. Nero's response to these scurrilous rumors of state terrorism had an equally familiar ring. The whole affair was blamed on an obscure and unpopular sect of religious fanatics influenced by foreign ideologies such as monotheism and millenialism. One of the victims of the resulting campaign of perscution was a Jewish fisherman named Simon Peter, who was crucified in the Imperial Circus and buried nearby, in a tomb hollowed out of the flank of the Vatican hill.

This stirring historical perspective, far from inspiring Aurelio Zen to a sense of wonder and pride, merely intensified his oppressive conviction that nothing ever changed. Being stuck for twenty minutes at Garbatella station because of a signaling fault hadn't exactly helped his mood. The work in progress to integrate the grubby old Ostia railway into the revamped *metropolitana* B line to EUR had resulted in the partial paralysis of service on both. Nevertheless, it would be wonderful when it was finished—until it started to fall apart like the A line, which had been open for less than a decade and already looked and smelled like a blocked sewer.

The short walk to the office where Tullio Bevilacqua worked helped restore Zen's spirits, although he wouldn't have dreamed of admitting this to anyone. For both political and aesthetic reasons, it was wholly unacceptable to admire the monumental EUR complex, conceived in the late thirties for a world's fair designed to show off the achievements of Fascist Italy. The war put an end to the prospects for an *Esposizione Universale di Roma,* but the architectural investment survived and, as usual in Rome, was recycled for purposes quite different from that intended by its creator.

The resulting complex—the only example of twentieth-century urban planning attempted in the capital since the first world war—had a freakish, hallucinogenic appearance at once monumental and two-dimensional, like a film set designed by Giorgio de Chirico for a production by Dino de Laurentis. The vast rectangular blocks of white masonry evenly distributed along either side of the broad straight thoroughfares locked together at right angles created a succession of perspectives that seemed designed at once to demonstrate and to subvert the laws of perspective. Despite the crushing scale and geometric regularity, the effect was curiously insubstantial, abstract, and ethereal, diametrically opposed both to the poky confines of the old city center and to the sprawling jumble of the unplanned *borgate* on the outskirts.

Tullio Bevilacqua looked like a caricature of his brother, the same features exaggerated into an extravagance larger than life. Tullio was not just overweight but grossly fat. His balding scalp was beaded with sweat, his nose glistened with grease, his moustache bristled and curled in anarchic abandon. Seeing him, Zen felt his first twinge of sympathy for fastidious, pedantic Mauro.

Zen introduced himself as Luigi Borsellino and outlined the cover story he had prepared.

"The case is still *sub judice,* of course, but without going into details I can tell you that it concerns a drug-smuggling ring that has been bringing in heroin in consignments of tinned tuna from Thailand destined for the Vatican supermarket. Such goods are exempt from inspection by our customs officials, of course. The box containing the hot tuna is then moved across the unguarded frontier into Italy for distribution."

Bevilacqua raised his eyebrows and whistled. Zen nodded.

"The problem is that the resulting scandal would be so damaging for the Vatican that unless we go to them with a watertight case, they might try and hush it up. What we're doing at the moment is assembling a jigsaw of apparently unrelated pieces, one of which consists of some papers we believe may be concealed in the Archives. But since we're not liaising officially with the Vatican, we have no way of getting at them. That's why your assistance would be invaluable—if you would be prepared to collaborate."

He needn't have worried. Tullio Bevilacqua was one of those men who are fascinated by police work. He clearly felt thrilled and privileged at the idea of becoming a part of this investigation, even on the basis of such a flimsy briefing. Zen had been prepared for awkward questions and hard bargaining, but Tullio had no more intention of quibbling about the details than a small boy who has been invited onto the foot-plate by the engine driver will stop to ask where the train is going.

"We believe that the papers have been concealed in or near the document filed under this reference," Zen explained.

He passed Bevilacqua a card on which he had written the sequence of numbers and letters Giovanni Grimaldi had noted in his diary.

"Do we know what it looks like?" asked the new recruit.

What a thrill that "we" gave him!

"It's probably a number of typed pages, possibly with a printed heading of some sort to make it look official. In any case, it should stand out like a sore thumb in the middle of all those medieval manuscripts. Don't worry about the contents. The information we need will be coded. Just get us the document and we'll take care of the rest."

Zen hoped that Grimaldi would have had the sense to remove any reference to Ruspanti on the cover of the transcript, and that the document itself would conform to the standard practice, identifying the telephone numbers involved rather than the speakers' names. At any rate, Tullio Bevilacqua gave every impression of having been convinced by the story Zen had told him, and promised to do everything he could to help. He gave Zen his home phone number and told him to ring between seven and eight that evening.

At the intersection just beyond the offices of the *assessorato alla cultura,* four sets of converging facades combined to produce a perspective of vertiginous symmetry. Zen stood motionless at the curb, gazing at the seemingly endless vistas on every side. In the even, pearly light, the outlines of the buildings seemed to blur and merge into the expanse of the sky. It was impossible to say how much time passed before the metallic gray Lancia Thema screeched to a halt beside him.

"Hop in," said Gilberto Nieddu.

The Sardinian had changed out of the jeans and polo shirt he had been wearing earlier that morning into a sleek suit with matching tie and display handkerchief.

"You look like a pimp at a wedding," Zen told him sourly as they swept off along the broad central boulevard running the length of EUR.

"I've got an important lunch coming up," explained Nieddu. "It's all very well for you, Aurelio. You can wear any old tat. In business, if you want to be rich and successful you have to look like you already are."

Zen flushed indignantly. His suits came from an elderly tailor in Venice who had once supplied his father. They might not be in the latest style, but they were sober, durable, well cut, and of excellent cloth. To hear them denigrated was like hearing someone speak ill of a friend.

"You sound like that jerk I saw on television yesterday," he retorted. "He claims that you are what you wear."

"Falco?" exclaimed Nieddu. "He's a genius."

"What!"

"Well he's done all right for himself, hasn't he? Which reminds me, have you got the cash?"

"Of course I've got it."

The envelope containing the five fifty-thousand-lire notes was safely lodged in his jacket pocket. At this rate he was going to be broke by the New Year. They left the confines of EUR and drove along a road whose original vocation as a winding country lane was still perceptible despite the encroaching sprawl of concrete towers and jerry-built shacks that continually spilled across it. Nieddu punched the buttons of the radio without finding anything that satisfied him.

"Want to hear a joke?" he said. "This priest is playing bowls with the village drunk. Every time the drunk misses his shot, he yells, 'Jesus wept!' 'Don't take Our Lord's name in vain,' the priest tells him. Next shot, the drunk is wide again. 'Jesus wept!' 'If you blaspheme like that, God will strike you dead,' warns the priest. They play again, again the drunk misses. 'Jesus wept!' Sure enough, a black thundercloud covers the sky, a bolt of lightning sizzles down and strikes dead . . . the priest. And from the heavens comes a tremendous cry, '*Jesus wept!*' "

Nieddu turned off onto a dirt track running through an enclave of shacks and shanties to the right of the tarred road. The Lancia bumped over dried mud ruts and a collapsed culvert. Three toddlers standing on the bed of a rusty pickup perched on concrete blocks watched solemnly as they passed by. Just before the track turned left to rejoin the road, Nieddu stopped the car.

Like its neighbors, the house at the corner had apparently been cobbled together out of materials scavenged from other jobs. The walls were formed from cinder blocks, roof tiles, bricks of varying shapes and shades, and sections of concrete and tile piping, all stuck together with plenty of rough, thick cement. The house seemed to have grown organically, like a souk, further sections being added as and when required. Some of these were roofed with tiles, others with corrugated iron or asbestos sheeting, one with a sagging tarpaulin. There were few windows, and one of these, its wooden frame painted a lurid shade of puce, was nailed to the outside of the wall, presumably for decorative effect. The house was surrounded by a large expanse of bare earth, every growing thing having been consumed by the pigs and goats that roamed the property freely except for a small fenced-off area of kitchen garden. The entire lot was surrounded by a mesh fence against which two savage-looking mongrels were hurling themselves, their fangs bared at the intruders.

Nieddu locked the car, having first set and tested an alarm that briefly silenced the dogs. As he and Zen walked up to the gate they renewed their aggressive clamor, only to be stilled again, this time by a voice from inside the house. The front door opened and a shapeless,

ageless creature appeared on the step. It was wearing a long robe of
bright yellow silk, a crimson sash, and a tiara set with green, blue, and
red stones.

Gilberto Nieddu raised his right hand in a gesture of salutation.

"Peace be with you, Signora!"

"And with you."

The voice was loud, coarse, hopelessly at odds with the archaic
formulas of greeting.

"We would fain speak with him that abideth here, yea, even with
Mago," intoned Gilberto in a fruity tone, before adding prosaically, "I
phoned earlier this morning."

The figure screamed incomprehensible abuse at the dogs, who
looked as though they might burst into tears at any moment, and slunk
off to the rear of the property. Gilberto opened the gate and led the way
across the yard to the door where the robed figure stood to one side,
gesturing to them to enter.

The interior of the house was cool and dark and smelled strongly
of animal odors. They walked along a passage that twisted and turned
past a succession of open doorways. In one room a young man stripped
to his underpants lay asleep on an unmade bed, in another an elderly
man pored over a newspaper with a magnifying glass, in a third two
teenagers wearing crinkly black acrylic shell suits with bold colored
panels sat watching a television set on top of which a cockerel perched,
watching them in turn.

The next doorway was covered by a heavy velvet curtain.

"Make ready your offering," hissed their guide.

Nieddu nudged Zen, who produced the envelope containing a
quarter of a million lire. A plump hand appeared, its sluglike fingers
bedecked with an assortment of jeweled rings, and the envelope vanished into the folds of the yellow robe.

"Wait here while I intercede with Mago, that he may suffer you to
enter in unto him."

The creature drew back one edge of the curtain a little, releasing
an overpowering whiff of fetor, and slipped inside. The curtain dropped
into place again.

"My grandfather used to move his bowels first thing every morning," Nieddu remarked conversationally. "Afterward, he'd inspect the

result carefully, then go outside and eat the appropriate herb or vegetable, raw, with the dirt still on it. He lived to be a hundred and four. He saw Garibaldi once."

There were muffled voices from behind the curtain, which twitched aside to reveal the robed figure.

"Mago is graciously pleased to grant your request for an audience."

As the two men stepped inside, the curtain fell shut behind them, leaving them in a darkness that was total except for a glow emanating from the far side of the room. Nauseating odors of unwashed flesh, stale sweat, and spilled urine made the air almost unbreathable. As Zen's eyes gradually adjusted, he made out the reclining figure bathed in the toneless radiance.

"Hi, Gilberto!"

"Nicolo! How's it going?"

Nieddu put his arm around Zen, forcing him forward.

"Let me introduce a friend of mine. This is Aurelio. Aurelio, meet Nicolo."

Propped up in bed lay a teenage boy with delicate features, flawless pale skin, and fine dark hair. His big expressive eyes rested briefly on Zen, and his slender hand stirred in welcome from the keyboard where it had been resting. A length of coiled wire connected the keyboard to a stack of electronic equipment on a table beside the bed. On an old chest of drawers at the foot of the bed stood a video screen.

"Aurelio's got rather an amusing little puzzle for you," said Nieddu.

"Oh goody!" the boy cried gleefully. "It's been a bit boring lately. Is it like that one I did for you last month, Gilberto, the one where you wanted to find out how much money? . . ."

"No, no," Nieddu interrupted, "it's nothing to do with that at all. Aurelio wants to break into a database at the Ministry of the Interior."

The boy's face fell.

"Government systems are easy-peasy."

Nieddu nudged Zen.

"Tell Nicolo what you want to know, Aurelio."

Zen was busy trying to block his nasal passages against the pervading stench.

"I want a copy of a confidential file on an organization called the Cabal."

The supine figure fluttered his fingers over the keyboard like a blind man reading braille.

"Like that?" asked Nicolo.

Zen followed his gaze to the glowing screen, which now read CABAL. He nodded.

"It's in a part of the database you need special security clearance to get into," Zen explained. "The problem is that it's quite urgent. Have you any idea how long it might take?"

Nicolo gave a contemptuous sniff.

"I could get the system on-line while you wait, but if this is restricted access data that isn't going to help."

He stared at the screen in silence for a while.

"There are various ways we could do it," he mused. "There are probably a few guest passwords left lying around in the system. We might be able to use one of those."

Zen shook his head.

"How do you mean?"

"Well, let's say some VIP like Craxi comes to visit the place, they'll set up a password customized just for him, for example . . ."

"Duce," suggested Nieddu.

Zen laughed. Bettino Craxi, the leader of the Socialist party, was notoriously sensitive about comments likening his appearance and style to that of Benito Mussolini. Nicolo paid no attention to the joke.

"Yes, that would do. After the visit, the guest password is supposed to be erased, but half the time people forget and it's left sitting in the control system, waiting to be used. And it's easier to guess passwords than you might think. They have to be relatively straightforward, otherwise the designated users can't remember them. Anyway, that's one possibility. Another would be to run a keystroke capture program, but if this level is classified, it may be accessed relatively infrequently, so that would take time."

"I need to know in the next day or two," Zen told him.

Nicolo nodded.

"In that case, we'd better go in via Brussels. I cracked the EEC system last month. This friend of mine in Glasgow and I had a bet with the Chaos crowd in Hamburg to see which of us could get in there first and leave a rude message for the others to find. We won. From Brussels we can log on to the antiterrorist data pool, and then access the Ministry from, say, London or Madrid. That way we circumvent the whole password procedure. If you're on-line from a high-level international source like that, you come in with automatic authorization."

Zen nodded as if all this made perfect sense.

"Oh, and just one other thing," he said. "If you do manage to access this area of the computer, I'd like to see the file on an official named Zen. Aurelio Zen."

Nieddu looked at him sharply but said nothing.

"Zen," said Nicolo, spelling the name on the screen. "I'll get to work on it right away. Give me a ring tomorrow. With any luck I should have something by then."

Gilberto bent over the bed and handed something to the boy, who slipped it hastily under the covers with a guilty grin as the curtain drew aside again and the robed figure reappeared to usher the visitors out.

Back in the car, Zen burst into the hysterical laughter he had been suppressing. Nieddu grinned as he slalomed the Lancia through the twists and turns of the narrow country road.

"I know, I know! But believe me, Nicolo's the best hacker in Italy, and one of the best in Europe. He's done things for me I didn't believe were possible. And when he says he'll get to work right away, he means exactly that. The boy lives and breathes computers. He's capable of going for forty-eight hours without sleep when he's on the job."

"But that . . . *thing* in the fancy dress!"

"That's his grandmother. Nicolo was born with a spinal deformity so severe he wasn't expected to live. The family's from a village near Isernia. Nicolo's parents had their hands full working the land and looking after their other seven children, so they handed him over to Adelaide, who'd moved up here to Rome with her other daughter. One of the grandsons was given a computer for Christmas, but he couldn't figure out how to work it properly, so they passed it on to Nicolo. The rest is history."

"But what's all this Mago business?" demanded Zen.

Nieddu laughed.

"Adelaide thinks the whole thing is a con. Well, what's she supposed to think? Here's this crippled adolescent invalid, never leaves his bed, can't control his bladder, kicks and screams when she tries to change the sheets, yet is supposedly capable of roaming the world at the speed of light, dodging in and out of buildings in Amsterdam, Paris, or New York, and bringing back accounts, sales figures, medical records, or personnel files. I mean *come on!* I'm in the electronics business and even I find it barely credible. What's a sixty-year-old peasant woman from the Molise to make of it all? Yet the punters keep rolling up to the door and pressing bundles of banknotes into her hand! It's a scam, she thinks, but it's a bloody good one. So she's doing her bit to help it along by dressing up like a sorcerer's assistant."

Zen lit cigarettes for them both.

"What did you give the boy at the end?"

"Butterscotch. It's some sort of speciality from Scotland. This friend of his in Glasgow—they've never met, needless to say—sent him a packet, and now Nicolo can't get enough. I've bought a supply from a specialist shop in Via Veneto and I take him some every time I go."

They had reached the Via Appia Nuova, and Gilberto turned left, heading back into the city. Zen felt totally disoriented at the sight of the shiny cars and modern shopping centers, as though he'd awakened from a dream more real than the reality that surrounded him.

"So what is this Cabal?" Nieddu said suddenly. "It was mentioned in that anonymous letter to the papers about the Ruspanti affair, wasn't it? Are you still investigating that?"

"No, this is private enterprize."

Nieddu glanced at him.

"So what is it?"

"Oh, something to do with the Knights of Malta," Zen replied vaguely.

Nieddu shook his head.

"Bad news, Aurelio. Bad news."

"Why do you say that?"

"Well for a start, the Knights of Malta work hand in glove with the American Central Intelligence Agency and our own Secret Services."

"How do you know that?"

"I get around, Aurelio. I keep my ears open. Now I don't know what you mean by private enterprize, but if you're thinking of trying anything at all risky, I would think again. From what I've heard, some of the stuff the Order of Malta has been involved in, especially in South America, makes Gelli and the P2 look small-time."

They drove in silence for a while. Zen felt his spirits sink as the city tightened its stranglehold around them once more.

"Like what?" he asked.

"Like funding the Nicaraguan Contras and mixing with Colombian drug barons," Nieddu replied promptly. "You remember the bomb that brought down that plane last year, killing a leading member of the Brazilian Indian Rights movement? Every item of luggage had been through a strict security check, except for a diplomatic pouch supposedly carrying documents to one of the Order's consulates."

Zen forced a laugh.

"Come on, Gilberto! This is like claiming that Leonardo Sciascia was a right-wing stooge because his name is an anagram of CIA, CIA, and SS! The Order of Malta is a respectable charitable organization."

Nieddu shrugged.

"It's your life, Aurelio. Just don't blame me if you end up under that train to Milan instead of on it."

Tania Biacis had said that she wouldn't be home until eight o'clock, so Zen got there at six-thirty. This time there were no problems with the electricity, but as he pushed the button of the entry phone to make sure the flat was in fact unoccupied, Zen couldn't help recalling the night when Ludovico Ruspanti had died and all the lights went out. As the darkness pressed in on him, Zen had thought of his colleague Carlo Romizi. That association of ideas now seemed sinister and emblematic.

There was no answer from the entry phone, and the unshuttered windows of the top floor flat were dark. Zen let himself in and trudged upstairs. On each landing, the front doors of the other apartments emitted tantalizing glints of light and snatches of conversation. Zen ignored them like the covers of books he knew he would never read, his mind on other intrigues, other mysteries. A series of loud raps at the front door of Tania's flat brought no response, so Zen got out his key and unlocked the door.

Once inside, he turned on the hall light and checked his watch. He had plenty of time to search the flat and then retire to the local bar-cum-pizzeria, run by a friendly Neapolitan couple, before returning at about ten past eight for his dinner date with the unsuspecting Tania. First, though, he phoned his mother to make sure that Maria Grazia had packed his suitcase. His train left at seven the next morning, and he didn't want to have to do it when he got home.

"There's a problem!" his mother told him. "I told Maria Grazia to pack the dark blue suit but she said she couldn't find it! She wanted to pack the black one or the dark gray, but I said no, the black is for funerals, God forbid, and the gray one for marriages and first communions. Only the blue will do, but we can't find it anywhere, I don't know where it's got to . . ."

"I'm wearing it, Mama."

". . . unless we find it you won't be able to go. We can't have you appearing at an official function looking less than your best . . ."

"Mama, I'm wearing the blue suit today!"

". . . so important to make a good impression if you want to get ahead, I always say. People judge you by your clothes, Aurelio, and if you're inappropriately dressed it doesn't matter what you do . . ."

"Mama!!!"

". . . watching on television while I was at Lucrezia's yesterday, ever so nice, and talented too! He's written this book called *You Are What You Wear,* which is precisely what I've been trying to say all along, not that anyone ever has me on TV or even listens to me for that . . ."

Zen depressed the rest of the telephone, cutting the connection. He counted slowly to ten, then dialed again.

"Sorry, Mama, we must have got cut off somehow. Listen, apart from the blue suit, is my case packed?"

"All except your suit, yes. We looked everywhere, Maria Grazia and I, but we just couldn't find it. Perhaps it's at the cleaners, I said, but she . . ."

"I've got to go now, Mama. I'll be back late. Don't wait up for me."

"Oh listen, Aurelio, I almost forgot, someone phoned for you. They were going to ring again tomorrow but I told them you were going to Milan on the early train and they said they needed to speak to you urgently and so they gave me a number you're to ring at seven-thirty tonight."

"Who was it, Mama?"

"I don't remember if he gave a name, but he said it was about something you had for sale. It's not any of the family belongings, I hope?"

Zen felt his heart beating quickly.

"No, no. No, it's just something to do with work. Give me the number."

He noted down the seven digits and stared at them for some time before setting to work. Like a burglar, he worked his way steadily through the flat, turning out drawers and searching cupboards, wardrobes, and shelves. He became much better acquainted with Tania's taste in clothes and jewelry, including a number of unfamiliar items bearing designer labels that even Zen had heard of. He had been allowed to see the Falco sweater, but the others had been concealed from him. None, he reckoned, could have cost much less than half a million lire.

As he passed by the extension phone in the hallway, he had an idea. He dialed the Ministry, quoted the Rome number his mother had passed on, and asked them to find out the subscriber's name and address. Then he went into the kitchen. Spreading an old newspaper over the floor, he lifted the plastic rubbish sack out of its bin and emptied out the contents. When the phone rang, he was on his hands and knees, separating long white worms of cold spaghetti from the ripe mess in which they were breeding, poring over fish bones, separating scraps of orange peel from the gutted hulks of burst tomatoes. Wiping his hands quickly on a towel, he took the call in the hallway. It was the Ministry with the information he had requested.

"The number is a public call box, Dottore, in the lobby of the Hotel Torlonia Palace. The address is . . ."

"It's all right, I know the address."

"Very good, Dottore. Will that be all?"

Zen closed his eyes.

"No. Contact the Questura and have a man sent over there to watch the phone. He's to take a full description of anyone using it around seven-thirty. If the person is a guest, he's to identify him. If not, follow him."

Back in the kitchen, he resumed his analysis of the mess on the floor. Deep in the ripest puree of all, which had been fermenting for days at the bottom of the sack, he found the first scrap of paper. Gradually he recovered the others, one by one, from a glutinous paste of coffee grounds moistened with the snot of bad egg white. In the end he traced all but two of the sixteen irregular patches into which the sheet had been torn, and carefully pieced it together again on the kitchen counter.

Dear Tania,

    It's great news that you can make it on the 17th. Let me know which flight you'll be on and I'll meet you. I have to take my wife to the opera that evening, but we can have lunch and then spend the afternoon together. I'm really looking forward to it.

    All the best,

    Primo

Zen crunched the fragments into a clammy wodge, which he tossed back onto the pile of smelly rubbish. Then he rolled up the sheets of newspaper and stuffed the bundles back into the plastic sack. The seventeenth was the following Saturday, when Tania claimed she was going back to Udine to spend the weekend with her cousin. When the rubbish was bagged, he opened the window to air out the kitchen. It was just after a quarter past seven, time to find out if his hunch about Giovanni Grimaldi's hiding place for the transcript had been correct. Going back to the living room, he phoned the number Tullio had given him. A girlish voice answered before being silenced by a rather older boy. A brief struggle for the phone ended with a slap and crying.

"Who is it?" asked the victor.

"Luigi Borsellino," said Zen. "Let me speak to your dad."

Cutlery and crockery pinged and jangled distantly above the chatter of a family mealtime, and then a gleeful voice in Zen's ear exclaimed "I've got it!"

"It was there?"

"Exactly where you said, interleaved between the pages of a four-teenth-century treatise on some obscure Syrian heresy."

"And you brought it out with you?"

"No problem. The security at that place is a joke. Anyway, if they'd tried to stop me I'd have pointed out that fourteenth-century Syrians didn't use typewriters."

"What does it look like?"

"There's about twenty pages. It starts with a list of what looks like telephone numbers."

"No, those will be the numbers of the bank accounts the gang uses to launder the money from the drug sales," Zen replied glibly. "Just read them out to me, will you? I'll pick up the document itself later on this evening, but we need to take action to freeze those accounts as soon as possible."

There were about twenty numbers altogether. Zen wrote them down in his notebook on the same page as the number his mother had passed on. To his surprise, one of the numbers Bevilacqua read out was the same, the pay phone in the lobby of the Hotel Torlonia Palace. But the Torlonia Palace was of course one of the leading luxury hotels in Rome. It was perfectly natural that the intimates and associates of Prince Ruspanti should choose to stay there, just like other eminent visitors to the city such as Antonio Simonelli.

". . . before nine o'clock, all right?" Tullio Bevilacqua was saying.

Zen glanced at his watch. Christ! Seven thirty-one!

"Yes, yes! I'll see you then! Bye!"

"But I haven't given you the address!" squawked Bevilacqua.

"I'll get it from . . ."

Zen broke off in confusion. "From Tania," he had been going to say.

". . . from the Ministry computer."

Bevilacqua gasped.

"You mean . . . you've got a file on me?"

"We've got a file on *everyone.*"

He hit the receiver rest repeatedly until he got a dial tone, then punched in the number that now figured twice on the notebook page open on his knee. It was answered immediately.

"You're late."

It was the voice that had spoken to Zen the night before from the confessional in St. Peter's. The man's arrogant tone triggered an instinctive response for which Zen was quite unprepared.

"I've cornered the market in the commodity you're interested in. I'll be as late as I fucking well choose."

"Can you prove you have possession?"

The voice was the same as the night before, but the background was now thoroughly worldly: a babble of voices competing for attention against the synthetic battery of a pop band.

"Well, I could read you a list of phone numbers, but that would be giving away information I could sell elsewhere. Just as a taster, though, one of the numbers Ruspanti phoned just before he died is the same as the one on which you are now speaking. But I expect you already knew that."

There was a brief pause.

"But now we know that *you* know. That makes all the difference."

Zen said nothing.

"Hello? Are you still there?" the man queried peevishly.

"I'm here. I'm waiting for you to say something worth listening to. I got an earful of your waffle last night."

"How much do you want?"

This was the crunch. If Zen had been bluffing, his bluff had been called. And what else could he have been doing? The idea of selling evidence to the highest bidder, never more than an idle speculation in the first place, was out of the question after what had happened to Carlo Romizi. It was unthinkable to imagine disposing of the transcript for his personal advantage, merely to restore his flagging finances and win Tania back from the rich young shit beside whom he looked drably impoverished, timidly conventional.

"How much?" prompted the voice impatiently.

"Rather more than Grimaldi asked, and rather less than he got."

The man laughed. He could relax, the deal was in the bag. Money would never be a problem for these people.

"We offered Grimaldi thirty million, but he tried to hold out for more. I think we would be prepared to improve the price this time, to let us say fifty. But I would very strongly urge you to accept."

Zen kept silent. What was the man talking about? The transcript wasn't for sale, not at any price. It was sacred, stained with the innocent blood of his colleague, Carlo Romizi.

"That figure of course applies only to the *original,"* the voice stressed. "As you rightly surmized, the contents are already known to us."

"Grimaldi showed you a photocopy, I suppose, to whet your appetite for the real thing?"

"We'll contact you in the next day or two, Dottore. I understand you're going to Milan tomorrow?"

"Yes, but . . ."

"We shall know how to contact you. *Buon viaggio."*

Zen replaced the phone slowly. Then he shrugged, as though shaking off a bad dream. Nothing would come of it. Tomorrow he would take the transcript to Milan and hand it over to Antonio Simonelli or his secretary. Then it would be out of his hands, and just as well, too. He didn't trust himself to do the right thing any longer.

The thought of Milan made him get out his notebook and look again at the list of phone numbers that Ruspanti had called from his hideaway in the Vatican. As he thought, in addition to those in Rome, there had been several calls prefixed 02, the code for Milan. Zen picked up the phone and dialed one of them, just out of curiosity. There was no answer. He tried another and got an answering machine.

"This is 879 4632 There is no one able to answer the phone at present. If you wish to leave a message . . ."

The voice sounded rather like the man he had just been speaking to a moment ago in the Hotel Torlonia Palace. Which all went to show that one person can sound much like another, particularly on the telephone. There was one other Milan number on the list, and Zen was just about to dial it when the phone suddenly started to ring.

"Yes?"

"This is the Questore, Dottore. The Ministry asked us to contact you about that phone you wanted watched. I'm afraid the situation was a bit confusing. Apparently there was some sort of publicity event being held at the hotel, a launch party for some book, so the place was thick with media people and the phones were in use all the time."

"I see. Thank you."

He had expected something of the kind. The men he was dealing with were too clever to allow themselves to be trapped in that way. Zen picked up the phone again and dialed the last of the Milan numbers Ludovico Ruspanti had called in the final week of his life.

"Yes?"

The voice was that of a young woman. She spoke hesitantly, as though expecting a reprimand. Zen realized that he had no idea what to say.

"It's me," he murmured finally.

There was a brief pause.

"Ludo?"

The woman sounded tentative, incredulous. Not half as incredulous as Zen, though.

"Who else?"

There was a stifled gasp.

"But they told me you'd had to go away. They told me I'd never see you again . . ."

Her voice trailed away. Perhaps she, too, had become aware of the altered acoustic on the line. Someone, somewhere, was listening in.

"Listen, can I see you tomorrow?" Zen went on quickly.

"You're coming here? To see *me?*"

"Yes! I'll ring when I arrive."

"But remember to let it ring and then call back, so that I have time to get rid of Carmela. You forgot this time, silly! Luckily her sister is visiting this week and they're out every evening. Well, she couldn't very well bring her here, could she?"

Zen caught sight of the clock on the sideboard opposite. It showed five to eight, long past time for him to be gone.

"Till tomorrow, then!"

"Oh, I can't wait, I can't wait!" the woman cried girlishly. "You promise?"

"I promise."

"Cross your heart and hope to die?"

A superstitious revulsion rose like nausea in Zen's throat.

"I'll ring you tomorrow," he said, and hung up.

He couldn't believe what had just happened. Seemingly the number in Milan belonged to one of "Ludo" Ruspanti's mistresses, and—

incredible as this seemed—she was apparently unaware that her lover was dead. His elation was briefly dimmed by the knowledge that someone had been eavesdropping on their conversation. Nevertheless, here was a golden opportunity, which, if he could only find the right way to handle it, might lead him to the heart of the . . .

"All right, Aurelio, who is she?"

Zen looked up to find Tania Biacis glowering at him from the doorway.

"Come on!" she shouted, advancing into the room. "Don't try palming me off with clever lies. I've seen you taking in too many other people to fall for it myself. Just tell me the truth, then get the hell out of here!"

He had never seen her like this, furious, overbearing, utterly sure of herself. He got up, gesturing weakly.

"You don't think . . ."

"I don't *think* anything!" she broke in brutally. "I just heard you speaking to her on the phone, fixing a rendezvous for tomorrow. "Oh, I can't wait, I can't wait!" Sounds like hot stuff, this lady of yours!"

"So it was *you* listening in, on the extension in the hallway!"

"I wasn't *listening in*. I was trying to use my phone. I had no idea you were here. How the hell did you get in, anyway? You've had a key all along, I suppose. I might have known!"

"The American gave me a spare key. I thought I'd hang on to it, just in case . . ."

"So I get home and pick up the phone, only to hear this woman practically sticking her tongue into your ear. So you're going away tomorrow, right? A sudden urgent mission of the highest importance to —where did you say she lives?"

"And what about you, my dear?" Zen retorted. "Who were you trying to phone so urgently the moment you got in? Was it that man who answered the phone when I called here on Tuesday?"

Tania held up her hands.

"All right, I admit it. It wasn't a wrong number. It was Aldo, my cousin Bettina's husband. He was here on business."

"Business? You told me he worked for the post office."

She flapped her hands in evident confusion.

"Well, there was some . . . conference or something."

The evident lie stung him to push things to the limit.

"All right, then, let's forget Aldo. But you still haven't told me who you were trying to phone. Was it Primo, by any chance?"

The pink flush around her high cheek bones revealed that the name had had its effect.

"It's too bad he's got to take his wife to the opera in the evening, isn't it?" Zen carried on. "Still, he's going to pick you up from the airport and take you out to lunch, and after that, who knows?"

"Is that why you broke in here? So that you could snoop around reading my mail? You . . . you . . . you COP!"

"I could think of an even more insulting epithet to apply to you, if I chose to use it!"

"Fuck off! Just fuck off out of my house!"

Zen measured her with a look.

"What do you mean, *your* house?"

Tania tossed her head contemptuously.

"Oh, you mean because you've been secretly paying someone to rent this place to me? Well, I'd guessed that, as it happens. I'm not *stupid*. The only reason I hadn't told you I knew was that I didn't want to hurt your feelings. Oh, it's so fucking pathetic, the whole thing . . ."

To Zen's utter consternation, she turned away and burst into tears. Not as a ploy; that he could have withstood. But she had moved beyond him, into uncharted areas of real grief. Yet how could it be real when she was false, and believed him to be? It didn't make sense. None of it made sense. So he fled, leaving her to her intolerable mysteries. The real world awaited him: his distraction, his toy.

SIX

The piazza in front of Rome's Stazione Termini, normally thronged with buses, cars, traders' vans, and lorries, with crowds of commuters, tourists, beggars, transients, and the forlorn Senghalese and Filippino immigrants who used the place as an informal clubhouse, information center, and canteen, was now a bleak, empty, rain-swept wasteland. As Zen stared out of the window of the taxi at the porticoed arcade to one side and the blank wall closing off the vista, he slipped back into the dream from which the alarm clock had saved him less than half an hour earlier.

He'd been walking across just such a piazza, but in broad daylight, beneath a brutal summer sun. The light flattened the ground at his feet, reducing it to a featureless expanse bordered by a row of broken columns, the last of which cast a perfect shadow of itself on the hot paving, like the hands of a clock showing one minute to twelve. That was indeed the time, and he would never manage to catch the train, which left on the hour from the station whose enormous facade sealed off the perspective. Already he could see the plume of smoke as the locomotive pulled away from the invisible platform, inaccessible behind a high wall . . .

The taxi hit one of the curbs delineating the bus lanes, jolting him awake again. The dream was still horribly vivid, though: the stillness, the stifling heat, the paralysis of his limbs, the sickening perspectives of the piazza, at once vertiginous and claustrophobic. He sat up straight, willing himself back to the here and now. It was only a dream, after all.

Having paid off the taxi, he carried his bag through the booking hall into the main concourse of the station. It was twenty past six. He'd spent a quarter of an hour blundering around the apartment, worrying that he'd remembered to pack everything except the one essential item, whatever it was, without which his journey would be in vain, and was just wondering whether to take the replica revolver when the taxi arrived, ten minutes early. In the end he'd thrown the thing into his suitcase along with a couple of spare shirts, grabbed his briefcase with the precious transcript, and rushed downstairs. As a result of that unnecessary haste, he now had forty minutes to hang around the drafty public spaces of the station.

The cafeteria was still closed, but a small kiosk was dispensing coffee to a huddle of early arrivals. Zen joined the queue, eventually obtaining a double expresso, which he knocked back like a shot of spirits. The warming glow of caffeine hit his bloodstream, adding the depth of memory to his two-dimensional consciousness. He winced, recalling his parting from Tania the night before, the unforgivable things said on both sides, the way he had walked out without any attempt at reconciliation. Well, what was the point? It was over, that was clear enough. Tania might be ludicrously mistaken about his supposed amours, but he certainly wasn't about hers. There was too much evidence, both material and circumstantial, and he was too experienced an investigator to be led astray. Besides, Tania had made it plain that after years of confinement in a joyless marriage to Mauro Bevilacqua she wasn't prepared to submit to the straitjacket of another exclusive relationship. Why insist on freedom and then leave it untasted?

Zen tossed the disposable plastic cup into the rubbish bag provided and turned to survey his fellow passengers. They looked bizarrely out of place, an elegant, wealthy throng clustered around the minibar like factory workers on the early shift. Power dressing was the order of the day, both men and the few women present discreetly flaunting an understated sartorial muscle based on cut, finish, and quality fabrics. The only exception was a tense-looking man wearing the undress uniform of the Church the world over, a plain clerical suit and white collar, clutching a locked attaché case under his arm. Zen instinctively glanced at his own battered leather briefcase, leaning against the overnight bag at his feet.

After storming out of Tania's apartment the night before, he had gone to the bar around the corner and shared some of his problems, suitably depersonalized, with the Neapolitans over a hot chocolate. Since he couldn't very well ask Tania for her brother-in-law's address, Zen looked it up in the phone book and then took a cab to pick up the transcript. Unfortunately, Tullio Bevilacqua was so proud of his part in the relentless struggle against organized crime that he had invited his brother to witness this historic event.

The last time Zen saw Tania's husband, Mauro Bevilacqua had been waving a gun in his face and threatening to exact revenge for the insult done to his family honor, so his unexpected appearance at this juncture seemed likely to result in all manner of problems, both professional and personal. In the event, the encounter was less fraught than it might have been. After a brief but violent internal tussle, Mauro opted for a pose of contemptuous indifference, as though to emphasize that the doings of his estranged wife were of no interest to him. Only at the end, when Zen was about to leave, did his mask slip for a moment.

"We mustn't detain our guest any longer, brother. He has important work to do keeping prostitution off the streets."

Tullio frowned.

"Dottor Borsellino isn't in the Vice Squad."

Mauro gave a smile of exquisite irony.

"Borsellino?" he enquired archly. "Ah, excuse me! I was confusing him with an official who used to work with all the sluts of the city. A slimy, venal little cunt by the name of Aurelio Zen."

He turned to face Zen.

"Do you know him by any chance, Dottore?"

Zen nodded.

"I'll tell him what you said."

"Yes, do that. Not that I've got anything personal against him, you understand. In fact he did me a favor once. Took this *whore* off my hands."

Mauro Bevilacqua smiled reminiscently.

"I wonder who she's with now!"

Since Zen was wondering almost exactly the same thing, he was unable to come up with a suitably crushing reply. Back home, his mother had kept him up late with a long and involved story about some childhood friend of hers who had moved to Milan with her husband and been killed during the war when an Allied bomb struck the laundry where she worked. By the time he extricated himself, Zen had felt too tired to do more than go straight to bed and hope he would feel better in the morning.

He walked over to the news stall, which had just opened, and looked over the magazines. The cover of the new issue of *Moda* showed an extraordinary peacock of a man, a shimmering apparition in heavy gray-and-gold silks, his guileless blue eyes turned levelly toward the camera. The caption read "Falco: A Philosopher in the Wardrobe." Just then a subliminal frisson spread through the group of men standing at the news stall, leaping from one to another like an electric charge. Zen turned his head along with all the others, but it was too late. The woman who had generated all this excitement had already passed by, and all he could see of her was her shoulder-length blonde hair and the back of her dark cream trenchcoat, the hem oscillating back and forth above her suede boots. With a sigh he picked up his luggage and followed her and the other passengers toward the platform where *"il pendolino,"* as the pride of the Ferrovie dello Stato was popularly known, was now boarding.

The eight carriages that made up the ETR 450 high-speed unit, with a bullet-shaped cab at each end, were mounted high above the bogies on which they tilted to maintain stability at speeds of up to 150 mph—whence its nickname, "the pendulum." All seats were reserved and first-class only. Zen's carriage was toward the middle of the train. In the vestibule, a uniformed attendant checked his ticket and directed him to his place. Two rows of reclining seats ran the length of the coach, just as in an airplane. Indeed, the *pendolino* was the next best thing to a plane, covering the four hundred miles between Rome and Milan in under four hours.

Zen had booked a single seat, so there was little danger of his being observed. Having stowed the suitcase in the luggage rack, he lowered the table attached to the back of the chair in front, opened his briefcase, and extracted a sheaf of papers. Apart from the initial reference list of phone numbers, the transcript consisted of twenty-two pages headed UFFICIO CENTRALE DI VIGILANZA and covered in single-spaced typing, divided into blocks each headed with a date, time, and telephone number. Each block represented one phone call Ruspanti had made. There were no incoming calls. Ruspanti presumably hadn't given his phone number to anyone, either because the 698 prefix would have revealed his presence in the Vatican City State, or because he knew or suspected that the line was being tapped.

There was a whistle blast from the platform outside, a whine as the automatic doors closed, then a slight jolt of movement. Zen glanced at his watch. Seven o'clock on the dot. A moment later the window was covered in a speckle of rain as the train emerged into the gray dawn. Inside, the broad strip of fluorescent paneling on the ceiling of the coach bathed everything in a coolly efficient radiance. Zen lowered his head over the papers again and started to read.

Some time later he sensed someone standing behind him, craning over him. He hastily covered the typewritten page, but it was only one of the stewards, offering him an airplane-style breakfast tray containing an assortment of sad pastries and unloved rolls in plastic shrouds. Zen waved it away, then reclaimed the cup and asked for coffee. Beyond the window, the flat expanses of the Tiber floodplain slipped past like a video being fast-forwarded. They were on the new *direttissima* line by now, the train humming purposefully along at its top speed on the custom-built track.

Zen read quickly through the rest of the transcript, then laid it on the table, face down, and sighed. Giovanni Grimaldi had been felled in his shower like a beast at the abattoir because he had threatened to reveal the contents of this document, yet Zen had just read it from cover to cover and it meant almost nothing to him.

He turned back to the beginning and read it through once more. Whether Ruspanti had been aware of the tap on his own line, or was concerned about possible eavesdroppers on the other end, he had gone to great pains to say nothing of any consequence. About half the calls amounted to little more than requests to be contacted "at the usual number" or "in the normal way." In others, Ruspanti referred to "the sum agreed" or "under discussion," or urged that "the measures previ-

ously outlined be put into immediate effect." Only twice did he mention anything more specific. The first instance occurred in the course of
the call to the pay phone in the lobby of the Hotel Torlonia Palace the
previous Thursday. His patience had finally run out, Ruspanti said. If
"Zeppegno" couldn't be persuaded to "do the decent thing" by the
weekend at the latest, then he would "have no alternative but to make
public the matter which you know about."

Given the timing, this might well have had some bearing on the
circumstances of Ruspanti's death. But as the nature of the secret he
threatened to make public was not even hinted at, and the name mentioned was presumably false, it did not amount to very significant evidence. The other call was to the last of the Milan numbers Zen had
tried the night before, but although it sounded an intimate note, perceptible even in the unrelievedly literal transcription, its significance
remained equally cryptic.

"Hello?"

"Ludo! Where are you? Are you coming here?"

"I'm not in Milan, my love."

"Where, then?"

"I'm . . . moving around a bit. Here today, gone tomorrow."

"Sounds like fun."

"In fact, I was talking to someone about you just the other day,
Ariana. Someone who works for a magazine."

"About *me?*"

"That's right. I told him all about your dolls. He sounded very
interested. In fact, he wants to write an article about them."

"Don't make fun of me, Ludo. It isn't fair."

"I'm not! This is quite serious."

"But why would anyone be interested in my dolls?"

"You'd be amazed, Ariana. So would your brother!"

"You haven't told him, have you?"

"No, I can't seem to get hold of him. Why don't *you* tell him? Tell
him to get in touch and let me know what he thinks about the idea. He
knows how to contact me, if he wants to."

"But when will I see you?"

"As soon as all this is over."

"All what? There's some problem, isn't there? I can feel it. What is it, Ludo? Tell me!"

"Oh, nothing. Just the silly games we boys play. Girls are more sensible, aren't they?"

Zen looked at the window, but the train was running through a tunnel, and all he could see was the reflection of his own features, baffled and haggard. Perhaps someone more familiar with the details of the case against Ruspanti might glean something more substantial from the transcript. Since someone had been prepared to kill Grimaldi and bribe Zen to obtain the damn thing, there must be some clue hidden there. The reference to "dolls" might be a code of some kind. What would Ruspanti's mistress be doing playing with dolls? Perhaps Antonio Simonelli would know what it meant.

The roar of the tunnel faded as the train emerged into bright sunshine. A moment later they had crossed the Arno and rejoined the old line running through the outskirts of Florence. Zen returned the transcript to his briefcase, which he locked and placed on his knees as the train drew into the suburban station of Rinfredi, which it used to avoid the time-wasting turnaround at the Florentine terminus of Santa Maria Novella. The stop was a brief one, and by the time he'd had a chance to skim *La Stampa* they were once again under way, along the fast straight stretch to Prato.

"Good morning, Dottore."

Zen looked up from his newspaper. The voice was both distinctive and familiar, but it still took him a moment to recognize the man standing beside his seat, an umbrella in one hand and a briefcase in the other, gazing down at him with a smile of complicity. It was the man who had been in his thoughts just a few minutes earlier, the man he was going to Milan to see, Antonio Simonelli.

"Have you brought the transcript?"

They had barely settled down in the seats to which Simonelli had led the way. When the magistrate suggested that Zen join him in the next carriage, he had at once agreed. Policemen are accustomed to obeying the instructions of the judiciary, and besides, seeing Simonelli was the reason for Zen's trip to Milan. This chance meeting—the magistrate had apparently just joined the train at Florence, where he had been attending a meeting—was simply a happy coincidence. Or so it had seemed, until Simonelli mentioned the transcript.

Zen instinctively tightened his grip on the briefcase, which was lying on his knees. The train rounded a curve, and sunlight suddenly streamed in through the window. In the lapel of Simonelli's jacket, something glimmered. Zen looked more closely. It was a small silver eight-pointed cross.

"You're a member?"

The magistrate glanced down as though noticing the insignia for the first time.

"I am, actually."

"Like Ruspanti."

Simonelli's laugh had an edge to it.

"Hardly! Ruspanti was a Knight of Honor and Devotion. You need at least three hundred years of nobility behind you to achieve that. I'm just a simple Donat, the lowest of the low."

"You weren't wearing it when we met in Rome the other day."

Simonelli stared back at him with ill-concealed hostility.

"So? I've just been attending a gathering where it happened to be appropriate."

It was only when Zen felt the magistrate's restraining hand on his wrist that he realized he had reached for his cigarettes. Simonelli indicated the sign on the window with a nicotine-stained finger.

"No smoking."

Beyond the dirt-flecked window with its prohibitory sign, the slanting winter light streaked the narrow gorge of the Bisenzio where road and railway run side by side until the river peters out in the southern flanks of the Apennines. Then the road, largely disused since the motorway was opened, begins the long climb to the pass thousands of feet above, while the railway plunges into the eleven-mile tunnel under the mountains.

Why had Simonelli reserved a seat in a nonsmoking section when he was himself a smoker? There were plenty of single seats available in the coach where Zen was sitting. There were no doubles, though, and if Simonelli had already known that the seat beside his would be unoccupied, it could only be because he had booked them both in advance.

The implications of this were so dizzying that he hardly heard Simonelli's next words.

"After all, it wouldn't do for a judge and a policeman to break the law, would it?"

Zen glanced round at him witlessly.

"Or at least," corrected Simonelli, "to be *seen* to do so."

"Seen to . . . How?"

"By smoking in a nonsmoking carriage."

Zen nodded. Antonio Simonelli joined in until both their heads were wagging in the same tempo. They understood each other perfectly.

"It *is* the original, I trust."

Once again the magistrate's nicotine-stained finger was extended, this time toward the briefcase Zen was hugging defensively to his body.

"As my colleague explained to you on the phone, we're not interested in purchasing a copy."

Zen's mouth opened. He laughed awkwardly.

"No, no. Of course not."

Simonelli glanced out the window at the landscape, which was growing ever more rugged as they approached the mountain chain that divides Italy in two. With its many curves and steep gradients, this difficult section of line was the slowest, and even the *pendolino* was reduced to the speed of a normal train. Simonelli consulted his watch.

"Do you think we're going to be late?" Zen asked.

"Late for what?"

The Maltese cross in the magistrate's lapel, its bifurcated points representing the eight beatitudes, glinted hypnotically as the contours of the valley brought the line into the sunlight.

"For whatever's going to happen."

Simonelli eyed him steadily.

"All that's going to happen is that you give me the transcript, and I take it to an associate who is seated in the next carriage. Once he has confirmed that it is the original, I return with the money."

Zen stared back at the magistrate. Marco Duranti had described the supposed maintenance man who hot-wired the shower to kill Giovanni Grimaldi as stocky, muscular, of average height, with a big round face and a pronounced nasal accent, "a real Northerner." The description fitted Simonelli perfectly. And would not such a humble task befit "a simple Donat, the lowest of the low"? Despite the almost oppressive warmth of the air-conditioned carriage, Zen found himself shivering uncontrollably.

Simonelli tugged at the briefcase again, more insistently this time. Zen held on tight.

"How do I know I'll get paid?"

"Of course you'll get paid! No one can get off the train until we reach Bologna anyway."

As the train glided through the Vernio station and entered the southern end of the long tunnel under the Apennines, Zen's attention was momentarily distracted by the woman who had caused such a stir at the terminus in Rome. She was making her way to the front of the carriage, and once again he saw only her clothes, a cowl-neck ribbed sweater and tightly cut skirt. She left a subtle trail of perfume behind her, as though shaken from the shoulder-length blonde hair like incense from a censer.

"If the transcript is safe with you, the money is safe with me," Zen found himself saying above the roaring of the tunnel. "So give it to me now, before you take the transcript."

He had hoped to disconcert Simonelli with this demand, to force him to consult his associate and thus give Zen more time to consider his next move. But as usual, he was a step behind. With a brief sigh of deprecation at this regrettable lack of trust on Zen's part, Simonelli opened his briefcase. It was filled with neat bundles of ten-thousand-lire notes.

"Fifty million," the magistrate said. "As we agreed."

He closed the lid and snapped the catches, locking the case, then stood up and laid it on his seat.

"Now give me the transcript, please."

Zen stared up at him. Why struggle? What difference did it make? He had been going to hand the transcript over to Simonelli anyway, in Milan. This way the result was the same, except that he came out of it fifty million lire better off. Even if he wanted to resist, there was nothing he could do, no effective action he could take. The only weapon he had was the fake revolver, which was buried inside his suitcase in the luggage rack at the end of the next carriage. But even if he had been armed to the teeth, it wouldn't have made any difference in the long run. The Cabal would get their way in the end. They always did.

He lifted his arm off his briefcase. Simonelli reached across, opened the case and removed the transcript.

"I shall be no more than five minutes," he said. "We have several men on the train. If you attempt to move from this seat during that time, I cannot be responsible for your safety."

He strode off along the carriage toward the vestibule where the blonde woman was now smoking a cigarette. The train seemed to be full of masochistic smokers, Zen reflected with a forlorn attempt at humor. He stared out the window, trying to think of something other than the humiliation he had just suffered. Although he had been traveling this line for years, the ten-and-a-half-minute transit of the Apennines was still something that awed him. His father had impressed the young Aurelio with the history of the epic project, which had gripped the imagination of the nation throughout the 1920s. Although marginally shorter than the Simplon, the Apennine tunnel had been infinitely more difficult and costly to construct, running as it did a nightmarish schist riddled with pockets of explosive gas and unmapped underground lakes that burst forth without warning, flooding the workings for months on end. Almost a hundred men had lost their lives in a struggle as grueling and far more glorious than the foreign wars with which Mussolini had later tried to galvanize the nation. It was one of these that had ultimately carried Zen's father away to his death in Russia, while his son rode through the Galleria dell'Apennino in an air-conditioned, high-suspension luxury that seemed an ironic comment on the past, with its excessive, sweaty heroism. He was still pursuing this thought when, just like the previous Friday, all the lights went out.

A moment later the secure warmth of the carriage was gutted by a roaring torrent of ice-cold air. The train shuddered violently as the brakes locked on. Cries of alarm and dismay filled the carriage, turning to screams of pain as the train jerked to a complete stop, throwing the passengers against each other and the seats in front.

Once Zen's eyes had adjusted to the darkness, he discovered that it was not quite total after all. Although the lights in this carriage had failed, those in the adjoining coaches reflected off the walls of the tunnel, creating a faint glimmer by which he could just make out the aisle, the seats, and the vague blurs of the other passengers moving about. Then two figures wielding torches like swords appeared at the end of the carriage. A moment later, the fluorescent strip on the ceiling of the carriage came on again.

It had been a perfect moment for a murder, Zen reflected afterward. The killers would be wearing sunglasses, and while everyone else was blinded by the sudden excess of light, they could carry out their assignment as though in total darkness. Fortunately, however, the men who had entered the carriage were not assassins but members of the train crew. Zen followed them to the vestibule at the front of the carriage, where he made himself known to the guard, a gray-haired man with the grooming and gravity of a senior executive.

The gale-force wind that had stripped all the warmth out of the carriage had diminished now that the train had come to a halt, but there was still a vicious draft streaming in through the open door. Zen asked what had happened. The *capotreno* indicated a red lever set in a recess in the wall nearby. Shouting to make himself heard over the banshee whining in the tunnel outside, he explained that the external doors on the train were opened and closed by the driver, but that this mechanism could be overridden manually to prevent people being trapped inside in the event of an emergency. The lever was normally secured in the up position with a loop of string sealed like a medieval parchment with a circle of lead embossed with the emblem of the State Railways. This now dangled, broken, from its grommet.

"As soon as this lever is thrown, a warning light comes on in the driver's cab, and he stops the train. Unfortunately some people like to kill themselves this way. I don't know why, but we get quite a few."

Just like St. Peter's, thought Zen.

"But why did the lights go off?" he asked.

The guard indicated a double row of fuses and switches on the wall opposite, protected by a plastic cover that now swung loose on its hinges.

"The fuse for the main lighting circuit was missing. We swapped over the one for the air-conditioning thermostat just to get the lights back on before the passengers started to panic. He must have done it himself, so he couldn't see what was going to happen to him."

The toilet door opened with a click and the blonde woman stepped out. She looked slightly flustered by so much male attention.

"Has something happened?" she asked.

Close to, her skin showed a slight roughness that made her seem older. Her pale blue eyes looked at Zen, who sniffed. Apart from her perfume, there seemed to be another new odor present—the smell of burning.

"Did you hear anything?" he said.

The flaxen hair trembled as she shook her head.

"Just the roaring noise when the lights went out. Has some-one? . . ."

The *capotreno* dismissed the woman with a wave and told two of his assistants to keep the passengers out of the vestibule.

"We'd better have a look on the track," he said.

The *pendolino* had never seemed more like an airplane to Aurelio Zen than when he stepped out of its lighted sanctuary into the howling storm outside. The Apennines form a continuous barrier running almost the entire length of the Italian peninsula, and the prevailing climatic conditions often differ dramatically from one side to the other. This man-made vent piercing the range thus forms a conduit for violent air currents flowing in one direction or the other as the contrasting weather systems try to find their level.

The high pressure was in Tuscany that day, so the wind was flowing north, battering the faces of the men as they walked back along the track. While they were still alongside the train, light streaming from the windows high overhead, Zen found the experience just about tolerable. But when they passed the final coach and struck out into the turbulent darkness that corroded the fragile beams of their torches, wearing them away, using them up, until they could hardly see the track in front of them, he was gripped by a terror so real it made anything else appear a flimsy dream of security, a collective delusion provoked by a reality too awful to be contemplated.

The noise was already deafening, but as they moved forward, breasting the black tide that threatened at every moment to sweep them away with it, it became clear that its source lay somewhere in front of them. The five men trudged slowly on, leaning forward as though pushing a laden sledge, their feeble torch beams scanning the ballast, sleepers, and rails. The occasional patch of toilet paper, a soft drink can or two, an ancient pack of cigarettes, and a newspaper were all they found at first. Then something brighter, a fresher patch of white, showed up. One of the train crew picked it up and passed it to the *capotreno,* who held up his torch, scanning the line of heavy type at the top: UFFICIO CENTRALE DI VIGILANZA.

As the clamor up ahead grew ever more distinct and concentrated, the movement of the air became stronger and more devious, no longer a single blast but a maelstrom of whirling currents and eddies fighting for supremacy. Without the slightest warning, a giant beacon appeared in the darkness behind them and swept past, forging south into the gale. As the locomotive passed, the darkness was briefly pushed aside like a curtain, revealing the vast extent of the cavity where they cowered, deafened by the howl of its siren. Then the darkness fell back, and all other sounds were ground out by the wheels of a seemingly endless succession of unlighted freight cars.

At length two red lights appeared, marking the last car. As it receded into the distance, the men started to move forward again and the original, primitive uproar reasserted itself, an infinitely powerful presence that was seemingly located somewhere in the heart of the solid rock above their heads. The train crew shone their torches upward revealing a huge circular opening in the roof of the tunnel. It was almost impossible to stand in the vortex of the vicious currents spiraling straight up the mountaintop thousands of feet above.

The *capotreno* beckoned to Zen, who lowered his ear to the man's mouth.

"Ventilation shaft!"

They found the body a little farther along, lying beside the track like another bit of rubbish dropped from a passing train in defiance of the prohibition in several languages. One leg had been amputated at the thigh and most of the left arm and shoulder was mangled beyond recognition, but by some freak the face had survived without so much as a scratch. The Maltese cross glinted proudly in the lapel of the plain blue suit, and the fingers of the right hand were still clutching several pages of the transcript, which now appeared to have claimed its second victim.

• • •

The power and influence of Milan—Italy's rightful capital, as it liked to call itself—had never appeared more impressive to Aurelio Zen than as he strode along the corridors of the Palazzo di Giustizia late that afternoon. The office to which he had been directed was in an annex built onto the rear of the main building, and its clean lines and uncluttered spaces, and still more the purposeful air of bustle and business, were as different as possible from other sites sacred to the judiciary. If Milan was capable of influencing, even superficially, an organization in which the bacillus of the Bourbonic plague was preserved in its purest and most virulent form, then what couldn't it do?

He rounded a corner to find a woman looking toward him from an open doorway. A helmet of lusterless black hair cropped at the nape framed her flat, open face, the bold cheeks and strong features blurred by menopausal turmoil like a damp-damaged fresco. She wore a slate-gray wool jacket with a matching skirt cut tight just below the knee.

"Antonia Simonelli," she said. "Come in."

He followed her into an office containing two teak desks. One, pushed into a corner, was almost invisible beneath a solid wall of stacked folders reaching to within a meter of the ceiling. The other was completely bare except for a laptop computer. At the other side of the room a large window afforded an excellent view of the Gothic fantastications of the cathedral and the glazed roofs and dome of the Galleria Vittorio Emanuele.

The woman sat at the bare desk and crossed her long legs. Zen on the only other seat, a hard wooden stool.

"I must apologize for the spartan furnishings," the woman said. "My office is in the part of the main building that is being renovated, and meanwhile I'm with a colleague whose tastes and habits are, as you can see, very different from mine. Gianfranco likes the blinds drawn and the lights on, even in high summer. That's his desk. I sometimes feel I'm going to go crazy just looking at it."

Zen looked at the rounded peak of her knee and the tip of her gray suede shoe, which rose above the sheeny expanse of the desktop like a tropical island in a calm sea.

"He didn't have any ID," he murmured.

The woman bent forward, frowning slightly.

"I beg your pardon?"

Zen looked up at her.

"The man on the train. He didn't have any identification. But I suppose you do."

He produced his own pass certifying him as a functionary of the Ministry of the Interior and laid it on the desk.

"Anyone could walk in here," he remarked earnestly. "We've never met before. How would you know it wasn't me?"

The woman regarded him fixedly.

"Are you feeling all right?" she asked guardedly.

Zen tapped the desk where his identification lay. The woman opened her black grained-leather bucket bag and passed over a laminated card with her photograph and an inscription to the effect that the holder was Simonelli, Antonia Natalia, investigating magistrate at the Procura of Milan. Zen nodded and handed it back.

"I'm sorry," he said. "I suppose I must have sounded a bit crazy."

The woman said nothing, but her expression did not contradict the idea.

"I've had a bit of a shock," Zen explained. "On the way here a man fell from the train. I had to help retrieve the body from the tunnel."

"That can't have been very pleasant," the magistrate murmured sympathetically.

"I had been talking to him just a few moments earlier."

"It was someone you knew, then?"

Zen nodded.

"Who?"

He looked at her.

"I thought it was you."

The woman's guarded manner intensified sharply.

"If that was intended as a joke . . ." she began.

"I don't think the people involved intended it as a joke."

She eyed him impatiently.

"You're speaking in riddles."

Zen nodded.

"Let me try and explain. On Wednesday I received a message at the Ministry asking me to call a certain Antonio Simonelli at a hotel in

Rome. When I did so, he identified himself as an investigating magistrate from Milan working on a case of fraud involving Ludovico Ruspanti, and asked me to meet him to discuss the circumstances of the latter's death."

The woman seemed about to say something, but after a moment she just waved her hand.

"Go on."

Zen sat silent a moment, considering how best to do so.

"At the time I thought he was trying to obtain information off the record that might help him prosecute the case against Ruspanti's associates. That risked placing me in a rather awkward position. When I was called in by the Vatican, they insisted I sign an undertaking not to disclose any information I came by as a result of my investigations. I therefore answered his questions as briefly as possible."

The woman opened a drawer of her desk and removed a slim file, which she opened.

"Go on," she repeated without looking up.

Zen pretended to look at the view for a moment. He decided to make no mention of the transcript of Ruspanti's phone calls. That was lost forever, scattered beyond any hope of retrieval by the gale that had sucked it away and strewn it the length of the eleven-mile tunnel. The only thing to do now was to pretend it had never existed.

"On the train up here this morning," he continued, "I was approached by the same man. He asked why I was traveling to Milan. I said I had an appointment with one of his colleagues at the Procura. He must have realized then that the game was up, I suppose. He went off toward the toilets, fused the lights, and threw himself out."

The woman looked steadily at Zen.

"Describe him."

"Burly, muscular. Big moon face, slightly dished. Strong nasal accent, from the Bergamo area, I should say. Smoked panatellas."

Antonia Simonelli selected a photograph from the file lying open on the desk and passed it to Zen. A paper sticker at the bottom read ZEPPEGNO, MARCO. Zen suppressed a gasp of surprise. There had been so many fakes and hoaxes in the case so far—including the fifty million lire, which had turned out to consist of a thin layer of real notes covering bundles of blank paper—that he had assumed the names appearing

in the transcript were also pseudonyms. But perhaps Ruspanti had deliberately raised the stakes by mentioning the real name of one of the
men he was threatening on a phone he knew to be tapped, making it
clear that he was ready to start playing dirty. That would certainly
explain why the individual concerned had been desperate to suppress
the transcript by any means, including the murder of Giovanni Grimaldi.

Zen handed the photograph back.

"You know about him, then?"

Antonia Simonelli nodded.

"I know *all* about him!"

"Including whether he is—was—a member of the Order of
Malta?"

She looked at him with surprise.

"What's that got to do with it?"

Zen said nothing. After a moment, the magistrate tapped the keyboard of the laptop computer.

"Since 1975," she said.

"It wasn't an aspect of his activities that concerned you?"

She gave a frown of what looked like genuine puzzlement.

"Only in that it was perfectly typical of him. Joining the Order is
something that businessmen like Zeppegno like to do at a certain point.
It provides social cachet and a range of useful contacts, and demonstrates
that your heart is in the right place and your bank account healthy. But
I repeat, why do you ask?"

Zen shrugged.

"He was wearing the badge on the train. I asked him if he was a
member, and he said he was. I just wondered if that was a lie too, like
everything else he had told me."

Antonia Simonelli wagged her finger at him.

"On the contrary, Dottore! Apart from the little matter of his
identity, everything he told you was true."

A smile unexpectedly appeared on the woman's face, softening her
features and providing a brief glimpse of the private person.

"Antonio Simonelli, indeed!" she exclaimed. "You have to hand it
to the old bastard. What nerve! Supposing we had been in touch before,
and you were aware of my gender?"

"He checked that by suggesting that we had. It was only when I said I didn't know him—you—that he asked to meet me."

She sighed.

"So he's dead?"

"Well, the identification still has to be confirmed, of course, but . . ."

"Who's handling the case?"

"Bologna. That took another half hour to work out. He jumped out right on the border between Tuscany and Emilia-Romagna. In the end we had to get a length of rope and measure the distance from the body to the nearest kilometer marker."

"But there's no question that it was suicide?"

Zen looked away. This was the question he had been asking himself ever since the torch beams picked out the corpse sprawled by the track side. The circumstances had conspired to prevent anything but the most cursory investigation at the scene. Short of closing the Apennine tunnel, and thus paralyzing rail travel throughout central Italy, the corpse could not be left in situ while the Carabinieri in Bologna dispatched their scene-of-crime experts. Fortunately there happened to be a doctor traveling on the train who was able to pronounce the victim dead. Zen then carried out a nominal inspection before authorizing the removal of the body. By the time the train reached Bologna, no one had the slightest interest in questioning that they were dealing with a case of suicide. The only remaining mystery was the victim's identity, since there were no papers or documents on the body.

Zen shook his head.

"The only person who was anywhere near him when he fell from the train was a woman who had gone to the toilet, and she wouldn't have had the strength. Anyway, she was a German tourist with no connection with the dead man. No, he must have done it himself. There's simply no other possibility."

Antonia Simonelli got up from her desk.

"I'm sure you're right, Dottore," she said. "It's just that I'd come to know Zeppegno quite well, and if you'd asked me, I'd have said he just wasn't someone who would ever commit suicide. He thought too highly of himself for that."

She waved at the file, the photographs, the computer.

"For the past five years I have been painstakingly building up a case against a cartel of Milanese businessmen. Zeppegno was typical. His family were provincial bourgeois with aspirations. His father ran an electrical business in a town near Bergamo. By a combination of graft and hard work, Marco gradually built up a chain of household appliance suppliers in small towns across Lombardy. As an individual unit, each of his outlets was modest enough, but taken together they represented a profitable slice of the market.

"Like other entrepreneurs, Zeppegno hated paying taxes and wanted to be able to invest his money freely. The answer was to cream off a percentage of his pretax profits and invest them abroad. The problem was how to do it. Big businesses have their own ways around the currency control laws, of course. You order a consignment of raw material from a foreign supplier who is prepared to play along. This is duly invoiced and paid for, but the goods in question are never shipped, and the money ends up in the off-shore bank account of your choice. There's an element of risk involved, but in a big outfit with a complex structure and a high volume of foreign trade the danger is minimal. The bogus orders can be hidden among a mass of legitimate transactions, and if all else fails *i finanzieri* have on occasion been known to look the other way."

Zen acknowledged the gibe with a blink. The venality of the Finance Ministry's enforcement officials was legendary.

"The turnover of a company like Zeppegno's was far too small to conceal that sort of scam successfully. Which is where the late Ludovico Ruspanti came in. It didn't hurt that he was an aristocrat, of course. Self-made provincials like Zeppegno tend to retain the prejudices of their class. A title like "prince" not only helped convince them that their money was safe in Ruspanti's hands, but reassured them that what they were doing was nothing much to be ashamed of, since a man like him was involved. The procedure itself couldn't have been simpler or more convenient. You simply wrote Ruspanti a check for whatever amount you wished to dispose of. If you preferred, of course, you could hand it over in cash. He deposited the money in his account at the Vatican bank, and it was then transferred—less his fee—to your foreign bank account.

"The fascinating thing about this arrangement is that while the ensemble constitutes a flagrant breach of the law, each of the individual operations is in itself perfectly legal. There is no law against one Italian citizen donating a large sum of money to another. If the recipient happens to be one of the privileged few who enjoy the right to an account at the Institute for the Works of Religion, it is perfectly in order for him to deposit the money there. And since that institution is extraterritorial, what subsequently happens to the money is of no concern to the Italian authorities."

She gave a bitter laugh.

"They talk about the rival claims of London and Frankfurt as the future financial capitals of Europe, but what about Rome? What other capital city can boast the convenience of an off-shore bank, completely unaccountable to the elected government, subject to no verifiable constraints or controls whatsoever, and located just a brief taxi ride from the center, with no customs controls or security checks to pass through? Ludovico Ruspanti could walk in there with a billion lire, and when he came out again that billion had effectively vanished! Poof!

"The only weak point in all this was Ruspanti himself. The cut he took counted as unearned income, and of course he couldn't declare it —even supposing he wanted to—without giving the game away. That was the lever I had hoped to use to squeeze Ruspanti for information on the whole operation, and I must say I was very hopeful of success. But without him, there is literally no case. I naturally couldn't help wondering whether this might not have occurred to some of the other interested parties. That's what I really want to know, Dottore. Forget Zeppegno for a moment. You investigated Ruspanti's death. Tell me, did he fall or was he pushed?"

Zen smiled.

"Funnily enough, those were exactly the words that Simonelli used when I spoke to him in Rome."

The magistrate stared at him coldly.

"*I* am Simonelli."

"Of course! Please excuse me! I meant Zeppegno, of course."

He tried to think clearly, but his experiences on the train and in the tunnel seemed to have left him incapable of anything other than reacting to immediate events. The only thing he was sure of was the single thread, flimsy but as yet unbroken, he still held in his hand. It might yet lead him to the heart of this affair, but it would not bear the weight of a judicial process. So, although he found himself warming to Antonia Simonelli, he was going to have to stall her for the moment.

"Ruspanti was murdered," he replied. "So was the minder the Vatican had assigned to him."

The magistrate stared at him fixedly.

"But you were quoted in the papers the other day as saying that the allegations of suspicious circumstances surrounding Ruspanti's death were mischievous and ill-informed."

"I wasn't consulted about the wording of that statement."

He had Simonelli hanging on his every word. The dirtier and more devious it got, the better she liked it. The case she thought was dead had miraculously sprung back to life before her eyes!

"The familiar tale," she said, nodding grimly.

Zen stood up and leaned across the desk toward her.

"Familiar, yes, but in this case also long and complex. I'm not sure this is the time to tackle it. As I said, I'm still in shock from what happened this morning, and you will naturally want to get in touch with the authorities in Bologna, and possibly even go there in person."

"Almost certainly."

"By tomorrow, I shall have recovered fully, and you will be fully informed about the death of Marco Zeppegno. I therefore suggest that we postpone further discussion of the matter until then."

She glanced at her watch.

"Very well," she said. "But please don't imagine that this is any more than a postponement, Dottore. I am determined to get to the bottom of this business, whatever the vested interests involved. I hope I shall have your full cooperation, but if I have any reason to suspect that it is not forthcoming, I shall have no hesitation in using my powers to compel you to testify."

Zen held up his hands in a protestation of innocence.

"There'll be no need for that. I've been put in an impossible position in this case, but basically I'm on the side of the angels."

Antonia Simonelli looked at him with a finely judged mixture of wariness and confidence.

"I'm not concerned with angels, Dottore. What I need is someone who's on the side of the law."

. . .

The house was not immediately recognizable as such. The address, in a back street just north of the Teatro alla Scala and west of the fashion alleys of Via Monte Napoleone and Via della Spiga, appeared at first to be nothing more than a slab of blind walling, slightly less high than the modern apartment buildings on either side. It was only as his taxi pulled away that Zen noticed the doors, windows, and balconies painted on the plaster, complete with painted shadows to give an illusion of depth. The facade of a severe late-eighteenth-century Austro-French *palazzo* had been re-created in considerable detail, and the fact that the third dimension was missing would doubtless have been less apparent by daylight than it was under the intense glare of the street lamps, diffused by the pall of fog that had descended on the city with the coming of dusk.

It took Zen some time to locate the real entrance, a plain wooden door inset in the huge trompe l'oeil gate framed by pillars at the center of the frontage. There was no nameplate, and the grille of the entry phone was disguised in the plumage of the hawk that rose in fake bas-relief above an illusory niche where the actual button figured as the nippled peak of a massive painted metal bellpull. Zen had barely touched the button when, without a challenge or a query, the door release buzzed to admit him. It was only when he stepped inside that he realized, from the shock he felt, what it was he had been expecting: some aggressively contemporary space defined by the complex interaction of concrete, steel, and glass. The punch line of the joke facade, he had tacitly assumed, must lie in its contrast with something as different as possible from historical gentility.

It was the smell that initially alerted him to his error. The viscous, musty odors that assailed him the moment he stepped over the threshold were quite incompatible with the processes of late twentieth-century life. Nor could they be reproduced or mocked up. Dense and mysterious, with overlapping strata of rot and mold and fume and smoke, they spoke of years of habitation, generations of neglect. He looked around the cavernous hallway, a huge, vaulted space feebly lit by a lamp dangling from a chain so thickly encased in dust and spiderwebs that it seemed to be this rather than the rusted metal that was supporting the yellowing bulb. He had a sudden urge to laugh. This was a much better joke than the predictable contrast he had imagined. It was a brilliant coup to have the fake and the real *correspond*. Evidently the house really was what it had been made to resemble, an aristocratic residence dating from the period when Milan was a city of the Austro-Hungarian Empire.

At one end of the hallway, an imposing stone staircase led upward into regions of murky obscurity. There was no sound, no one in sight. "You remember how to get here?" the voice on the phone had asked when he rang that afternoon from his hotel. The same girlish tones as before. For her part, though, she had remarked this time that he "sounded different, somehow." He had gotten the address from SIP, the telephone company, via the Ministry in Rome. They had also supplied the names of the other two subscribers whom Ruspanti had called in Milan. One, predictably enough, was his cousin, Raimondo Falcone. The other was Marco Zeppegno. The woman had told him to arrive at eight o'clock. Apparently Carmela was taking her sister to the opera that night and would have left by then.

The stairs led to a gallery running the length of the building on the first floor, which was conceived on a scale such as Zen had seen only in museums and government offices. Stripped of the trappings and booty it had been designed to show off, the gallery looked pointless and slightly macabre, like a drained swimming pool. Such furnishings as there were related neither to use nor comfort. There were no chairs, but a wealth of wooden chests. A fireplace the size of a normal room took up much of one wall, but there was no heating. Acres of bare plaster were relieved only by a series of portraits of men with almost identical beards, whiskers, cravats, and expressions of earnest insolence.

"You're not Ludo!"

He whirled around. The voice had come from the other side of the gallery, but there seemed to be no one there. Then he noticed what looked at first like a full-length oil portrait of the woman he had seen on the train, her light blue eyes turned toward him, her head surrounded by a nimbus of fine flaxen hair. He squinted at her. The air seemed thick and syrupy, as though the fog outside were seeping into the house, distorting distances and blurring detail.

"He couldn't come," Zen ventured.

"But he *promised!*"

He saw now that the supposed canvas was in fact a lighted doorway from which the woman was observing his advance, without any alarm but with an expression of intense disappointment, which she made no effort to disguise.

"I spoke to him just this afternoon, and he promised he would come!"

She was wearing a shapeless dress of heavy black material that accentuated the pallor of her skin. Her manner was unnervingly direct, and she held Zen's gaze without any apparent embarrassment.

"He *promised!*" she repeated.

"That's quite right. But he's not feeling very well."

"Is it his tummy?" the woman asked serenely.

Zen blinked.

"Yes. Yes, his tummy, yes. So he asked me to come instead."

She moved toward him, her candid blue gaze locked to his face.

"It was you," she said.

Had she recognized him from the train?

"Me?" he replied vaguely.

She nodded, certain now.

"It wasn't Ludo who rang. It was you."

He smiled sheepishly.

"Ludo couldn't come himself, so he sent me."

"And who are *you?*" she asked, like a princess in a fairy story addressing the odd little man who has materialized in her bedchamber.

Zen could smell her now. The odor was almost overpowering, a heady blend of bodily secretions that was far from unpleasant. Combined with the woman's full figure and air of childish candor, it produced an overall effect that was extremely erotic. Zen began to understand the prince's attraction to his cousin in Milan.

"Do you remember Ludo mentioning that he'd spoken to someone who worked for a magazine?" he said.

The woman's face creased into a scowl, as if recalling the events of the previous week was a mental feat equivalent to playing chess without a board. Then her frown suddenly cleared and she beamed a smile of pure joy.

"About my dolls!"

Zen smiled and nodded.

"Exactly."

"It was you? You want to write about them?" she exclaimed.

She bit her lower lip and wrung her thin hands in agitation.

"Will there be photographs? I'll need time to get them all looking their best. To tell you the truth, I thought Ludo was only joking."

She smiled a little wistfully.

"He has such a queer sense of humor sometimes."

Zen explained that although they would of course want to take photographs at some later stage, this was just an introductory visit to get acquainted. But Ariana Falcone didn't seem to be listening. She turned and led the way through the doorway as though lost in the intensity of her excitement.

"Just think! In the magazines!"

By contrast with the cold, formal, antiquated expanses of the gallery, the room beyond—although about the size of a soccer field—was reassuringly normal in appearance. The architectural imperatives of the great house had been attenuated by the skillful use of paint and light, and the furnishings were comfortable, bright, and contemporary. But to Zen's dismay, the place was filled with a crowd numbering perhaps fifty or sixty people, standing and sitting in complete silence, singly or in groups.

Their presence struck Zen with panic. Ariana might have accepted his story at face value, but it was unlikely to bear scrutiny by this sophisticated host. Never had Zen been so conscious of himself as the dowdy government functionary, encased in his anonymous suit as though in armor, as when he ran the gauntlet of that fashionable throng, each flaunting an outfit so stylish and exotic that you hardly noticed the person wearing it. And in fact it was not until Ariana swung around with a grand gesture and announced, "Well, here they are!", that Zen realized they were all mannequins.

"Some of them are upstairs, being fitted," she went on. "Raimondo gave me a copy of *Women's Wear Daily* recently. I got lots of ideas from that. Which magazine do you work for, by the way?"

"Er . . . *Gente.*"

"Never heard of it."

You must be the only person in Italy who hasn't, thought Zen. She didn't know what had happened to Ludovico Ruspanti, either. Was there a connection?

"It's about famous people," he explained. "Stars."

"All Raimondo brings me are fashion magazines. And I can't go out, of course, because of my illness. Anyway, what do you think?"

She pointed around the room, watching anxiously for Zen's reaction.

"It's magnificent," he replied simply.

He meant it! Whatever the implications of this peculiar ensemble, the scale of the conception and the quality of the execution were quite astonishing. Each of the "dolls"—a full-size figure of articulated wood—was fitted out with a costume like nothing Zen had ever seen. Sometimes the fabrics and colors were boldly contrasted, sometimes artfully complementary. The construction often involved a witty miracle in which heavy velvets apparently depended on gossamer-fine voile, or tweed braces supported a skirt that might have been made of beaten egg whites. Even to someone as deeply ignorant of fashion as Zen, it was clear that these garments were very special indeed.

"Raimondo is your brother?" he asked.

Ariana's face, which had been beaming with pleasure at his compliment, crumpled up. She nodded mutely.

"And what does he do?" Zen enquired.

"Do? He doesn't do anything. Neither of us *do* anything."

Zen laughed lightly and pointed to the dolls.

"What about all this?"

She made a moue.

"Oh, that's play, not work."

He walked about through the throng of figures inclined in a variety of lifelike poses. One costume in particular caught his eye, a clinging cardigan of stretch panne velvet textured to resemble suede and dyed in clashing patches of brilliant primary colors. He had seen it before, and not on a mannequin.

"Do you really make them all yourself?" he asked.

"Of course! I used to have little dolls, but that was too fiddly, so Raimondo got me these."

She pointed to a male figure on Zen's right.

"I made that outfit last year. It's based on something I saw in a men's fashion magazine Raimondo left lying around, a leather blouson and jeans. I thought that was a bit boring, so I let those panels into the suede to reveal a false lining made of blue-shot silk, which looks like bleached denim. The slacks are in brushed silk, mimicking the suede."

Zen looked at it admiringly.

"It's wonderful."

Her pixie face collapsed into a scowl.

"He doesn't think so."

"Your brother?"

She nodded.

"I'm surprised he agreed to let you come, actually. I think he's a bit ashamed of my dolls. When I told him what Ludo had said about the magazine when he phoned last week, Raimondo got terribly angry."

Zen gazed at the stretch panne velvet cardigan, his mind racing. Was it possible?

"And where is he now?" he asked.

"Raimondo? Oh, he's away in Africa, hunting lions."

Zen nodded sagely.

"That must be dangerous."

"That's just what *I* said when he told me. And do you know what he replied? 'Only for the lion!' "

He looked at her, and then at the mannequins. The contrast between their astonishing garments and the woman's shapeless black apparel, imbued with the heady reek of the living body within, could not have been more marked.

"Do you ever wear any of the clothes yourself?" Zen asked.

She frowned, as though he'd said something that made no sense.

"They're *dolls'* clothes!"

"They look quite real to me."

She shrugged jerkily.

"It's just something to keep me amused while I'm ill. When I get better again, and Mummy and Daddy come back, we'll put them all away."

He gestured around the room.

"What a huge house!"

She looked at him blankly.

"Is it?"

He was about to say something else when she went on, "Daddy

used to say it was like a doll's house, with the windows and doors painted on the front."

"Why is it like that?"

She made an effort to remember.

"It happened in the war," she said at last. "A bomb."

"Ah. And do you and Raimondo live here all alone?"

"No, he's got a place of his own somewhere. He doesn't want to catch my illness, you see."

Zen nodded as though this made perfect sense.

"Is it infectious, then?"

"So he says. He told me that if he stayed here any longer he'd end up as crazy as I am. That's why Mummy and Daddy left, too. I drive people away. I can't help it. It's my illness . . ."

Her voice trailed away.

"What is it?" asked Zen.

She stood listening, her head tilted to one side. He peered at her.

"Is something? . . ."

"Ssshhh!"

She started trembling all over.

"Someone's coming!"

Zen strained his ears, but couldn't detect the slightest sound.

"It must be Carmela! I don't know what's happened! The opera can't be over yet."

She clapped her hands together in sheer panic.

"Oh, what are we going to do? What are we going to do?"

Zen stood looking around uncertainly. Suddenly Ariana looked at him intently, sizing him up.

"Take off your coat and jacket!" she hissed.

She darted to the mannequin nearby, removed the blouson he was wearing and tossed it to Zen. Then she bundled up his overcoat and jacket and stuffed them hurriedly under a chair. Feeling absolutely ridiculous, Zen struggled into the blouson. Ariana snatched a sort of fisherman's cap off another dummy and put it on him.

"Now stand there and *don't move!*"

There was a sound of footsteps.

"Ariana? Ah, there you are!"

Zen recognized the voice at once. Indeed, it seemed as if he'd been hearing nothing else for the past week. The speaker was out of sight from the position in which Zen was frozen, but he could clearly hear the tremor in Ariana's voice.

"Raimondo!"

"Who were you expecting?"

"Expecting? No one! No one ever comes here."

You're overdoing it, thought Zen. But the man's brusque tone revealed no trace of suspicion.

"Can you blame them?"

The woman moved away from Zen.

"I thought you were in Africa," she said. "Hunting lions."

He laughed shortly.

"I killed them all."

Zen's posture already felt painfully cramped and rigid. To distract himself, he stared at the costume of the mannequin opposite him, an extraordinary collage of fur, leather, velvet, and silk apparently torn into ribbons and then reassembled in layers to form a waterfall of jagged, clashing fabrics.

"Did you see Ludo?" the woman demanded suddenly.

The eagerness in her voice was unmistakable.

"Cousin Ludovico?" the man drawled negligently. "Yes, I saw him."

"When? Where? How is he? When is he coming back?"

"Oh, not for some time, I'm afraid. Not for a long, long time."

His voice was deliberately hard and hurtful.

"Did a lion hurt him?"

She sounded utterly desolate. The man laughed.

"What nonsense you talk! It wasn't a lion, it was *you*. He can't stand being around you, Ariana. It's your own fault! You drive everyone away with your mad babbling. Everyone except your dolls. They're the only ones who can put up with you any longer."

There was a sound of crying.

"I hope you've kept yourself busy while I've been away," the man continued.

"Yes."

"Then stop blubbering and show me. Where are they? Upstairs in the workroom?"

"Yes."

"Come on then."

Suddenly the man was there, close enough for Zen to touch. The woman followed, her head lowered, sobbing. She gave no sign of being aware of Zen's presence.

"I'll have to keep an eye on you, Ariana," the man remarked coldly. "It looks to me as if you might be going to have one of your bad patches again."

"That's not true! I've felt ever so well for ages now."

"Rubbish! You have no idea whether you're well or not, Ariana. You never did and you never will."

They went out of a door at the far side of the room, closing it behind them. Zen hastily removed the blouson and cap, retrieved his coat and jacket, and put them on again. The gallery was as cold and silent as a crypt. Zen tiptoed across it and pattered downstairs to the hallway, where he opened the wooden door set in the painted gate and let himself out. The fog was thicker and denser by now, an intangible barrier that emerged vampirelike every night, draining substance and solidity from the surroundings to feed its own illusory reality. Zen vanished into it like a figment of the city's imagination.

SEVEN

*Z*en's hotel was next to the station, a thirty-story tower topped with an impressive array of aerials and satellite dishes. The next morning, shaved and showered, his body pleasantly massaged by the whirlpool bath, clad in a gown of heavy white toweling with the name of the hotel embroidered in red, he sat looking out of the window at the streets far below, where the Milanese were industriously going about their business beneath a sky of flawless gray.

Opposite Zen's window, a gang of workers were welding and bolting steel beams into place to form the framework of what, according to the sign on the scaffolding around the site, was to be another hotel. Judging by the violence of their gestures, there must have been a good deal of noise involved, but within the double layer of toughened glass the only sounds were the hiss of the air conditioning, the murmur of a newscaster on the American cable network to which the television was tuned, and a ringing tone in the receiver of the telephone Zen was holding to his ear.

"Peace be with you, Signora," he said solemnly, as the phone was answered with an incomprehensible yelp.

"And with you."

"This is the friend of Signor Nieddu. I would fain speak with Mago."

"Hold on."

The receiver was banged hollowly against something. Zen turned to the television. He picked up the remote control and shuffled randomly through a variety of game shows, old films, panel discussions, direct selling pitches, and all-day sportscasts. Spotting a familiar face in the welter of images, he vectored up the sound.

". . . whatsoever. Would you agree with that?"

"I agree with no one but myself."

"What's your position on the hemline debate?"

"It's an irrelevance. My clothes are based on the simple complexities at the heart of all natural processes. Nature doesn't ask whether hemlines are long or short this season. I seek to echo in fabric the regular irregularity of windblown sand, the orderly chaos of breaking waves . . ."

Zen pressed the "mute" button as the receiver was picked up again.

"Mago is graciously pleased to grant your request. Lo, hearken unto the words of Mago."

There was a click as the extension was picked up.

"Hello?" said a boyish voice.

"Nicolo, this is Aurelio, the friend of Gilberto. Have you had any luck with the little puzzle I set you?"

"Just a moment."

Zen closed his eyes and saw again the casbahlike shack amid the sprawling suburbs of Rome's Third World archipelago and the fetid stall at its heart, dark but for the glowing screen from which the bedridden boy with the etiolated grace of an angel played fast and loose with the secrets of the material world.

"It's dated Wednesday, the day before you came to see me," said Nicolo, picking up the receiver again. "The text reads as follows. 'Anonymous sources in the Vatican allegedly assert that there is a secret group within the Order of Malta, called the Cabal. The existence of this group was allegedly revealed to the Curia by Ludovico Ruspanti in exchange for asylum in the weeks preceding his death. Reported verbally to RL by Zen, Aurelio.' "

There was a long silence. Then Zen began to laugh, slowly and quietly, a series of rhythmic whoops that might almost have been sobbing. So this was the information he had supposed so sensitive that Carlo Romizi had been killed to preserve its confidentiality! The Ministry had no "parallel" file on the Cabal. All they knew about it was what they had been told by Zen, who knew only what he had been told by the Vatican, who knew only what they had been told by Ludovico Ruspanti, who had made it up.

"I did a series of searches for the classified file on this Aurelio Zen," Nicolo continued, "but I didn't come up with anything."

"You mean it's inaccessible?"

"No, it doesn't exist. There's an *open* file, in the main body of the database. I made a copy of that. You can have it if you're interested, although frankly it sounds like he's had a pretty boring life . . ."

Zen spluttered into the mouthpiece.

"Thank you for your help, Nicolo."

"It's all been a bit of a waste of time, I'm afraid."

"Not at all. On the contrary. Everything's clear now."

He put the phone down with an obscure sense of depression. Everything was clear, and hateful. Perhaps that was why everything normally remained obscure, because people secretly preferred it that way. It was certainly a very mixed pleasure to discover that he was considered so unimportant that the powers that be hadn't even bothered to keep tabs on him. Any relief he felt was overwhelmed by shame, anger, and hurt. Was he worth no more than that? Evidently not. Well, it served him right for wanting to read his own obituary. He had just done so: *a pretty boring life.*

On the table lay a message that had been brought up with his breakfast, telling him that Antonia Simonelli expected to see him in her office at eleven o'clock that morning. Zen looked at it, and then at the television, where "the philosopher in the wardrobe" was still holding forth. He identified the name of the station—a private channel, based in the city—and got the number from directory inquiries. It was answered by a young woman who sounded quite overwhelmed by the excitement of working in television.

"Yes!"

"This talk show you've got on now, is it going out live?"

"Live! Live!"

"I need to speak to your guest."

"Our guest!"

"Tell him to leave a number where I can contact him later this morning."

"Later! Later!"

"Tell him it's urgent. A matter of life and death."

"Life! Death!"

"Yes. The name is Marco Zeppegno."

Before getting dressed, Zen made one more call, this time to Rome. Gilberto Nieddu was initially extremely unenthusiastic about doing what Zen wanted, particularly on a Saturday, but Zen said he'd pay for everything, even a courier to the airport.

After leaving the hotel, Zen strolled down the broad boulevard leading from the fantastic mausoleum of the Central Station to the traffic-ridden expanses of Piazza della Repubblica. This was in fact one of the least propitious parts of the city for a pleasant walk. Because of its proximity to the railway yards, Allied bombers had given it their full attention during the closing stages of the war, and the subsequent reconstruction had taken place at a time when Italian architecture was still heavily influenced by the brutal triumphalism of the Fascist era. Zen wasn't concerned about his surroundings, however. He just needed to kill a little time.

He idled along, staring in the shop windows, studying the passersby, lingering in front of an establishment that sold or rented Carnival costumes. Eventually he reached Piazza della Repubblica, whose oval and rectangular panels of greenery still showed signs of the damage they had incurred during the building of the new "C" underground line. At a discreet distance from the piazza, beyond a buffer zone of meticulously trimmed and tended lawns, stood one of the city's oldest and most luxurious hotels. As Zen turned back, his attention was attracted by a young couple walking down the strip of carpet beneath the long green awning toward the waiting line of taxis. The woman looked radiant in a cream two-piece suit that effortlessly combined eroticism and efficiency, while the man, his cherubic face set off by a mass of curls, was a lively and attentive escort. Zen stopped, quite shamelessly gawking. The woman looked mysteriously familiar, like a half-forgotten memory. So bewitching was the vision that it was only at the very last moment, as the taxi swept past, bearing the woman and her young admirer from the scene of past pleasures to that of future delights, that Zen recognized her as Tania Biacis.

He promptly sprinted up the drive toward the next taxi in line, which was coming alongside the awning to pick up a pair of Japanese men who had just emerged from the hotel. Ignoring the shouts of the doorman, an imposing figure clad in something resembling the dress uniform of a Latin American general, Zen opened the passenger door and got in.

"Follow that taxi!" he cried.

The driver turned to him with a weary expression.

"You've been watching too many movies, *dottò.*"

"This rank is for the use of our guests only!" thundered the doorman, opening the door again.

The two Japanese looked on with an air of polite bewilderment. It was too late now anyway. The other vehicle was already lost among the yellow cabs swarming in every direction across the piazza. Zen got out of the taxi and walked slowly back down the drive, shaking his head. At the corner of the block opposite, beneath the high portico, a red neon sign advertised the Bar Capri. Whether intentionally or not, the interior, a bare concrete shell, vividly evoked the horrors of the speculative building that had virtually extinguished the magic of that fabled isle. Zen went to the pay phone and dialed the number that had been left for him at the television studio. There was no ringing tone, but almost at once the acoustic background changed to a loud hum and a familiar voice barked, "Yes?"

Until that moment, Zen had had no clear idea of what he was going to say, but the encounter outside the hotel seemed to have made up his mind for him. The sight of Tania and her young admirer had inspired him with a fierce determination to win her back at any cost. And cost—money—was the key. If Primo could afford to take her to a hotel like that, he must be *loaded!* He had probably paid for her flight, too. Of course, Primo had personal attractions as well, but then so had Zen. What he didn't have was cash, and that was going to change. He had been a sucker for long enough, beavering away at a meaningless job without either thanks or reward. It was success people respected, not diligence or rectitude. Gilberto patronized him, his colleagues patronized him, and now it turned out that Tania was having a fling with some married man with enough money to offer her a good time. And quite right, too, he thought. He didn't blame her. What was the point in playing safe when you could end up like Carlo Romizi at any moment? Would it be any consolation, in that final instant of consciousness, to reflect on how *correctly* one had behaved?

"Good morning, Dottore," he said, putting on the singsong accent of an Istrian schoolmaster whom he and his schoolfriends had once delighted in imitating. "I saw you on television this morning. A very fine performance, if I may say so."

"Who is this?"

"The name I gave earlier was Marco Zeppegno, but as you know, Dottore, Marco's phone has been disconnected."

In the background there was the constant hum of what sounded like a car's engine.

"I wonder why," Zen continued. "Didn't he pay his bills? Or had he started to make nuisance calls, like Ludovico Ruspanti?"

"Who are you? What do you want?"

Zen chuckled.

"Bearing in mind recent experiences, I'm sure you'll understand if I decline to answer just now. Tapping a phone in the Vatican is a matter for professionals like Grimaldi, but any radio ham can listen in to a mobile phone."

The connection went dead. For a moment Zen thought the man had hung up, but he came back at once, calling "Hello? Hello?"

"It was only interference," Zen assured him. "Don't worry, you won't get rid of me that easily!"

"What is it you want?"

"I'll tell you when we meet this afternoon."

"Impossible! I have a . . ."

Once again the connection was broken for several moments.

". . . until six-thirty or seven. I could see you then."

"Very well."

"Come to my office," the man said after a long pause. "It's just off Piazza del Duomo. The main entrance is closed at that time, but you can come in the emergency exit at the back. The place was burgled last week and the lock hasn't been repaired yet. It's in Via Foscolo, next to the chemist's, the green door without a number. My offices are on the top floor."

In Piazza della Repubblica, Zen boarded a two-coach orange tram marked "Porta Vittoria." A notice above the large wooden-framed windows set out in considerable detail the conditions governing the transport of live fish and fowl. Goldfish and chicks, Zen learned, would be conveyed (up to a maximum of two per passenger) providing the containers, which might under no circumstances be larger than a "normal parcel or shoe box," were neither rough nor splintery, dirty nor foul-smelling, nor yet of such a form as to cause injury to other passengers. The remainder of the text, which laid down the penalties for flauting these regulations, was too small to read with the naked eye, but the implication was that any anarchistic hothead who took it upon himself to carry goldfish or chicks on trams without due regard for the provisions heretofore mentioned would be prosecuted with the full rigor of the law.

Zen recalled the bewilderment of the Japanese businessmen as he barged in like a truculent drunk and attempted to commandeer their taxi. "Is it always like this?" they were clearly asking themselves. "Is this the rule, or just an exception?" If they really wanted to understand Italy, they could do worse than give up taxis, take to public transport, and ponder the mysteries of a system that legislated for circumstances verging on the surreal while yet unable to ensure that the majority of its users even bought a ticket.

He got off at the stop opposite the Palazzo di Giustizia and ran the gauntlet of the traffic speeding across the herringbone pattern of smooth stone slabs. As he reached the safety of the curb, a taxi drew up and Antonia Simonelli got out. She looked severe and tense.

"It was Zeppegno all right," she nodded. "There doesn't seem any question that it was suicide."

There was a squeal of tires and someone called his name. Turning around, he found himself face to face with Tania Biacis. Another taxi had pulled up behind the first. The young man who had left the hotel with Tania sat watching from the rear seat of the taxi with an expression of alarm.

"Okay, Aurelio," shouted Tania, thrusting a finger aggressively toward Antonia Simonelli. "I've asked you before and I ask you again. Who is she?"

Arm in arm, visibly reconciled, Tania and Zen walked across the pedestrianized expanses of Piazza del Duomo. At the far end, the upper stories of several buildings were completely hidden behind a huge billboard displaying three faces represented on the gargantuan scale Zen associated with the images of Marx, Lenin, and Stalin that had once looked down on May Day parades in Moscow's Red Square. But like Catholicism, its old rival, communism was no longer a serious contender in the ideological battle for hearts and minds. The icon dominating Milan's Cathedral Square was that of the United Colors of Benetton, the vast, unsmiling features of a Nordic woman, a black woman, and an Asian baby. These avatars of the new order, representatives of a world united by the ascendant creed of consumerism, gazed down on the masses whose aspirations they embodied with a look that was at once intense and vapid.

"They're suing the hospital," said Tania.

"Good for them."

"This is all between us, but apparently Romizi's wife was having an affair with Bernardo Travaglini."

"You're joking!"

"Once she'd got over the shock of Carlo's death, she got in touch with Bernardo and told him her suspicions about what had happened. He and De Angelis went to the hospital with a couple of uniformed men and put the fear of God into the director."

Zen could easily picture the scene, the two plainclothes officials wandering menacingly about the director's office, their words a mixture of bureaucratic minutiae and paranoia-inducing innuendo, while their uniformed cohorts guarded the door. Yes, Giorgio and Bernardo would have had the director eating out of their hands in no time at all. The irony was that Zen might have done something of the sort himself if he hadn't been so convinced that Carlo had been the victim of the Cabal. But it now appeared that Romizi's death had been caused by a different sort of plot.

"Under pressure from Travaglini and De Angelis, the director came up with the name of the intern who visited Romizi that night,"

Tania continued. "When they called on him, the intern claimed he had been acting on orders. He'd never been trained to use life-support equipment, and had no idea what the effect would be. He was told to reset such-and-such a knob to such-and-such a setting, and that's what he did."

"They needed the bed?"

Tania shrugged.

"That's what it looks like. The hospital is denying the whole thing, of course. Signora Romizi's suing the hospital. The intern and the doctor in charge have been suspended, and the Procura has opened a file on the affair."

They crossed the square and entered the glazed main aisle of the Galleria Vittorio Emanuele. The elegant mall was almost empty, the offices on the upper floors and the exclusive shops at ground level both shut. Tania lingered for some time in front of a window displaying the latest creations from the teeming imagination of the legendary Falco. With a shove half-playful, half-serious, Zen propelled her toward the one establishment still open for business, the Cafè Biffi. They sat outside, under the awning whose function here was purely decorative, in an area cordoned off from the aisle by a row of potted plants on stands. Tania opted for a breaded veal cutlet and salad. Zen said he'd have the same.

"But if you specialize in products from the Friuli," Zen asked, picking up their earlier conversation, "what are you doing here?"

"We want to diversify, keeping the original concept of tradition-ally made items from small producers whom a big export company won't handle because they can't deliver in quantity. Primo is based here in Milan, so . . ."

"Don't tell me he's a farmer!"

"God, you don't let up, do you?"

Her look wavered on the brink of real challenge. Don't push me too hard, it said. Zen grinned in a way he knew she found irresistible.

"You know what the police are like."

"Yes," she said. "They're bastards."

Their food arrived, and for a while everything else was forgotten. It was almost two o'clock by now, and they were starving. Once the embarrassment and confusion of the initial confrontation in front of the law courts had been cleared up, there had been no time to do anything but arrange to meet later. Then Zen had accompanied Antonia Simonelli to her office, where he provided her with a detailed and largely accurate account of the circumstances in which Ludovico Ruspanti had died, while Tania had gone off to "talk business" with Primo.

Now they were together again, other commitments suspended for an hour. But although both seemed eager to dispel the suspicions that had arisen as a result of past evasions, the explanations and revelations came unevenly, in fits and starts, a narrative line deflected by questions and digressions, forging ahead toward the truth but leaving pockets of ambiguity and equivocation to be mopped up afterward. Among these was the one Zen had just tackled, and to which he returned once they had satisfied their immediate hunger.

"So, about Primo . . ."

Tania wiped her lips with a napkin that looked as though it had been carved from marble.

"Primo is an agent representing a network of small producers stretching from Naples to Catanzaro."

Zen nodded slowly.

"Oh, you mean he works for the mob! No wonder he can afford to stay at that fancy hotel. They probably own it."

Tania twitched the hem of her cream skirt.

"Aurelio, I'm going to get really angry in a moment. Quite apart from anything else, it so happens that *I'm* the one who's staying there."

Zen raised his eyebrows, genuinely disconcerted.

"Well, well."

"It's my little indulgence."

"Not *that* little. You must be doing well."

She nodded.

"We are. Very well. But I'm increasingly realizing that the future is in the south. Up here, agriculture is getting more and more commercialized, more industrialized and centralized. You're no longer dealing with individual producers but with large agribusinesses or cooperatives whose managers think in terms of consistency and volume. The south has been spared all that. It's just too poor, too fragmented, too disorganized, too far from the center of Europe. Those factors are all drawbacks for bulk produce, but once you're talking designer food the negatives become positives . . ."

She broke off, catching sight of his abstracted look.

"I'm boring you."

He quickly feigned vivacity.

"No, no."

"It's all right, Aurelio. There's no reason why you should be interested in the wholesale food business."

He pushed the last piece of veal cutlet around his plate for a moment, then laid down his knife and fork.

"It's just a shock to find that you're so . . . so successful and high-powered. It makes me feel a bit dowdy by comparison."

If his words sounded slightly self-pitying, the look he gave her immediately afterward was full of determination.

"But that's going to change."

"Of course. You'll soon get used to it."

"I don't mean that."

"Then what do you mean?"

"You'll see."

A pair of Carabinieri officers in full dress uniform strode by, murmuring to each other in a discreet undertone. With their tricorn hats and black capes trimmed with red piping, they might have passed for clergy promenading down the apse of this secular basilica, oriented not eastward, like the crumbling Gothic pile in the square outside, but toward the north, source of industry, finance, and progress.

"So he works for you?" asked Zen, lighting a cigarette.

Tania pushed her plate aside.

"Primo? No, no, we don't pay salaries. Piece rates and low overheads, that's the secret of success. Look at Benetton. That's how they started out. Run by a woman, too."

She took one of her own cigarettes, a low-tar menthol brand. Zen had tried one once. It was like smoking paper tissues smeared with toothpaste.

"No, Primo works for the EEC," she said. "He goes around to farms assessing their claims for grants. We pay him on a commission basis to put us in touch with possible suppliers."

He nodded vaguely. She was right, of course. He wasn't interested in the details of the business she was running. He *was* interested in the results, though. Tania had rejected the idea of moving in with Zen on the grounds that his flat was too small. But if he could bring off the little coup he had planned for that evening, he would have the cash for a down payment on something much larger, perhaps with a separate flat for his mother across the landing. And as a two-income couple, they could pay off the mortgage with no difficulty.

He looked around the Galleria, smoking contentedly and running over the idea in his mind. This was a new venture for him. He had cut corners before, of course. He had bent the rules, turned a blind eye, and connived at various mild degrees of fraud and felony. But never before had he cold-bloodedly contemplated extorting a large sum of money for his personal gain. Still, better late than never. Who the hell did he think he was, anyway, Mother Theresa? Not that there was any great moral issue involved. Antonia Simonelli might succeed in embarrassing the Vatican, but she had no real chance of making a case against those responsible for killing Ludovico Ruspanti. One of them, Marco Zeppegno, was already dead, and with his death the other man had put himself beyond the reach of justice. But not beyond the reach of the Cabal, thought Zen.

He leaned back, looking up at the magnificent glass cupola, a masterpiece of nineteenth-century engineering consisting of thousands of rectangular panes supported by a framework of wrought-iron ribs soaring up a hundred and fifty feet above the junction of the two arcaded aisles. The resemblance to a church was clearly deliberate: the four aisles arranged like an apse, choir, and transepts, the upper walls decorated with frescoed lunettes, the richly inlaid marble flooring, the vaulted ceilings, the central cupola. Here is *our* temple, said the prophets of the Risorgimento, a place of light and air, dedicated to commerce, liberty, and civic pride. Compare it with that oppressive, dilapidated pile outside, reeking of ignorance and superstition, and then make your choice.

"What are you going to do now?" asked Tania.

He gave a deep frown, which cleared as he realized she meant the question literally.

"I've got to go to the airport."

"You're not leaving already?"

"No, no. I have to pick up something that's being air-freighted up here. Something I need for my work."

"What are you doing here, anyway?"

He shrugged.

"Just following up some loose ends in the Ruspanti affair. Nothing very interesting."

She signaled the waiter and asked for two coffees and the bill. Zen raised his eyebrows slightly.

"I'll put it on expenses," she said.

"Fiddling already?"

"Actually I'm saving money. If I hadn't bumped into you, I'd be lunching Primo instead, the full five courses somewhere they really know how to charge."

"Whereas I get a snack in a café, eh?" he retorted in a mock-surly tone.

Tania smiled broadly and stroked his hand.

"I'll make it up to you tonight, sweetheart."

His face clouded over.

"Is there a problem?" she asked.

"Well, I may not be free until nineish."

She patted his hand reassuringly.

"That's all right. I'll just have to go and buy some very expensive clothes to while away the time. There's a wonderful new outfit by Falco I just *crave*. Jagged strips of suede and silk and fur arranged in layers like a pile of scraps, just odds and ends, but somehow holding together, though you can't see how. Did you see it in that shop, toward the back?"

He smiled mysteriously.

"I've seen it, but not in a shop."

She looked at him with interest.

"You've seen someone wearing it?"

"Not exactly."

The waiter arrived with their coffee, and Zen took advantage of the interruption to change tack slightly.

"Are his clothes very expensive?"

"Hideously!" she cried. "But each one is an original creation. It's an investment as well as a luxury, like buying a work of art."

Zen's mysterious smile intensified.

"All the same, if I were you I'd put my money into something else. I have a feeling that the market in Falco creations is about to take a tumble."

Tania patted his hand indulgently.

"Aurelio, you're a dear, sweet man, but you haven't a clue about fashion."

The man stepped off the exercise bicycle and surveyed himself in the mirror. His lithe, slender body was covered with a pleasing sheen of sweat, creating highlights and chiaroscuro and emphasizing the contours of his evenly tanned flesh, hardened and sculpted by workouts such as the one he had just completed. So satisfied was he by what the mirror showed him that he lingered a moment longer under the spell of that unattainable object of desire.

His private life, he knew, was a topic of much gossip. If he himself encouraged the wildest and most colorful rumors, it was simply to deflect attention from a truth that—as so often in this imperfect world —paled by comparison. In fact his sexual activities amounted to no more than brisk sessions of manual relief whenever that part of his anatomy started to draw attention to itself. It was true that the images that came to his mind at these moments were male rather than female, but this did not indicate a preference for his own sex, which would have been perfectly normal in the world in which he now moved. The writhing male body, tormented by desire, that he visualized at such moments was not one of the various acquaintances who had cruised him more or less openly, nor yet some ideal partner he hoped to meet one day. It was quite simply his own.

"Without my clothes, I feel naked," he had once remarked to an interviewer, who had laughed uproariously at this witticism. It was in fact the literal truth. Even his own nudity was only tolerable when reflected back to him from the mirror. The idea of other people's bodies was quite repugnant to him. His secret fantasy was to *become* that glistening image, to break through the glass and merge with that substanceless child of light, for whom being and seeming were one and the same. As for the others, as imperfect as himself, and a good deal less fastidious in most cases, he did not particularly care to share a room with most of them, never mind anything more intimate. With a final, flirtatious glance at the mirror, he turned away and flounced off to the bathroom.

Ten minutes later, dressed in jeans and a leather jacket, he walked through to the adjoining suite of offices. The clock on the wall showed twenty to seven. The suite was located on the top floor of a block backing onto the Galleria Vittorio Emanuele, and commanded a striking view of the great glazed cupola, swelling up into the night sky like a luminous balloon. He had switched off all the lights, and this background glimmer, softened by the thickening fog, was the only source of illumination. Feeling a prickle of sweat break out on his stomach and back, he opened the window slightly. Coolness was the key to everything. The secret of his success lay in the ability to remain perfectly calm whatever happened, to manipulate events and perceptions so that people saw only what he wished them to see.

He picked up a canvas bag lying on the desk and went into the workroom next door. The walls were covered with sketches and photographs, the floor littered with irregular off-cuts of the fine paper used for sizing garments. Only a tiny fraction of the light from the Galleria penetrated to this internal room, but he moved through it with total confidence, skirting pin-studded mannequins and sidestepping the benches draped with silk and velvet, cashmere and wool, leather and tweed. As he passed each one, he let his fingers run over the material, and shivered sensuously.

The one way in which he revealed himself to be his father's son was in his passion for materials, the way they looked, the way they felt, the way they smelled. His mother had later revealed that Umberto used to bring samples home from the mills at Como and stroke the boy's infant cheeks with them. The idea was to train Raimondo from the earliest possible age for his future role as heir to the family textile business. But the child had misunderstood, as children are so prone to do. He thought his father was caressing him, expressing a love that rarely manifested itself on other occasions.

At the door leading to the hallway, he paused briefly and listened.

All was quiet. He unlocked the door, went out, and closed it behind him, pulling until the lock engaged with a precise click. He removed a pair of disposable rubber gloves from the bag and put them on, then took out the cold chisel and hammer. Working the chisel into the crack between the lock and the jamb, he struck it repeatedly until the lock shattered. Then he replaced the chisel and hammer in the bag, peeled off the rubber gloves with a shudder of disgust—they reminded him of condoms—and went back inside, leaving the door slightly ajar.

As he passed one of the worktables, his fingers touched a garment he could not for a moment identify. He paused to stroke it delicately, caressing the surface of the fabric like a lover exploring the contours of his partner's body. A languid smile of recognition softened the normally rigid contours of his lips. Of course! It was the model for the new line of jeans he was going to unleash on the world next year, a move calculated to reaffirm the atelier's revolutionary reputation. Not that demand for the existing lines had in any way slackened. On the contrary, business was booming. But he knew that the time to abandon a successful formula was before it began to pall. That way, you retained the initiative. You weren't running for cover, you were "making a statement."

In the present instance, this meant abandoning the complex, multilayered pyrotechnics for which he'd become famous in favor of something plain and popular, something strong and simple, something *ecological*. Jeans were all these things, of course, but their appeal was fatally diminished by the fact that they were also durable and cheap. The response of the leading designers had been to price them up, to sell the price rather than the garment.

Such a solution was worthy of the shallow, conventional minds who ran the major fashion houses. Anyone could license a line of designer denims and sell them at a 500 percent markup—at least, anyone with a name like Armani or Valentino could. It had been left to him, the newcomer, to achieve a truly creative breakthrough. His fingertips caressed the soft brushed silk he'd had dyed to resemble worn and faded denim. Naturally no one in his right mind would be prepared to pay Falco prices for real denim, which would last for years. These, on the other hand, although virtually indistinguishable from the real thing to the naked eye, would tolerate only the most limited wear before falling apart. People were going to *kill* for them.

Back in his private sanctum, he sat down at his desk and held his watch up to the glimmer from the window. Five to seven. He opened the middle drawer of the desk and took out the pistol he had brought from home. The gun had belonged to his father, a service-issue revolver that he had retained illegally as a souvenir at the end of the war. As far as he knew, Umberto had never used the weapon in anger, not that it would have done him much good against the Red Brigades' Kalashnikovs. But that would just make the authorities more sympathetic when his son acted a trifle hastily in a similar situation. Not that anyone was likely to think twice about the matter anyway. Break-ins and muggings were everyday events in the junkie-ridden center of Milan. What was more natural than for him to keep his father's old service pistol at the office, where he often worked late and alone? Or indeed for him to use it when the need arose?

"I was walking toward my desk, Officer, when I heard a sound in the outer office. I'd just had a shower. I suppose that's why I hadn't heard the noise of the door being forced. I ran to the desk and got out the pistol I've kept there since the building was broken into last week . . ." After that, it would depend on whether his visitor proved to have been armed, something he could easily verify after shooting him dead. If he wasn't, it might be marginally more difficult, although accidents did notoriously happen in these circumstances. But that was unlikely. The overwhelming probability was that the intruder would have a gun, too. He sounded like Zeppegno, a wannabee thug full of tough talk and cheap threats. To scum like that, a gun was like an American Express card. It said something about you. People treated you with respect and said, "That'll do nicely, sir." You didn't leave home without it. All he needed to do was put on the rubber gloves and fire a few rounds from the victim's gun into the walls and furniture, then transfer the gloves to the dead man's hands, thus explaining the lack of fingerprints, and call the police. If he got anything more than a fine for possessing an unregistered firearm, there would be a universal outcry among the good burghers of Milan. What, an eminent designer could be threatened by some doped-up hoodlum in his own office without even being permitted to defend himself? What was the world coming to?

He placed the gun on the desk within easy reach and sat back in his swivel chair, thinking about his father. His parents were not often in his thoughts. Indeed, people had called him cold and unnatural at the time of the tragedy, but it would be truer to say that he felt little or nothing, and refused—this was the scandal, of course—to pretend that he did. He had never tried to get anyone else to understand his views on the subject, which all came down to the fact that he did not consider Umberto and Chiara to be his parents at all, except in the most reductive genetic sense. Their children were Raimondo and his sister Ariana. He, Falco, owed them nothing.

His cousin Ludovico Ruspanti had been an early inspiration. There was no natural way to be an aristocrat in the late twentieth century. The aristocracy had been about land and war, horses and hunting, privilege, philistinism, and irresponsibility. That world had long gone, destroyed by the mercantile class to which the Falcone family belonged. Ludovico Ruspanti's response was to carry on as though nothing had changed, feckless and selfish to the last, asserting a reality that had no substance beyond his own performance of it. He had made everyone else in Raimondo's circle seem wan and insipid. When Umberto and Chiara became martyrs of the class struggle, his father dying in a hail of machine-gun fire sprayed through the windshield of their Mercedes, his mother succumbing to her injuries a few days later, he had remembered Ludovico's deportment on the occasion of his own bereavement. He must have handled it badly, though. No one had criticized Ludovico's playacting, even though he had turned to wink broadly at his cousin after making some fulsome comments about his elder brother, as though to say "We know better, don't we?" He, on the other hand, had made the mistake of being frank about his feelings, or lack of them, and for this he had never been forgiven.

What no one could ever deny was that he had coped extremely well with orphanhood, while his sister Ariana had been broken. She had worshiped her parents, particularly her mother, to whom she had always been close. Raimondo had made no secret of the fact that he disapproved of her childlike dependency, of that physical intimacy prolonged well into adolescence. He found it cloying and excessive, and he had been proved right. When the walls of her emotional hothouse were so brutally shattered by the terrorists' bullets, Ariana had collapsed into something very close to madness.

It had all been hushed up by the services of exclusive and discreet private "nursing homes," which existed for just this very purpose, and by the use of such euphemisms as "prostrated by grief" and "emotionally overwrought." The plain truth was that Ariana Falcone had gone crazy, as her brother had not scrupled to tell her to her face shortly after the funeral. Enough was enough! He had always resented the exaggerated fuss that had been made of Ariana, the way her every wish and whim was pandered to. This excessive display of temperament was just another blatant example of attention-seeking, and in extremely poor taste, too, trading on their parents' violent deaths for her own selfish ends, and trying—with a certain amount of success, to make matters worse—to make him look cold and heartless by comparison. The sooner she faced up to the realities of their new situation the better. Their parents were dead and he was in charge. What Ariana needed was a series of short, sharp shocks to bring this home to her, and it was this he had set out to provide.

Although he had applied his treatment rigorously, Ariana stubbornly refused to respond. On the first anniversary of the killings, he had given her one last chance, ordering her to appear at a memorial service that was being held at their local church. Not only had she refused, but the only reason she deigned to give was that she wanted to play with her collection of dolls, which were kept in the beautiful wooden toy house her parents had given her for her eighth birthday. Her brother's response had been swift and decisive. Tying her to a chair, he had doused the dollhouse in paraffin and set fire to it before her eyes, with the dolls inside.

But Ariana's petulance seemingly knew no bounds. Far from accepting that it was time to stop these embarrassing and self-indulgent games, she had sunk into a condition verging on catatonia. The resulting course of treatment at one of the private clinics had proved so prolonged and expensive that Raimondo had eventually been forced to give in, very much against his own better judgment. He found a doctor who was prepared to pronounce Ariana fit to return home and prescribe an indefinite course of tranquilizers that kept her more or less amenable. Their Aunt Carmela, a despotic old bat who had been eking out a spinster's existence in a cold and leaky villa for as long as anyone could remember, was brought in to replace the professional minders.

Raimondo moved out to a small modern flat near the university, where he had been reenrolling for years without ever taking his exams. The huge palazzo that Umberto's father had bought in the twenties to add a bit of class to the family fortunes was turned over to Carmela and Ariana. A new playhouse was obtained and stocked with dolls. It was not quite the same, but Ariana fortunately showed no sign of noticing the difference, or of remembering what had happened to the original. She spent her days happily sewing doll's clothes based on ideas culled from Carmela's discarded magazines.

What happened next was completely unpredictable. Appropriately enough, the whole thing had been intended as a joke. Paolo, one of Raimondo's student acquaintances, had always dreamed of becoming a fashion designer, much against his parents' wishes. It was he who told Raimondo about the competition being run by a leading fashion magazine to find the "designers of tomorrow." He was submitting a portfolio of drawings and sketches, which he described to his friends at every opportunity. If he won, he explained, his parents would be obliged to let him follow his genius instead of taking a job in a bank. Paolo went on at such length about it that Raimondo finally decided to play a trick on him. One evening when Ariana had gone to bed, he borrowed a dozen of her dolls, complete with the miniature costumes she had made for them, removed the heads to make them look like dressmaker's mannequins, and then photographed them carefully with a close-up lens. Next he took the prints to a commercial art studio and had them reproduced as fashion sketches, which he triumphantly showed to Paolo as *his* entry.

If Paolo had taken the thing in the spirit it had been intended, Raimondo would have admitted the truth, had a good laugh, and that would have been that. To his amazement, however, Paolo reacted with a torrent of vituperative abuse. Raimondo's designs were impractical nonsense, he claimed. No one could ever make such things, let alone wear them. In short, it would be an insult to submit them for the competition. Until that moment, Raimondo had not had the slightest intention of doing so, but Paolo had been so unpleasant that he sent the drawings in to spite him. When the results were announced three months later, Raimondo was awarded first prize.

His first reaction was one of incredulity. The joke had gone far enough—much too far, in fact. He must put a stop to it at once. But that wasn't so easy, not with all Milan beating a path to the door. Paolo couldn't have been more wrong, it seemed. The designs Raimondo had submitted were judged to be daring but accessible, refreshingly different, striking just the right balance between novelty and practicality. He was offered contracts, more or less on his own terms, with several of the city's top fashion houses.

If Ariana had been in her right mind, he would have let her take the prize and the fame and fortune that went with it. At least, he liked to think he would. He could certainly have considered doing so. As it was, this was out of the question. His sister was quite incapable of sustaining the ordeal of public exposure. Apart from Aunt Carmela and Raimondo himself, the only person she ever saw was her cousin Ludovico, on whom she seemed to have developed a silly schoolgirlish crush. She was always brighter just before, during, and immediately after his visits, which had grown quite frequent. Apparently Ludo had some kind of business interests in Milan, although it was never quite clear what they were. At any rate, when he was around, Ariana could almost pass for normal. But this was an illusion, of course. Ariana lived in a self-contained world, talking to no one but her dolls. She had not watched television since the day a report about some terrorist atrocity had caused a lengthy relapse. She didn't listen to the radio or see the papers. Her world had a lot to recommend it, from her point of view. It was warm, stable, and quiet. There were no nasty surprises. Indeed, apart from Ludovico's visits there were no surprises at all. Love might safely be invested, secure in the knowledge that no harm could befall it.

For Raimondo to admit the truth would only have served to kill a goose whose eggs, it seemed, were of solid gold. But it wasn't really a question of money. The Falcone family fortunes, although no longer quite what they had been when Umberto was running the business, were still in an altogether different league from those of their Roman cousins. No, it was the original element—that of the practical joke, the elaborate prank—that swayed him in the end. If fooling Paolo had seemed a worthwhile thing to do, the chance of fooling *everybody* was completely irresistible.

It took him a while to find his feet. The freelance contract didn't work out in the end. When the house involved requested small changes in various details, he'd had to refuse, for the simple reason that he was unable to draw. His arrogance and intransigence attracted criticism at the time, but in the long run the episode merely strengthened his hand, increasing his reputation as a wayward, uncompromising genius who worked alone by night and then appeared with a sheaf of sketches and said, "Take it or leave it!"

When he launched his own ready-to-wear line the following March, it was only a modest success. The fashion world in Italy is dominated by a handful of big names whose control is exercised through exclusive contracts with textile producers, insider deals in which the fashion press allocate editorial space in direct proportion to the amount of advertising bought, and licensing arrangements for perfumes, watches, lighters, glasses, scarves, and luggage that make such "concession tycoons" multimillionaires without their having to lift a finger. What was being sold was an image created by the designers' haute couture collections, shown three times a year in Rome and abroad. Such garments, selling for tens of billions of lire, were out of reach to anyone but the superrich, most of them in America and the Gulf oil states, but the image of luxury and exclusivity was available to anyone prepared to pay a modest sum for a "designer labeled" product that might in fact have been produced in a Korean sweatshop. The sweat didn't stick, the chic did. That was the trick of it.

As sole owner of a large textile mill, Raimondo Falcone was in a unique position to break the cartel on raw materials. The problem lay in generating the desirable image. He clearly couldn't go into couture. As the word implies, this means being able to cut, to go into a fitting room with the client, pick up a length of cloth and a pair of scissors, and produce something that looked like it had grown there. This was clearly not a possibility for someone who couldn't cut a slice of panettone without leaving the cake looking as though someone had sat on it. Then he had his inspiration, which happened when he was being interviewed on television one day. His sudden eruption onto the fashion scene, as though from nowhere, was already the stuff of legend. People were naturally curious about him, his background, his working methods, his philosophy. While he was telling the interviewer a pack of lies —"I always thought of it as a hobby really, I used to scribble ideas on the back of an envelope and then lose it somewhere . . ."—it occurred to him that what people really wanted from their clothes was a kind of miraculous transformation like the one that fascinated them about Falco. They wanted to be able to put on a new personality like putting on a shirt. Fashion wasn't just about attracting sexual partners or showing off your wealth. It was a search for metamorphosis, for transcendence. And who better to offer it than a man who appeared to be unfettered by the constraints within which ordinary mortals were forced to operate?

From that moment, he had never looked back. It took no more than an occasional grudging, condescending word of praise from him to keep Ariana busy. Censored extracts from fashion magazines, from which all reference to Falco designs had of course been removed, kept her fantasy world in touch with the colors, lines, and fabrics that were currently in vogue. Once he had succeeded in convincing her that she needed big dolls to play with now, being a big girl herself, the trick photography and out-of-house sketches could be dispensed with. From time to time he removed a selection of the garments she'd made and handed them over to his subordinates, a tight, highly paid, and very loyal team who relieved the maestro of the tiresome day-to-day business of putting his creations into production from the original models. All he had to do was tour the country, appearing at shops and on television, telling people that they were what they wore, and that in the late twentieth century it was ideologically gauche to suggest otherwise.

He sat up suddenly, listening intently. Then he heard it again, a distant metallic sound somewhere far below. Once again, a smile bent his lips. He knew what it was: the discarded filing cabinet that had been sitting on the landing of the first floor for as long as anyone could remember. When he arrived, having smashed off the padlock used since the break-in to secure the emergency exit, he had pulled the metal cabinet out from the wall so that it all but blocked the way upstairs. Its faint tintinnabulation was as good as a burglar alarm to him.

He picked up the pistol and walked with rapid, light steps into the workroom, where he knelt down behind one of the tables with a clear view of the door. The moment it opened, the intruder would be framed in a rectangle of light, peering into a dark, unfamiliar territory where the only recognizable targets were the mannequins. But *he* would be ready, his eyes perfectly adjusted to the fog-muted glimmer from the

Galleria outside, the pistol steadied against the edge of the table and trained on its target. It would be like shooting rabbits leaving their burrow.

Then a miracle occurred. That, at least, is how he explained it to himself in that initial instant of wordless awe. After that it was pure sensation, pure experience. Later he realized that the whole thing could have taken no more than a few seconds, but while it lasted there was nothing else, only the noise and the light. The light was the kind you might see if they skinned your eyeballs, pickled them in acid, and trained lasers on them. As for the *noise* . . .

When he was a boy, he had once been allowed up the campanile of the family church. After endless windings, the spiral staircase broadened into a chamber where the bells hung, great lumps of dull metal, seeming no more resonant than so many rocks. Yet when the clapper struck, they could be heard over half the city. He had wondered ever after what it would have sounded like if they'd started pealing while he was standing there. Now he knew. His whole body thrilled and jangled, every cell and fiber quivering in exquisite agony as the overtones and reverberations of that blow died away. Another such would kill him, he thought as he lay in a heap on the floor, clutching his head. But there wasn't another. This puzzled him at first. Once the clapper was set swinging with that kind of violence, it was bound to come back to strike the other side, just when you were least expecting it.

Hands moved lightly and rapidly all over his body, like a couturier fitting a client. He opened his eyes. A tall figure wearing a black clerical suit stood looking down at him, a revolver in each hand. Above the trim white collar rose a garish latex carnival mask representing the bluff, benign features of John Paul II.

From the other side of the latex mask, Aurelio Zen surveyed the situation with a sense of satisfaction and relief. Ever since picking up the package that afternoon at Linate, he had been extremely dubious about the outcome of this adventure. He had no idea what stun grenades looked like, but given what Gilberto had told him they were going to cost, he was expecting something pretty impressive. Gleaming stainless-steel canisters with spring-action triggers and time-delay settings, slightly greasy to the touch—that sort of thing. Above all, he was expecting them to *weigh*. "We are the goods," he expected them to tell him as he staggered away from the airline counter with a metal case marked DANGER—HIGH EXPLOSIVES.

Instead of which the clerk had casually tossed him a padded envelope that felt almost empty. Zen left feeling like the victim of a confidence trick. Matters did not improve when he opened the envelope in the taxi on the way back to the city. Inside, he found two gray plastic tubes, each about the size of a toothpaste dispenser, lashed together by a rubber band looped over on itself. At one end, a red plastic peg with a ridged grip protruded a few centimeters from the body of the tube, the junction being sealed with a pull tab. There was also a note in Gilberto's jauntily precise writing.

> *To avoid accidents, remove seal at last moment. After pulling out the red pin, you have 3 seconds to deliver the grenade and get out. The effects last 5 seconds or more, depending on the physical condition of the opposition, their degree of preparation and training, etc. One pack is enough for an average-sized room: larger areas may require two.*

Just like air freshener, thought Zen disgustedly. Four hundred thousand lire each, Gilberto was charging him for these! "And that's cost price, Aurelio. In fact *below* cost, because it's what I paid three months ago. God knows what the replacement cost will be." As an added irony, the source was one of Zen's colleagues. The reason the grenades were so expensive was that very few came on to the market. Any equipment of general military or police issue could be had at massive discounts, for that was very much a buyer's market. But stun grenades were supplied only to a few specialist units in the police and Carabinieri. Nieddu's supplier was connected to the Interior Ministry's DIGOS antiterrorist squad, whose morale was at an all-time low these days—which no doubt explained why they were resorting to private enterprise, like everyone else.

In the event, though, Zen had to admit that his doubts had been decisively confounded. The grenades might not look like much, but they packed one hell of a punch. Even from the other side of the door, the effect had been that of the firework to end all fireworks. He hadn't been sure how large the room was, but at almost half a million lire a go, Zen decided one was going to have to be enough. Which it certainly had been. When he charged in, Falcone was lying on the floor, his hands to his head and his knees drawn up, like one of the victims of Pompeii. Setting down his replica revolver, Zen grabbed the pistol the man had been holding and swiftly frisked him for other weapons. Then he picked up his toy gun and stepped back.

After a few seconds, Falcone moaned and rubbed his eyes as though stirring from sleep. He stared incredulously at Zen, who smiled behind the privacy of his latex mask. The costume had been another aspect of the affair that he had been unsure about. Some disguise was certainly necessary. He didn't want to give his game away too soon, not without finding out as much as he could first. This was his first deliberate attempt at criminal extortion, and he didn't want to bungle it. The single card he had to play should certainly be enough to extract a cash settlement, but if his victim could be kept in suspense about who he was and what he wanted, other potentially profitable facts might well emerge. At the very least, the aura of psychological domination thus established would work strongly to Zen's advantage when it came to negotiating terms.

The moment he thought of disguises, he recalled the fancy dress shop he had seen that morning in Via Pisani. At that time of year, they had an extensive selection available, but in the end Zen had opted for a clerical outfit. The mask, a pudgy parody of Wojtyla's Slavic features, had then been an obvious accessory. Nevertheless, it remained to be seen what effect it would have. As it turned out, there were no worries on that score either. Falcone couldn't keep his eyes off it.

"You're a bit early for Carnival," he eventually remarked with a brave attempt at reasserting himself.

"It's for your protection," Zen replied in the singsong accent he had used on the phone.

"For *yours,* you mean."

The plastic pope's face moved from side to side in a gesture of negation that made a macabre contrast with its expression of benevolent paternalism.

"If I were not masked, you might recognize me," Zen explained. "Then we would have to kill you."

He waited a moment for this to sink in.

"We may decide to do so anyway in the end, of course. That depends on you, and on whether you are able to furnish a satisfactory explanation of your conduct with regard to the Ruspanti affair."

Falcone tried a laugh.

"What have *I* to do with that? There's absolutely no evidence linking me to the Ruspanti affair."

"Evidence is for judges. I am not a judge, I am an executioner. Sentence has already been passed. Unless you can persuade me otherwise in the next few minutes, it will be carried out."

In the pools of shadow on the floor, Falcone squirmed like a stranded fish.

"But what have I done, for God's sake? What have I done?"

"You have taken our name in vain! You have slandered our organization and circulated lies about our aims and activities. You have stirred up a hornet's nest of speculation and rumor that is causing us considerable embarrassment. In short, you have attempted to make use of us."

The black holes of the mask's eyes bored into Falcone.

"The Cabal does not allow itself to be made use of."

Once again Falcone tried to laugh, but it broke from him like a belch, uncontrolled and shameful.

"Listen, there's been a terrible mistake! I had no idea that any such organization as the Cabal even existed! Ruspanti told me he had dreamed it up as a way of getting the Vatican to give him refuge. He was very proud of how clever he'd been, of how the priests were swallowing it all and coming back for more. I thought that's all it was, just something he'd made up!"

"That's not what you told the police."

At this, Falcone visibly shrank.

"What?"

"The police official from the Ministry of the Interior who was called in by the Vatican to investigate the Ruspanti affair. You didn't tell *him* that you thought the whole thing was a hoax. On the contrary, you went to great lengths to ensure that he thought the Cabal was behind the whole affair."

Falcone gasped.

"You know about that?"

"It will save a lot of time if you just assume that we know *every-thing*. Now answer my question! Why did you go to such extraordinary lengths—breaking into a confessional in St. Peter's, setting up a short-wave radio link—just to smear an organization whose existence you now say you didn't believe in?"

"I never intended to smear anyone . . ."

"Well, you certainly succeeded! The Ministry of the Interior even opened a file on us. Fortunately, one of our men was able to have it suppressed, but the effects could have been incalculable. For the last time, *why?*"

Falcone looked up at the pistol in the man's right hand. It was now pointing directly toward him. For the first time, he realized that he was going to die—and by his own gun, or rather his father's.

"It was just a bluff!" he cried. "We suspected that the police knew more than they were officially admitting. The idea was to convince the officer in charge that Ruspanti's death was not a criminal matter but a political one, and that the guilty party might include anyone and every-one from his own boss to the President of the Republic."

The papal mask nodded like an obscene parody of a priest hearing confession.

"But who is this 'we'? And why should you care what line the police were taking?"

"I meant the Falcone family. Ruspanti was a distant cousin of ours, and we were worried that . . ."

A harsh cackle from the lips of the plastic pope cut him off.

"Oh come, now! You had rather more reason to worry than the family connection, didn't you?"

"I don't know what you mean."

"Then let me fill you in. Last Friday, you and Marco Zeppegno murdered Ludovico Ruspanti by throwing him from the upper gallery in St. Peter's . . ."

"We didn't *throw* him!"

Too late, he realized the trap he had fallen into.

"Quite right," the intruder continued gloatingly. "You lashed him to the railings with a length of fishing twine fastened in such a way that once he regained consciousness, his own struggles precipitated him to his death. Four days later, you electrocuted Giovanni Grimaldi in his shower . . ."

"I had nothing to do with that!"

The cry was spontaneous, an affirmation of an innocence he really felt. Although it had been he who had connected the electric cable to the mains and listened to the dying man's screams, the elimination of Grimaldi had served only Zeppegno's interests. The photocopy of the transcript he had been shown on Monday afternoon confirmed that there was nothing to compromise him, particularly since Grimaldi had obviously been totally taken in by his female clothing—even to the extent of doing a half-hearted number on him!

To be honest, it might have been that which sealed the Vigilanza man's fate. He'd been shocked to find himself the object of that kind of attention, just because he'd put on a skirt and blouse. Of course this merely confirmed what he'd claimed all along—fixed categories were an illusion, you were what you appeared to be—but it was one thing to theorize about such things, quite another to see a man eye you up and down in that smug, knowing way. There was nothing remotely sexual about his cross-dressing. It was just an extension of the possibilities open to him, that was all, a blurring of distinctions he had already proclaimed meaningless. He would even more happily have dressed as a child, if that had been possible.

But Giovanni Grimaldi had made the mistake of making sexual advances to him, and when Marco had said they were going to have to move, he had agreed, even though he himself was not at risk. The telephone call from Ludovico to Ariana that had originally forced him to intervene was recorded in the transcript, but Ludo was still being careful at that point, and he had said nothing that would make any sense to an outsider. But by the eve of his death, Ruspanti had thrown caution to the winds, and Zeppegno's name appeared in black and white. If the police got hold of it, they'd beat the truth out of Marco in no time at all. That was another reason he'd decided to play along. It was only later that he realized his own interests would have been better served by killing Zeppegno himself.

"I had nothing to do with that!" he repeated.

The intruder seemed at first to understand.

" 'You are what you wear.' I didn't realize you took your own slogan so seriously! Very well then, Zeppegno's accomplice wasn't you but a woman of similar build and bone structure. Oddly enough, yesterday yet another young woman—clearly no relation, because she was wearing brown instead of black—pushed Marco Zeppegno out of a train in the middle of the Apennine tunnel. Quite an eventful week they've had, these girls, whoever they may be."

Raimondo Falcone had once watched a pig gutted, out at the villa where Carmela used to live. The beast was suspended by its hind trotters from a hook. The knife was plunged in below the pink puckered anus and tugged down like the tag of a zipper, opening the animal's belly, releasing its heavy load of innards. The plastic pope's words had a similar effect on him now. The man had not exaggerated. He *did* know everything.

Well, not *every*thing. He knew about Ruspanti and Grimaldi. He even knew about Zeppegno. But that was only the wrapping on the real secret, the key to all the others and the reason why he had originally suggested to Zeppegno that they join forces and pay a visit to the prince in Rome. Ironically enough, it was Ruspanti himself who had brought Falcone and Zeppegno together in the first place, when he learned that his cousin had abandoned the derelict family mansion to mad Ariana and moved into a smart new apartment building that also happened to house one of the former clients in his currency export business. At first the prince had merely asked Falcone to pass on his demands and menaces to Marco Zeppegno, who could in turn relay them to the other men under investigation by Antonia Simonelli. When Raimondo balked, his cousin had reminded him that it was in his own interest to see the affair settled quietly. A major scandal would reflect badly on everyone in the family, especially a young designer at such a delicate stage of his career, just starting to rise in the world, but still within reach of jealous rivals who would seize on any excuse to burst the bubble of his success.

At the time Falcone had understood it as an observation, not a threat, and had agreed to act as go-between. Zeppegno, for his part, refused to be drawn on the specific commitments Ruspanti wanted, claiming that he needed more time, and that dramatic interventions by influential people were just around the corner. To Falcone he was less diplomatic, perhaps hoping that some echo of this might get back to the prince. "It was a business arrangement. He did the job, we paid him well. If the bastard's in the shit now, let him look after himself. I've got problems of my own without adding conspiracy to pervert the course of justice." Raimondo took little interest in the matter one way or the other until the day Ruspanti dropped an oblique reference to Ariana's dolls. A few days later, he mentioned the dolls again, this time referring to their "extraordinarily inventive" costumes. In a panic, Falcone hung up. When the phone rang again, he did not answer it. He did not answer it for the next week, but when he dropped in to pick up a consignment of costumes from Ariana, she told him Ludovico's story about meeting a reporter who was interested in writing an article about her and her dolls. The implication was clear. If his demands were not met, Ruspanti would reveal to the world that Falco was a fake, a pretentious posturer who had deceived everyone by cynically exploiting the talents of the traumatized sibling he kept locked up at home.

It was then he had decided that his cousin must die. Ruspanti had in fact seriously miscalculated. Not for a moment did Falcone think of agreeing to the prince's demands, which now included private planes to smuggle him out of the country and secret hideouts in Switzerland or Austria where he could lie low until the affair blew over. It was not just his commercial success that was at stake, but his very self! He was no longer Falcone, but Falco. If Falco were to be revealed as a sham, an illusion, then what would become of *him*? As long as Ludovico Ruspanti had remained alive, Falco's existence had hung in the balance.

As it did now, he thought. The intruder stood quite still, pistols aimed at Raimondo's queasily yawing head.

"Until this moment, I had no idea that any such organization as the Cabal existed," Falcone said wearily. "If I have inadvertently offended or inconvenienced you, I apologize. If there is any way I can make reparations, I am more than willing to do so."

The man in clerical costume raised his hands slowly.

"No!" shrieked Falcone in sheer terror. "For the love of God forgive me, I beg of you!"

The empty eyes of the mask stared at him.

"I? I have nothing to do with it."

Falcone groveled on the floor, abasing himself utterly.

"I meant the Cabal."

The intruder laughed.

"The Cabal doesn't exist." And he raised his mask like a visor.

The effect was as stunning as the detonation of the grenade. Slack-jawed, pale, seemingly paralyzed, Falcone just stared and stared. He, who had fooled everyone around him for so long, had now himself been made a fool of—and by a dowdy creep whose suits looked as though they were made by his mother! How was it possible? Why had it been permitted? The world had stopped making sense.

"Don't worry, Dottore, you're in good company," said Zen, tossing the latex mask aside. "The best minds in the Vatican fell for it when Ruspanti spun them the tale. The press and the public fell for it when Grimaldi wrote his anonymous letter. I fell for it myself when the Vatican seemed to be covering the matter up, and the top men at the Ministry did when I passed the story on."

Falcone studied him watchfully from the floor.

"The shock's wearing off now, isn't it?" Zen continued. "You're starting to ask yourself why I bothered going to all this trouble. After all, everyone else has had a reason. Ruspanti used the Cabal to get into the Vatican. Grimaldi used it to stir up speculation about Ruspanti's death, so that he could put the squeeze on you and Zeppegno. You two used it to try and lead me up a blind alley. But what's in it for me? That's what you're asking yourself, isn't it, Dottore?"

He took out his pack of Nazionali and lit up.

"Of course, I could say that I'm just getting even for that session in the confessional. My knees just about seized up solid! Where were you, anyway?"

Falcone gave a pallid grin. He didn't know what this man wanted, but he sensed that his life was no longer in danger.

"In a car on the Gianicolo hill. It was Marco's idea. He provided the gadgetry and set it all up. Mind you, we had a few tricky moments, like when that police car passed by with its siren going."

"What you told me about the Vatican—the schisms and feuds, all the various groups jockeying for position—sounded very authentic."

"I got all that from Ludovico. He knew all the right-wing weirdos and religious eccentics in Rome, of course. These people are actually quite harmless, of course, like the ones who want to restore the monarchy. All I did was make them seem a significant threat."

Zen nodded.

"It sounds like you were on quite good terms with your cousin. And Ariana is still in love with him, isn't she?"

A chill ripple passed over Falcone's skin.

"What?" he croaked.

Zen waved a pistol casually.

"Look, let's get one thing clear. I'm not here in my professional capacity."

Falcone stared at him.

"You mean . . ."

"I mean I'm on the make," Zen replied. "I'm a corrupt cop. You've read about them in the papers, you've seen them on television. Now, for a limited period only, you can have one in your own home or office."

Raimondo Falcone stood up, facing Zen.

"How much?"

Zen let his cigarette fall to the floor and stubbed it out with the toe of his right shoe. Falcone watched anxiously to make sure it was properly extinguished. Fire in the atelier was the great terror of every designer.

"How much do you think it's worth?"

Falcone's eyes narrowed.

"How much *what's* worth?"

Zen looked past him at the window of the inner office, where the lighted dome of the Galleria rose into the gathering fog.

"You killed your cousin to keep it secret," he said as though to himself. "That would seem to make it quite valuable."

Again the chill spread over Falcone, eating into his complacency like acid. With an effort, he pulled himself together. There was no need to panic. He was in no danger. All this crooked, taunting bastard wanted was money. Give it to him, promise him whatever he wanted, and get him the hell out of here.

"We agreed fifty million for the transcript," he said decisively, the businessman in him taking charge.

"I no longer have the transcript."

Falcone couldn't help smiling. He knew that, having wrested most of it from Zeppegno before pushing him out of the train. Instead of hanging on to the door, poor obtuse Zeppegno had clutched the transcript, still believing it was the real object of the exercise. The idea had been that Zeppegno would join the *pendolino* at Florence, engage Zen in conversation, and get hold of the transcript. Falcone, in drag again, would go to the vestibule as they approached the Apennine tunnel and turn off the lights. While Zeppegno walked through to the next carriage with the transcript, Falcone was to go back to the seat where Zen was sitting and shoot him dead.

At least, that's what Zeppegno thought was going to happen. Falcone had quite different ideas, and in the event, they prevailed. Once he'd opened the door and pushed his startled accomplice out, he'd taken the part of the transcript he'd managed to seize back to the lavatory. Luckily, it included the page where Ruspanti phoned Ariana. He'd burnt that and flushed the ashes down the toilet. This was no doubt an unnecessary precaution, but he preferred to err on the safe side. Then he'd pushed the other pages out the window, checked his appearance in the mirror, and gone out to face Zen and the train crew. As he'd expected, all they'd looked at was his bum.

"I'm not interested in the transcript," he said.

"There's no reason why you should be," agreed Zen. "You weren't even mentioned."

"I was simply using that figure as a benchmark."

"Your sister was, though."

For a moment Falcone hoped he'd misheard, even though he knew perfectly well he hadn't.

"And her dolls," added Zen. "And the journalist who supposedly wanted to write about them. That's who she thought I was when I went there yesterday. What really shook me was that she seemed to think Ruspanti was still alive."

Falcone stood perfectly still, his hands clasped and his eyes raised to the ceiling, like a plaster statue of one of the lesser saints.

"Of course, given the isolation in which she lives, there's no reason why she should ever find out. Unless someone told her."

There was no reaction apart from a fractional heightening of Falcone's expression of transcendental sublimity.

"I'm no psychologist," Zen admitted, "but I'd be prepared to bet that if Ariana were told her beloved cousin Ludo was dead, and exactly how he died, the consequences would be extremely grave."

He waved casually around the workshop.

"At the very least, the supply of new Falco designs would be likely to dry up for some considerable . . ."

Then the other man was on him, grabbing the pistol in his right hand. Zen tried to shake him off, but Falcone hung on like a terrier. In the end he had to crack him across the head with the other pistol before he would let go.

"There's no need for this," Zen told him. "All I want is a reasonable settlement. We can come to terms. I'm not greedy."

But Falcone was beyond reach. Shaking his woozy head like a boxer, he came forward again. Zen cocked the replica revolver and pointed it at him.

"Keep your distance!"

There was a deafening bang. This time both men looked stunned, but Zen recovered first. He wasn't still groggy from the first time, for one thing. But the main point was that he had felt the revolver rear up in his hand, and realized what had happened. Falcone didn't seem to have been hit, thank God, but his face was that of a man in hell.

"It was a mistake!" Zen assured him. "I got the pistols mixed up. I fired yours by mistake. Mine's just a replica."

But Falcone was gone, turning on his heel and sprinting through to the next room.

"Come back!" yelled Zen, chasing him. "You're in no danger! All I want is money!"

When he reached the door of the office, it was empty. He searched the gymnasium and bathroom beyond, but there was no sign of Falcone. Only then did he notice the open window. The offices formed part of the south end of the Galleria's main aisle, the lower floors having windows that opened directly onto it, at the base of the glazed barrel-vaulted roof. This floor was at roof level, and it was only a short drop from the window to one of the iron girders that supported the large panes of glass. Catwalks ran the length of the main supporting struts, giving access to the roof for cleaning and maintenance. Along one of these, Raimondo Falcone was now running for his life.

"*Merda!*" shouted Zen.

He was disgusted with his clumsiness, his unbelievable gaucheness, his limitless ineptitude. Couldn't he do *anything* right? What would Tania think of him, after all his proud boasts about things changing? Nothing had changed. Nothing would ever change. In sheer frustration he fired the pistol again and again, blasting away as though to punch new stars in the night sky.

The renewed firing made Falcone run even faster. He had reached the cupola now, and started to climb the metal ladder that led from the catwalk up the curving glass slope of the dome to the ventilation lantern at the top. Through the shifting panels of fog, Zen could just see Falcone moving rapidly across the panes of lighted glass like a nimble skater on a luminous mountain of ice. It thus seemed no great surprise when, in total silence and with no fuss whatsoever, he abruptly disappeared from view.

Down in the Galleria itself, Christmas was in the air. The shops, cafés, and travel agencies were all doing a thriving business. Giving and receiving, eating and drinking, skiing and sunning, and all the other rituals and observances of this festive season insured that money was changing hands in a manner calculated to gladden the hearts of the traders. Any modern Christ who had attempted to intervene would have been expelled in short order by the security guards employed to keep this temple of commerce free of beggars, junkies, buskers, religious fanatics, and other such riff-raff.

Nevertheless, it was some such gesture of protest that sprang to most people's minds when they heard the sound of breaking glass. The shop windows were a powerful symbol of the socioeconomic barriers against which the poor were constantly being brought up short. They could gawk at the goodies as much as they liked, but they couldn't get at them. Sometimes, especially around Christmas, the disparity between the way of life on display and the one they actually lived became too much to bear, and some crazed soul would pick up a hammer and have a go.

Even the screaming seemed at first to fit this scenario, until some people, more acute of hearing, realized it was not coming from onlookers in the immediate vicinity of the presumed outrage, but from somewhere altogether elsewhere—in fact from *above*. When they raised their eyes to the roof to see what it could be, the expression of amazement on their faces made their neighbors do the same, until in no time at all everyone in the Galleria was looking up. It must have looked extraordinary, seen from above, this crowd of faces all tilted up like a crop of sunflowers.

Until then, the distribution of people in the aisles of the Galleria had been fairly even, but they now began to scatter and press back, forming clusters near the walls and rapidly evacuating the space at the center of the building, where the arms of the House of Savoy were displayed in inlaid marble. The clearing thus formed might have been destined for an impromptu performance of some kind, a display of acrobatics or some similar feat of skill or daring. But the crowd's attention was high above, where the vast, dark opacity of the cupola weighed down on the lighted space below. Now that the shock was over, they were reassured to realize that the body plummeting to earth amid a debris of broken glass must be a spectacle of some kind got up to divert the shoppers, an optical illusion, a fake. Clearly no one could have *fallen* through the enclosure overhead, as solid and heavy as vaulted masonry. It was all a trick. A moment before impact the plunging body would pull up short, restrained by hidden wires, while the accompanying shoal of jagged icicles tinkled prettily to pieces on the marble floor before melting harmlessly away.

In the event, though, it turned out to be real.